FUMBLING PERFECT

A Raymere Grove Novel

Nikki Kwiatkowski

Cover designed by Karis Drake

This book is a work of fiction. Names, characters, places, and incidents either are products of the author's imagination or are used fictitiously. Any resemblance to actual persons, living or dead, events, or locales is entirely coincidental.

Nikki Kwiatkowski
Visit my website at www.NikkiKAuthor.com

Printed in the United States of America

First Printing: August 2020

ISBN-13 978-1-7332165-1-7

To my husband, Chris, and son, Lochlan

To my parents, Angie and Raymond

With loving memory, to Kevin and Kaci

CONTENTS

CHAPTER 1

Lilah blinked a few times, her face expressionless as she tried to process what Principal Willis was asking her. She should have known better to come into his office with such optimism on the second week of school.

While Lilah had been called in by Principal Willis several times over the previous three years, usually to be informed of academic excellence and awards, she knew something about this time would be different as soon as she saw the presence of Coach Turner hovering nearby, clearly annoyed and impatient.

"I'm sorry. I don't think I'm following," Lilah lied, her blood gradually beginning to boil at their suggestion.

"Miss McCallister, you're one of the best students in this year's senior class," Principal Willis began, only to be cut off.

"I am the best. I'll be valedictorian," Lilah coldly corrected.

Willis ignored her overly proud statement and continued. "Coach Turner needs someone who will have time to commit to this until the end of the season.

While you're above and beyond with academics, compared to others, you could use a few extracurricular items on your application."

"I'm in the honor society. I do volunteer work for them. With all due respect, being in a club here or helping an idiot jock there isn't going to matter once I'm in college."

"It will help you get recommendations from myself, Mr. Hughes, and I'm sure even Coach Turner here would be willing to write one up for you."

Lilah laughed and crossed her arms over her chest. "I'm seventeen. I'm well-aware as to how things work. My dad is Steven McCallister. Do you honestly think that I won't be able to get into whatever university I want?"

"I have to say, with that comment, I'm extremely disappointed by your attitude. I only hope that your university of choosing doesn't hear how little you think of the admission process," Willis sighed. "Anyway," he began again, shuffling through some papers. "Thank you for your time, you may return to second period."

Lilah rose from her seat, feeling a little sick. She tried to tell them she wasn't interested in tutoring from the beginning. This year she planned to see her friends a little more and keep up with the grueling studying. She was already enrolled in classes online so that she could knock out silly basic courses like college level history. Seriously, who needed to learn about the Civil War both in middle school, high school, and college? History was nothing more than memorization.

Just as she was about to reach the door, she heard Coach Turner speak for the first time.

"What about that other smart kid, Sophie or something?"

Lilah clenched the handle so hard that her knuckles turned white. While a tiny voice inside her head laughed and told her how funny it was, Sophie, a second choice to herself, another part, a much more competitive part, silenced the laughter.

Lilah turned back to face Principal Willis and Coach Turner. They had stopped talking after realizing that she was still in the room. Both held looks of bewilderment, wondering what else would continue to spew from the mouth of such an egotistical young lady.

She took a deep breath and finally unclenched her gritted teeth. "How long does the season last?"

* * *

"You could have always joined the science club this year," Alice pointed out as she sat her tray down at the same lunch table going on four years now.

"Or you could help with theatre productions after school. We always need volunteers," Jolee chimed in, reaching in her bag for a protein bar and some green liquid in a glass bottle.

"I don't need any extra activities. I just want to study, get a couple college courses under my belt, and I don't know, maybe hang out with the two of you, like we did before the pressures of everything," Lilah huffed, poking at her grilled chicken salad.

"No prospects of dating then," Alice asked through a mouthful of pizza.

"Come on, what is it with you? I swear, it's as though boys consume ninety percent of the female thought at our age," Jolee pointed out. To say that Jolee was a feminist was an understatement.

"I have no more prospects than either of you."

"Are you kidding me? Most of the science club are guys, and this year, I'm their queen," Alice giggled teasingly.

Lilah and Jolee had lost count the number of times since school started that Alice made comments, some subtle, others not so much, about being the president of the science club their senior year.

"Regardless, if I have time to date, I have time to take on another online entry course," Lilah said. Realistically she knew that there wasn't a guy in the school who would come near her like that.

Lilah's father was entrepreneur Steven McCallister of McCallister Industries, one of the fastest growing technological companies. He had founded the company shortly after marrying Lilah's mother, Jenna, and while the first ten years were a struggle at times, the last ten had been enough to move them into a mansion outside of the city.

Raymere Grove was a decent sized town. It had everything one needed, with the exception of big city shopping, and Lilah's mother was quick to make the hour drive into the city at least once a week for what she called her therapy. The town was more on the wealthy side, but when it came to the wealthiest of all, that was by far the McCallisters.

Who her father was should have been enough to deter Lilah from getting any dates, but the fact that she was the most pretentious snob in the whole school really did it. She was smart, and while she worked very hard, she was also sure to let everyone know just how smart she was. Perhaps her wealth and beauty could be overlooked when it came to an intimidation factor; however, the attitude that she was somehow better than everyone rubbed most everyone the wrong way, except of course for Alice and Jolee.

"You know the only reason you're stuck doing this is because you couldn't stand that their next choice of tutor was Sophie," Jolee said, bringing the subject back, before boys were mentioned.

Lilah stabbed at a piece of chicken. "She's always so competitive, thinking she's better than me."

"Yeah, but this has nothing to do with being valedictorian," Alice chimed in.

They were right. She should never have turned around. She should have left Principal Willis' office and gone back to second period without another word.

Lilah was forced to lift her eyes from the plate before her at Alice's next words. "Who do you think it is?"

Lilah had told them that Willis nor Coach Turner had given her a name, only that she had a brief meeting that afternoon. As the three girls turned their attention to the table flooded by testosterone, they were only left to speculate.

"Hopefully it's one of the cuter ones," Alice sighed.

Jolee gave her a hard nudge. "You're hopeless. If anything, Lilah better hope he has a pretty good attention span and can read beyond a third-grade level."

Lilah glanced from player to player, feeling more defeated by the second. "Considering that he's failing English two weeks into the year..."

"Hopefully it's Dawson," Alice gasped.

Lilah groaned. "No. It's not going to be Dawson. If he put a little more energy into studying, he'd be my biggest competition. Sadly for him, simply making an A is good enough." It wasn't like Lilah could blame him to an extent. He was in every AP class she could think of.

"It's probably an idiot like Sean, or one of his even more ridiculous followers," Jolee speculated.

They watched as Louis, one of Sean's lackeys chugged a thirty-two-ounce sports beverage, purple liquid seeping from the sides of his mouth and onto his shirt, as Sean and Cash cheered him on.

"If so, there's not a chance. There is no way that I could spend a second with that jerk." Lilah was adamant about that.

For the most part, the football players weren't horrible. Did a lot of them think that they were better than the other students at Raymere High? Of course. Sean, however, was the stereotypical bully of the team. The only person that gave him a run for his money was Miss Head Cheerleader herself, Sarah. The irony.

As they began to gather their bags, with two minutes before the bell to fifth period, "Just look on the bright side."

Lilah gave Alice a skeptical look. "Which is?"

"Well, I don't know yet," she whined at the attention being directed on her. "I thought maybe you did."

✳ ✳ ✳

"West! Get over here," Coach Turner called out as soon as he heard the last bell.

Kyler West casually jogged away from the group on the field. Upon taking off his helmet, "What's up, Coach?"

Coach Turner signaled for his assistant to continue without both he and their star quarterback. He began walking away as a confused Kyler followed closely.

"You know if you're not passing you can't play," Coach Turner began, not feeling the need to make small talk.

Kyler sighed. He had hoped to avoid this conversation a little longer.

"You had straight A's freshman, sophomore, and hell, most of your junior year. This isn't like you."

"Look it's only the second week of school; mid six weeks' grades don't come out until Monday after next," Kyler felt the need to point out; however, knowing that he probably wouldn't have time to make up his grade in English.

"I talked with Willis, while the mid-report will only be a warning, if you're failing at the end of the six-weeks, you're not playing," Coach Turner sighed.

"But, Coach," Kyler began.

"That's not my decision or his. That's the state. You've worked so hard all these years and I really can't stand to see you throw it all away. I mean, gosh boy, you've had scouts looking at you after freshman year. Your GPA is even good enough, and you're going to let this fall semester take that all away from you." He shook his head. "The smart thing for me to do would be to take you out now, until your grades get back up."

Kyler jumped in immediately. "No, you can't do that. Don't do that to the team. Our first game is tomorrow!"

"I know, which is why I came up with something else."

Kyler didn't like the smirk on Coach Turner's face. He was half hoping that there was a way to bribe Mr. Hughes on simply giving him a passing grade. Of all the English teachers, he had to get stuck with the one who took his job way too seriously.

"I'm sorry, what?!"

Turner grumbled at the idea of having to repeat himself. "Just head over to the library now. You two set up arrangements based on your schedules."

"I'm not having a tutor! I can do this on my own. I always have," Kyler insisted.

"Well, that's not working out too well. Keep your gear on. It shouldn't take long. Then get back over here. Practice until six on days before a game," Coach quickly spouted out, dismissing any protest by Kyler.

Kyler was still in shock, gasping like a fish in search of words as Coach Turner departed at a rapid speed back toward the field.

"Who am I even meeting," he shouted as quietly as he could. The last thing he needed was Sean finding out that he had a tutor.

"The name slips my mind," Coach Turner lied. He was well-aware of McCallister's reputation and somehow had the assumption that the two would rub each other the wrong way. Maybe that's what Kyler needed, someone who wouldn't let him skate by. "She's a real sweetheart. This will be a piece of cake." He quickly turned before Kyler could see his grin breaking out in the distance.

CHAPTER 2

As soon as Kyler signed in at the library and the parent volunteer at the desk pointed him toward the girl waiting for him, his stomach clenched, and he was unable to stifle back the groan of agony.

Lilah McCallister.

Of course, it had to be Lilah McCallister.

Rich.

Beautiful.

Genius.

Total know-it-all brat.

Kyler had her in several classes over the years, though he doubt she'd remember. She always sat at the front of the class, her hand up every few minutes, more often than not, correcting the teacher.

With every step he took through the near empty library, he tried to think of a reason to bolt. Having a tutor was already bad enough, but someone like her was downright impossible. He'd never be able to work with her. One snotty comment and he'd be done. That's when an idea came to him.

Lilah was engrossed with a book about the stock market crash of 1929 when darkness overtook the light streaming from a nearby window. Upon looking away from the cream pages, she became aware of the beast in front of her.

Kyler West.

Popular.

Gorgeous.

Athletic.

Total pretty boy who thought he was a gift to the female population.

Lilah would have been disappointed regardless of the person standing before her. Kyler wasn't the worst, but he had this cocky aura about him that made most girls swoon like imbeciles. Lilah was not an imbecile, and she certainly didn't find one thing charming about Kyler West. How he was Mr. Perfect of the school was beyond her, after all, he was failing at least one class.

Without meaning to, Lilah let out a sigh of annoyance.

"Problem?"

Lilah closed her book and placed it on a stack that she planned to check out. Kyler had not taken a seat, so she rose rather than stare up at him like the tiny mouse he probably thought her to be.

"You couldn't even bother to change," she snobbishly pointed out.

"Coach only gave me a few minutes. I have to get back to practice."

Lilah rolled her eyes. "Right." How someone could put so much effort into a stupid game and not their studies was inconceivable in her eyes. "Okay, I have a schedule of days and times when I'd be available to meet. Since the school library closes at five, we'd have to meet at the public library a good portion of the time. I have it color coded," she explained as she withdrew a piece of laminated paper from her bag, having prepared the schedule during one of her electives.

Kyler's eyes bulged. Laminated. What was wrong with this girl?

"My contact information is at the top, and–"

"Let me stop you," Kyler interrupted, pushing the shiny plastic sheet back across the table. He found humor in how shocked Lilah became at his cold rudeness. He was only about to make it better. "I don't need a tutor, certainly not you." He watched as her lips became thin wrinkled lines and her normally big and bright green eyes turned to nothing more than slits. Something about her reminded him of an angry kitten. While she appeared too cute to be terrifying, he most definitely knew that she still had claws. "I get it, I'm failing English. I just haven't had time to read that junk–"

"*Hamlet* is not junk." Her arms were now crossed.

"Yeah, sure, whatever. My point is, my overall GPA is pretty good, but that doesn't matter to the state when it comes to playing. All I have to do is barely pass English and I get to play. More likely than not, in the coming months I'll have a scholarship to college for football. I don't need to waste both of our time with all this studying. I'll get it above a 70 before the first six weeks' report card, and I'll do that on my own."

Lilah was extremely annoyed but hid it well as she began shoving a few of her things in her bag and gathering the books she planned to check out.

"Thank you for informing me of that, but it seems you've already wasted a great deal of my time," she huffed.

Kyler concealed the smile begging to get out at how much she was fuming at being rejected for help. Before he could say anything else, she spun on her designer heels and childishly stomped away to the check-out desk.

He couldn't help but watch her. He was a guy after all. If he was honest, she was cute. He knew other guys thought that as well. While he didn't feel the need to engage in locker room gossip, that didn't stop him from listening. Lilah was pretty much the definition of perfection in the school, that is, if the whole package didn't include the attitude that came with it.

Kyler waited for her to leave so that he wouldn't have even the faintest encounter with her. Also, it was hot outside, and as it stood right now, the team's defense needed the most practice, not him.

He glanced down at the table. In her haste, Lilah had left behind her availability schedule. For a moment he thought that it may have been intentional, in case he changed his mind, but the little he knew of Lilah, he couldn't imagine her caring enough about his grades for that.

Knowing that the sheet had her contact information, he grabbed it from the table and made his way to the nearest trash can. A sickening feeling came over him as the paper, still in his hand, hovered over the trash can.

He didn't need her help. He didn't need anyone's help. He just had to find the time to begin reading that stupid play and catch up on a few worksheets. He could do that just fine on his own. All he really needed was time.

* * *

11 days later.

After two wins in a row on back to back Fridays, though exhausted from the weekend, Kyler was excited to get on the field Monday morning. Everyone's spirits were high in hopes that they could go out with a bang their senior year. There was already premature talk of going to state.

"Not so fast, West," a booming voice called out before Kyler's cleat could even touch the field.

"Yeah, Coach?"

When Kyler turned around, he saw right away that something was wrong. It helped none that Coach Turner could barely look him in the eyes.

More quietly, "Go ahead and change back. Head on inside to the library and get some work done."

Kyler's stomach sank. He took several steps in the coach's direction so that they were less than an arm's length away, hoping that the rest of the team wouldn't hear what was being discussed.

"Coach, what's going on?"

"Grades were sent out to staff early this morning. Can you tell me why I'm a little pissed?"

Kyler sighed. He tried to give a little more effort in the direction of his English class, but *Hamlet* was one of the most boring things he had ever read. At least when they did *Romeo and Juliet* in sophomore year the teacher was nice enough to read along with them and explain what all those weird words meant. Not Mr. Hughes.

"It's only the middle of the first six weeks. You said Principal–"

"This is my call, not his," Coach Turner insisted, much to Kyler's shock. "It's still early in the season. We can make it without you. What I'm not going to do is risk losing the only person out there who can hit his men halfway into the season, or heaven forbid should we make state. Fix this now, West," Coach Turner demanded, the anger in his voice shaking Kyler to the core.

"Yes, sir," was all Kyler could manage in response.

Coach Turner wasn't done however. "Are things not working out with McCallister? I heard she can be a little tough when it comes to–"

"I told her I didn't need her help," Kyler quickly admitted.

Red flashed across Coach Turner's eyes. "You what?!"

Kyler could feel the eyes of some of the players on the field. At this point he welcomed the escape to the library.

"I went out of my way to go to both Hughes and Willis to see what we could do before you screwed up too badly, and this is how you repay me?"

"I thought I could handle it myself, but you know how difficult of a teacher Mr. Hughes is," Kyler replied, desperately hoping to deescalate the growing anger of an already fuming former linebacker.

"Kyler," Coach Turner began through gritted teeth. That's how Kyler knew he had had it. Coach never called him by his first name, others perhaps, but not him. "Four days," he said coldly.

"Excuse me?"

"Monday. Tuesday. Wednesday. Thursday. Four days," he repeated, this time holding up his hand with four fingers and shoving it in Kyler's face. "If I don't hear that something has changed come Friday, you're out for Friday's game."

Oddly, that gave Kyler a little bit of hope. He fully thought he was out for this week's upcoming game.

"You'll be at morning practice and last period after today, but that's it. After eighth period practice, you're done. The rest of the afternoon is for your studies. Got it?"

"Yes, sir," Kyler replied eagerly. For once he couldn't wait to get to the library. If he could turn in his missing assignments to Hughes, he'd be in the clear.

"Remember, I'll be checking in with McCallister about your progress first thing Friday," Coach Turner called out as he made his way onto the field.

Kyler's face went a ghostly white. He had to be kidding. Coach still expected him to use Lilah as a tutor? There wasn't a chance in hell that she would even speak to him after that day in the library.

CHAPTER 3

Kyler had managed to avoid his teammates both in class and during passing periods. Lunch, however, was one time he couldn't avoid them. He thought about sneaking off campus during lunch, despite the school's strict rules that under no circumstances were students allowed off property during school hours without guardian consent. That applied to even those such as himself who were already eighteen. Of course, there were special circumstances, but none of which benefited him.

"Hey, man," Miles greeted as he took his place next to Kyler at the table. "I tried texting you earlier."

"Sorry, my phone was on silent and I didn't have time between classes," Kyler lied.

Miles of course wasn't an idiot. "Whatever. I know something is up."

Miles was Kyler's best friend, followed by Gavin and Dawson; however, of the three, Miles knew him best.

"What happened this morning before practice? Don't think we didn't notice you bailing on us," Miles pressed on in a quiet voice so that Sean wouldn't hear. He knew that if it was anything serious, that was the last person on the team that needed to know anything.

Kyler decided to play his situation down at first. "Coach just got on me about my grades."

"That's not so bad," Gavin, who was on his other side chimed in. "He's been getting on me about that since freshman year," he laughed.

It was different for Gavin. Gavin simply liked to play football to play. He had been benched several times in the past. It didn't bother him too much. He had no desire to actually go to college on a football scholarship. In fact, lately he had been talking more along the lines of a technical school.

"No, he's not telling us everything," Miles hinted with a nudge in Kyler's side. The smile faded from his face when he got no reaction from Kyler.

Across from them, Dawson sat down and quickly pulled out his calculus notebook.

"Overachiever," Gavin teased, as he threw a fry.

Dawson simply brushed it off. "Real mature."

"Guys, shut up," Miles huffed. "Come on, Ky. What aren't you telling us?"

Kyler leaned into the table and the other three followed suit, creating a secluded bubble in a bustling jungle of chaos.

"Unless I make some major changes in Hughes' class, Coach is threatening to keep me from playing Friday."

They all gasped in shock as they processed.

Miles was the first to speak up. "Dude, that's crazy. That sucks! Cash is the backup. If he takes your spot, we all might as well sit on the bench."

"It's *Hamlet*," Gavin sighed. "I get half of my information online for each chapter. Not to mention my dad is a huge Mel Gibson fan." He made a gagging noise. "That movie was the worst."

Kyler refrained from pointing out that of the four of them, he was the only one who had the unfortunate placement into Mr. Hughes' class. His curriculum was completely different than the other senior English teachers. Sadly, Kyler also knew that they were acts and scenes, not chapters, yet between the two of them, Gavin was managing to pass.

He decided to tell them everything, Lilah McCallister included.

Their eyes all darted to a far-off table as soon as Kyler finished.

He watched her. From a distance, with her friends, a smile on her face that appeared very rarely, she looked like she could be a nice person.

"Dawson, why don't you be Kyler's wingman in English," Gavin suggested.

Dawson raised a brow. "First of all, that comment alone sounds stupid. Secondly, unlike Lilah, I'm not only in the honor society and football, but I'm in the technology club, math club, and future medical professionals club. Not to mention–"

"Okay," Miles interrupted. "We get it."

Eventually everyone, except for Kyler, went back to their regularly scheduled conversations. Kyler, however, found it difficult to focus, suddenly very aware of Lilah McCallister's presence.

* * *

"My vote, of course, was for *Sweeney Todd*. Watch the fall play be something stupid from middle school, like *Seussical*," Jolee ranted.

In a brief pause in conversation, Lilah heard her phone vibrate from her bag on the seat next to her. Though she was at lunch, she was mortified that she hadn't put it on silent for the day. It would have been so embarrassing if it would have gone off in a silent classroom during a quiz. She quickly reached for it to ensure that it would be on silent for the rest of the day, and in doing so, saw the message that had just appeared.

Unknown: Can you still meet today?

Lilah's brows crinkled at the ambiguity. She thought back to the prior week, but couldn't recall any meetings. She thought about not replying but finally informed the sender that they had the wrong number; however, glancing down at the screen from a second text, proved her wrong.

Unknown: Lilah McCallister?

Lilah was just about to say something about the strange message to her friends, but after seeing that they were deep in conversation about *Frankenstein*, Jolee from a play perspective and Alice from a scientific one, Lilah thought it best to let them debate and deal with the mysterious stranger behind the screen.

Lilah: Who is this?

Kyler watched her confusion from afar. Had he not needed her help that afternoon, he could have had a ton of fun with his newfound anonymity; however, he wouldn't make Lilah suffer past lunch.

Unknown: Wow. Did I fail to make any impression on you?

Lilah completely ignored the almost flirtatious way the text came across. For all she knew, it could be someone like Sarah playing a cruel prank.

Lilah: How did you get my number?

Unknown: You gave it to me.

Lilah laughed. That was absurd. She didn't give her number to anyone. She had a hard-enough time keeping up with Jolee and Alice when it came to socializing. She didn't need random classmates asking her what she was doing at ten at night simply because they were bored.

Lilah: You're a liar and I don't have time for any games. Please don't text this number again.

Unknown: You're so uptight.

Lilah had a few words that she wanted to say in response to the last text, but she was above that. Instead she opened her bag to place her now silent phone away, though curiously withdrew it when it lit up in the darkness between her books.

Unknown: Look up.

Lilah looked around their table. There was no one.

She casually glanced throughout the tables in the distance, noticing that everyone was buried in their own select cliques. It wasn't until she made her way down the football table that a set of blue eyes met hers. Even from far away she could tell that they were blue, but not only that, she remembered the cold and callous way they looked at her in the library not quite two weeks ago.

He had to be joking. He could not be asking for her help right now, not after how cocky he was, insisting that he could do it on his own, *especially* not needing her of all people, if she remembered the conversation correctly.

Kyler watched as Lilah angrily tapped her fingers over her phone. He forced himself not to laugh at how easily offended she got. Sure enough, not even thirty seconds later, he felt his phone go off.

Lilah: You have got to be kidding?! And how did you get my number?!

Kyler: Relax. It was on the laminated and color-coded schedule you gave me the other day.

Lilah: That was over a week ago, and you should throw that away.

Kyler: So, can you meet today?

Lilah: No!

Kyler sighed in frustration, aware that working with Lilah was no longer an option.

"That bad," Miles speculated, quickly reading the texts over Kyler's shoulder.

"She's pissed."

Just then the bell rang, and they all began gathering their things, Gavin scrounging up any food that hadn't been eaten on anyone's tray in hopes of scarfing it down on his way to his next class.

Ever the wisest, "You insulted her. I can't say I blame her."

"Seriously," Kyler gasped.

"Come on, Dawson. Who could say no to this adorable face," Miles teased as he pinched Kyler's cheeks, only to be swatted away instantly.

Dawson snorted as he neatly placed his calculus book back into the perfect place in his backpack. It was disturbing how organized he was. "Lilah isn't like...Well, someone like Sarah," he began.

"Dude," Gavin screeched. "Sarah is hot. I mean, head cheerleader, killer body."

"With a brain activity completely susceptible to Kyler's charisma," Dawson finished.

"So, what are you saying," Kyler asked, all joking aside.

"You really think you can just text her and she's going to come scampering to you like a wounded puppy? In no way does helping you benefit her, and no offense because you're my friend, but you were a little rude to her."

"She's the biggest snob in the school, and I'm the rude one?!"

"Regardless of that, she's the one on schedule for valedictorian, and she's the one Turner is talking to Friday," Dawson concluded.

Kyler knew Dawson was right. It didn't matter what he thought of Lilah. Right now, all that mattered was that she tell Turner that he was truly working hard and improving, and he had four afternoons to do that. All he had to do was convince her.

* * *

"Hey," Kyler quietly announced as he fell into step next to Lilah. Immediately after Dawson's words soaked in, he managed to make his way through the crowd to catch up to her, knowing that texting would no longer work, and needing her to agree to help him as soon as possible. "Can I talk to you a second," he asked when she gave no greeting back.

"I'm on my way to class."

"Aren't we all," he scoffed.

Lilah picked up her pace and went around a couple sauntering along in front of her. Kyler quickly realized his mistake and caught up to her.

"Okay, sorry about that, but seriously, can we talk?"

"Fine, talk."

Lilah was stunned when Kyler gently pulled her from the crowded hallway and into the nook of a classroom. The door was closed and the lights were off, which meant the next period was an off period. At least there wouldn't be a line of students surrounding them waiting to get into the room.

"Excuse you," Lilah spat.

Kyler glanced around at the passing students, growing fewer and fewer as the seconds ticked by before the tardy bell.

"I just thought the hall was a little loud to–"

"Wrong," Lilah interrupted. "You didn't want to be seen talking to me, or should I say begging me to help you with your ridiculous English grade."

They both knew she was right. While Lilah wasn't the typical looking nerd, she and Kyler were definitely in different circles when it came to the social ladder.

"Fine, whatever." He didn't have time to get into a lengthy explanation, including the fact that he really didn't want to be seen with her. However, judging from the way she was looking at him, the feeling was probably mutual. "Can you help me out?"

"I already told you, no," Lilah nearly shouted.

She turned to leave but Kyler put his arm on the wall in front of her, blocking her in the small area leading to the classroom behind her. It was in no way threatening, but somehow it shook Lilah, disarming her completely, as Kyler stepped into her bubble.

"Look, meet with me this afternoon. I'll apologize and everything."

Lilah saw right through the innocent look in the face that was far too close to her liking.

"No. Sorry," she insisted.

Kyler glared at her. Neither of them moved, only stared each other down as if it were a contest.

"Why," he found himself asking.

Lilah was actually glad that he asked that. Now she could set him straight. "Because, you're a jerk. I know guys like you. You think the word tutor means that I'll do all your work for you, simply because you're some fancy idol in the school. Well, you're wrong, and your charms won't convince me any differently."

At that, Lilah slipped past Kyler on the other side, the side he hadn't blocked with his outstretched arm. Much to her surprise, he willingly let her, not having another word to say on the matter.

She had never been late to class, but there was a first for everything, and upon glancing at one of the many digital clocks that adorned the hallways, today was that day.

"You think I'm charming," a soft and deep voice from behind casually asked.

Lilah huffed. Completely ignoring the question, although realizing the embarrassment that crept along her skin, "Are you following me now?"

"You really need to relax. No, I'm not following you. I have criminal justice next."

Lilah shot him a strange look as he now walked beside her.

"I needed a few lighter electives for senior year. We basically watch documentaries on serial killers," he admitted.

"You do realize that we can continue to our respective classes in silence," Lilah coldly responded.

Kyler rolled his eyes and took a deep breath. He had hoped to at least get some sort of confirmation on Lilah's part, but it looked like he'd be spending Monday afternoon on his own, starting *Hamlet* from the beginning.

"Mr. West and Miss McCallister," a voice called from behind, causing both to stop and turn.

Principal Willis stood a few yards before them in the now empty hallway. He glanced up at the nearest clock and shook his head. He began reaching in his pocket, no doubt for detention slips for being caught in the hallway minutes after the tardy bell.

Lilah was beyond infuriated with Kyler for keeping her for so long, but utterly shocked when he spoke up.

"I'm sorry, Principal Willis. Lilah was helping me catch up with all those assignments and by the time the bell rang we had a lot of packing up to do," Kyler smoothly began.

Principal Willis looked slightly surprised. "Then the tutoring is going well," he asked, directing his question to Lilah.

Lilah momentarily glanced at the concocting presence beside her, a satisfactory smirk plastered across his face that some might easily mistake for a sincere smile.

"Yes, sir. It's taking him a while to grasp the concepts, but no doubt he can improve with my help." She couldn't help it, she had to take a dig at Kyler where she could.

Though Principal Willis appeared skeptical, he let it go and reached into a different pocket. He quickly scribbled his initials on two green passes, tardy passes, that would get them into their next classes without grief from the teacher. He handed one to each of the students before him.

"Try not to make it a habit. Work on your time management in the future." He then turned and went back down the hall in the opposite direction.

Kyler and Lilah set back off in silence. Lilah's business class was first, Kyler's criminal justice class being slightly farther down and across the hall. There was an awkwardness once Lilah reached the room but didn't immediately go in. Kyler, on the other hand, slowed his steps and lingered a little longer than he should have.

Lilah let out a deep breath and sank into the wall behind her. "Thanks for that, with Willis," she clarified.

Kyler slightly nodded but didn't say anything, only watched as the girl before him seemed to battle an internal mess somewhere deep within.

"Fine," she sighed.

Kyler raised a brow for her to continue. It appeared that talking to him was the most difficult thing in the world for her at the moment.

Without giving any explanation, "I can do the public library at five. Don't be late, and don't waste my time."

Before the words had a chance to sink in for Kyler, Lilah quickly turned and slipped into the classroom behind her, leaving him alone in the empty hall.

A sincere smile spread across his face as he turned and made his way the short distance to his room.

CHAPTER 4

Lilah was shocked when she walked around one of the bookshelves to her preferred area to find Kyler already there and unpacking a few things from his bag.

He glanced up to meet her eyes, somehow sensing her presence immediately. "You look like you've seen a ghost," he laughed, already aware as to what she must be thinking.

He had to be on his best behavior, at least for the next few days, after that he was uncertain. Surely, he didn't actually need a tutor the entire season.

Lilah noticed things. The Kyler before her seemed different than what she was used to. Given, they had spoken more today than they ever had, but something about him seemed off, and she wasn't going to be taken for a fool.

She tossed her bag on one chair and sat in another directly across from Kyler.

When he looked up again, he was knocked off his feet, except for the fact that he was sitting down. She was glaring at him. She had her arms crossed and she was actually glaring at him. He couldn't imagine what he could have done in one statement to offend her so badly.

Before Kyler opened his mouth, "Cut the act."

His jaw dropped, not believing what was happening. Was he really that transparent?

"You're here early. You're forcing yourself to be nice. You're freshly showered," Lilah began.

"First of all, eighth period is athletics. I showered to spare you," he insisted. Then, just in hopes of rubbing her the wrong way, "And I may or may not have a date after this. So, shall we get started?"

There was that cocky grin again. Lilah had never wanted to slap it off his face more. He acted like he needed so badly to focus on his studies, yet here he was, desperately trying to finish up so he could go on a date. Unbelievable, and yet, exactly as she expected.

"Not until you tell me what's your deal," Lilah insisted.

If he were to be honest, he never did think that Lilah was like most of the girls he was used to. Looks and money aside, she was smart, absolutely brilliant. Of course, he'd never tell her that.

"Honestly?"

Her pursed lips were all the confirmation he needed.

"Apparently Coach Turner went out of his way trying to get me help, and he was livid that I turned you away." Lilah didn't seem to care at all as to what he was telling her, and why should she? "I have until Friday morning to make some sort of progress to show that I'll have a passing grade for the first report card in three weeks."

"I thought you could do all that on your own," Lilah spat. "Why do you need my help all of a sudden?"

Kyler hated how smart she was. Any other girl would be thankful to be spending time around him. He thought of all the lies he could tell, but quickly realized when it came to Lilah, the only way was going to be to shoot it straight.

"Coach is going to talk to you Friday morning about how I'm progressing. He'll probably talk to Hughes as well, but I doubt that he'll have all my assignments graded by–"

"I knew it," Lilah interrupted, more loudly than intended. She briefly sank back in her chair, a bit embarrassed by her outburst.

"Yeah, fine," Kyler admitted as he threw up his hands. At least he didn't have to pretend about anything anymore.

Lilah shook her head and quietly laughed. "And what? You thought you'd come here a few days, be nice, act like you're interested in anything I have to say, maybe flirt a little, thinking that I'd turn to a puddle of goo and give your coach a stellar report?"

"I never have, nor do I ever intend to flirt with you," Kyler scoffed in disgust.

Lilah shook her head, a smile of confidence still plastered to her face. She placed her hands on the table and rose from her seat. She reached for her bag with one hand when she felt the strangest and most unknown feeling singe through the one still on the table steadying herself.

"Wait," was the only word Kyler managed to get out as he instinctively reached for her.

He only meant to stop her from leaving, but something about her skin beneath the palm of his hand stopped any thoughts he had. A tingling sensation ran from his hand up his arm.

As if in unison, they both glanced down at the contact. A moment that may as well have been an eternity passed. Neither knew which pulled away first, but a second more and both of their hands were gone from the table. A brief silence followed, Lilah's bag dangling from her other hand, though she hadn't taken a step in the way of departing.

"What," she asked, more softly than she wanted.

"What?"

Lilah narrowed her eyes, noticing that Kyler had momentarily lost his confidence. "You're the one who said to wait. I thought we were done."

Kyler scrambled for a response. "No. You got an attitude after I told you the truth." There it was. He was back.

Realizing that they were going nowhere, Lilah cut to the chase. "Do you actually want me to tutor you, or do you just need me to tell your coach something nice come Friday?"

While the correct answer should have been both, "I'd really like it if you could help get me through this." He couldn't help but add, "Just until Friday."

Deep down, Lilah still doubted him, but if he knew even the slightest bit about her, he should know that no matter what he did or said, she would be telling his coach the absolute truth Friday.

* * *

Around 6:40, an alarm on Kyler's phone went off, interrupting a strangely productive but exhausting session. He quickly silenced it, but was painfully aware how long they had been going over the first act. Lilah had helped him complete two of the worksheets that went with it, and prior to the interruption, they were about to start on the third.

"I'm sorry," he sincerely apologized. "I didn't realize the time. I have to be getting out of here."

Lilah rubbed her eyes and yawned. After nearly two hours, she could use a break from the pages of black and white.

"Same thing tomorrow," Kyler asked.

Lilah ached as she rose from her seat. Generally, when she came to the library, she preferred to study on the couches near the windows, unless her studies required the use of a table. She wasn't quite sure why, but studying on a couch with Kyler didn't seem like the best idea.

"Sure," was all she said as she reached for her things.

Lilah left before he could say anything else on the matter. She and Kyler were not friends, and she didn't want to give him any indication that they would ever be.

The phone only rang twice before Antonio answered.

"Hey, Antonio. I'm done at the library. Can you pick me up," Lilah asked.

"I'm sorry, Miss Lilah. Shortly after I dropped you off, your father got a call for an emergency meeting out-of-town, in the city."

"So, what am I supposed to do?"

Antonio paused for a moment. When he was hired as Steven McCallister's driver, he was unaware that there were three, now two, children that would be using him as a shuttle service to and from school activities.

"I believe your brother is at a neighbor's or friend's, so I'm not sure if your mother..."

Lilah stopped listening as soon as he informed her of her brother's whereabouts. Of course, that meant that her mother wouldn't be home. There was no point in even calling her.

"It's okay, Antonio. I'll find another way home. Thanks."

Lilah was startled by the presence making its way down the library steps as she closed out her call.

"Boyfriend?"

"Eavesdrop much," she hissed.

Lilah immediately went to a group conversation with Jolee and Alice in hopes that one of them would be able to give her a ride home, but stopped before sending the message. She knew right away that Jolee was at a theater function.

She could always just walk home. It would easily take half an hour or better, but there was still plenty of daylight.

Her thoughts were soon interrupted.

"Do you need a ride," Kyler sighed in annoyance.

Lilah's facial expression was enough of an answer. Her eyes nearly fell from their sockets at the suggestion.

He didn't have time to entertain her any longer. "Fine. I'll see you tomorrow." He then pulled his bag over his shoulder and started back down the few remaining steps.

This was going to take everything in her, but as of right now, she could think of no definite and dependable way of getting home. "Okay, yes," she shouted out.

Kyler dreaded those words. He glanced down at the time on his phone. There was no doubt that he'd be late.

CHAPTER 5

For the most part, the short ride had gone in silence, the longest amount of talking being that of Kyler teasing Lilah for being seventeen and not having a driver's license.

Lilah was surprised to find her mother's car in the driveway as she walked from the gated entry; however, when she opened the door, she knew that wouldn't last long.

No sooner than she closed the door, Lilah glanced up the staircase, her mother in a dress she had never seen before, rushing down.

"Sweetheart, how was school? You're home early," Jenna squealed excitedly, though Lilah felt some of the emotion was lacking.

"It's already 7," Lilah pointed out.

Jenna gasped. "Oh dear, then I'm running late."

"Dinner with your girl friends?"

Jenna stopped rummaging through her purse for a second and kissed Lilah on the forehead as she continued to make her way to the door. Completely ignoring Lilah's question, "I should be home before 11. See to it that your brother turns off the video games by 9."

That was it. Just like that her mother was gone. At first it hadn't been as frequent, but it seemed like she had plans nearly every night now, and none of them included Lilah or her brother.

* * *

"So you're seeing him every single day after school now," Alice slowly asked as she sipped on her chocolate milk.

Lilah quickly swallowed her bite of lunch so that she could correct Alice before she got any absurd ideas. "Just through Thursday, so only three more days."

"How was it," Alice asked excitedly, to which Jolee groaned in pain.

"I mean, it's *Hamlet* so–"

Alice interrupted with a huff. "Stop it. You know what I mean. What's it like being one-on-one with Kyler West?"

Lilah shrugged. "I don't really know. We got through two worksheets, so at least he has some level of comprehension."

"That's it? That's all you've got?"

Lilah made a barely audible noise, desperately wanting to stop any talk of Kyler or the tutoring. She had to give him credit, he had tried. For most people, especially people her age, Shakespeare wasn't the easiest of readings. While she preferred her texts to contain some amount of depth, for the most part if she saw girls her age with an actual book, it was usually about brooding vampires.

After the mentioning of Kyler, Lilah couldn't help but glance over at the table where he and most of the other players ate. Today several of the cheerleaders had joined them. Everyone seemed to be in high spirits, laughing and joking, except for Dawson. Dawson had his head buried in a large textbook.

She rolled her eyes when she got to Kyler. Leaning on his shoulder was none other than Sarah. Lilah had to find humor in it. It was such a cliché. The quarterback and cheerleader.

It was at that moment that Kyler's attention was lost on whatever Miles was talking about and he met a pair of green eyes across the room. They held no emotion other than perhaps a little humor, but just as soon as he looked up, her eyes furrowed and returned to the two girls in front of her.

Kyler clenched and unclenched his left hand. Something still ran through his skin after the previous afternoon, something he couldn't quite place.

* * *

As Lilah headed to her honor society meeting right after school that Thursday, she was a little disappointed when she thought about what she'd have to tell Coach Turner. Monday started off a little rocky with Kyler, but the last two days it appeared that he was sincerely trying. He was easy to read; she could tell when he was turning on the charm to get his way, but it hadn't been like that. While he still made rude comments and rubbed her the wrong way, for the most part he was strictly business from 5:00 until when their sessions concluded, which generally happened when his alarm went off at 6:40. Although Kyler was still behind by a few assignments, he had two weeks before the first report card went out, and Lilah had no doubt that he'd be passing enough to play.

A voice startled Lilah, awakening her from her thoughts of her last tutoring session with Kyler and her conversation with Coach Turner the following morning.

"Is this seat taken?"

Lilah was a little speechless when she looked up to see Simon towering over her. He was like a Greek god of academics. His jet-black hair was never out of place, always sporting a fresh cut. His outfits looked like something picked out of a men's magazine. What did it most of all for Lilah were the glasses. Something about them didn't make him look nerdy at all. Instead he looked refined and educated. He was like a male version of Lilah, but with a better personality.

Lilah moved her bag that she had placed on the empty chair next to her. "No, not at all."

Simon sat down and tapped at his phone before the meeting started. Lilah glanced at hers to check the time and noticed a message.

Kyler: How late can you stay tonight?

Lilah: Why are you asking?

Kyler: I don't have plans, so I was hoping you could catch me up with the rest of my assignments.

Lilah groaned at the idea. Two hours was long enough. Did he not think that she had a life?

Lilah: I'll have to see. I might have plans.

Kyler: Yeah, right. Antonio can wait.

Lilah was furious by his assumption. Since he overheard her conversation on Monday, he had already teased her more than once about Antonio. She hadn't bothered to tell him the truth. Kyler had called her a snob twice that she could remember. She didn't want to parade around the fact that she used her daddy's driver to get around.

Before she could get a chance to respond, "Did you sign up for any of your volunteer work?"

Oddly, Lilah looked around to make sure that Simon was addressing her and not someone else.

"No, I guess I'll do that after the meeting today," Lilah admitted, already knowing that Simon probably had his volunteer days covered for the entire semester.

"Same here."

Lilah would have said more, but just then the meeting started. Actual conversation with Simon and virtual conversation with Kyler would both have to wait.

For once, Lilah didn't care to ask a million questions like she generally did. Ever since Kyler beat her to the library that first day, she was determined to always be there first. As soon as the meeting ended, she intended to rush to the signup board for her required hours for the first six weeks; however, Sophie had different plans. She continued with question after question, infuriating not only Lilah, but the sponsors as well.

Lilah was saddened when she saw that there were still a few openings for the animal shelter. Every year it had been a place she desperately wanted to volunteer at, but she knew leaving would break her heart. She and her siblings had begged their parents for a dog for years to no avail. It would kill her to go there, fall in love, only to be disappointed at having to say goodbye.

Instead, Lilah scribbled her name down for a slot at the hospital's gift shop. Generally, it was run by retired women that simply needed to get out of the house, but last year they had partnered up with the school, allowing for several weekends set aside for student volunteers.

* * *

"You're late," Kyler grumbled, not bothering to look up from his work.

"I had a meeting."

Kyler raised a seductive eyebrow full of insinuations.

"For the honor society," Lilah pointed out, though she owed him no explanation.

Going back to the pages before him, "You never answered my question."

"We should be able to accomplish enough in the two hours, especially if you take all your rudeness and criticism and put that energy into your work."

Kyler dropped his pen and stared Lilah down, not saying a word. His face held no emotion, which was unnerving to Lilah. She couldn't tell what he might be thinking.

She finally snapped. "Let me guess, you don't have a date tonight, so you want to suck the life out of me? Believe it or not, I have better things to do besides help you on something you messed up to begin with."

Kyler shook his head. "You really are a narcissistic brat."

Somehow, that comment stung a little more this time, but Lilah didn't allow him to see how his words affected her.

Shortly after that, they fell into common ground, the insults disappearing, and the only talk being that of *Hamlet*. It wasn't until Kyler bothered looking out the nearby windows that he saw that daylight had faded. He was quite surprised that Lilah had not complained so far. He wondered how long she would stay there with him. Regardless what he might think of her, he didn't intend to put her through anymore.

The few times their eyes had met in conversation, he could see the tiredness washing over hers.

He cleared his throat in the silence. "I think that should do it."

"Are you sure? This is our last session."

Something about that was a little disappointing to hear. "Yeah. I just have to find time to focus on this, as well as my other classes, and not screw up in the next two weeks."

As they began to gather their things, Lilah checked her phone. Kyler had no idea why she continued to keep it silenced after school was out. Upon reading something, her brows furrowed, and she took in a silent deep breath.

"Everything okay," Kyler found himself asking.

Maybe it was the tiredness, but Lilah didn't have a snarky comment in her. "Yeah...no, not really." She sighed before continuing. "Apparently, I was supposed to take Rover to the park, although my mother forgot to tell me that. She had a thing to go to tonight, and now I need to stop at the neighbors to bring him home."

Kyler hesitated. "He can't stay home alone for a few hours."

"He could. She's just over-protective of him," Lilah told Kyler as they began making their way to the exit doors. "He's too smart for his own good. There's no telling what all he'd get into if left alone."

"What kind is he?"

Lilah's steps faltered and she shot Kyler a look of disgust. "Kind?"

"Breed. Whatever," he clarified.

Lilah didn't answer as they approached the door. Kyler exited first, and much to her surprise held it open for her. It didn't help. She was still annoyed.

"Why do you look so cranky all of a sudden," he pointed out.

"Rover is not a dog! He's my little brother," she screamed, as if he should have known that.

Kyler's jaw dropped. Who in the world named a kid Rover?

He tried to begin an apology but a ding from Lilah's phone, that she must have only recently turned the volume up on, came through and interrupted.

Another deep and frustrating breath came from her. This time her eyes clenched shut and her nose wrinkled up in disgust.

Before Kyler could inquire as to what was wrong, "Can I get a ride home?"

Kyler tried to hide his amusement. That had to have been the hardest thing in the world for her to ask. There were so many ways he could have teased her or pushed her buttons, but for some reason, he didn't feel like it, at least not tonight.

"Sure." As they made their way to his truck, "Do you want me to stop somewhere to get you and your brother supper?"

Lilah laughed.

Kyler took offense. "What's that for?"

"I know what you're doing," she said with narrowed eyes as she approached his passenger door.

He took a step closer, slightly throwing her off. "And what is that?"

Though his presence was closer than she would have liked, Lilah quickly recovered from the initial surprise of having him near. "You're trying to be nice because you know that I have to talk to your coach tomorrow."

"Actually, for the last hour I've listened to your stomach make noises like it's about to give birth to a monster. I figured you might be hungry, and if your parents aren't home, you might not have a hot meal waiting for you."

Lilah held her breath as Kyler stepped even closer. She could smell whatever body wash he had showered with after football practice. It sent chills through her that she desperately wanted to stop. She nearly fell into his truck when his arm reached out and she forced herself to take a step back.

When she awoke from whatever hellish daze she had allowed herself to fall into, Kyler stood there, the passenger door open, waiting for her to get in. "That's fine though," he concluded. "Believe what you want."

The drive was awkward this time, maybe not for Kyler, but definitely for Lilah. She had to shake the feeling, the idea. Kyler was just trying to get into her head before she talked to his coach. Offering to get her dinner, or supper as he called it, opening her door, taking her home without one rude comment, it was all a game to him to get what he needed. The sad thing about it all, she had absolutely no reason to give his coach a bad report, aside from the fact that she disliked Kyler. He had genuinely tried the last few days. Would he continue after this week? Who could say.

CHAPTER 6

Lilah fully intended to wait until the end of the day before talking to Coach Turner; however, after she checked her school email Thursday night, she knew that wasn't an option. Therefore, Friday morning, Lilah woke a little earlier than usual. She wanted to be sure to talk with Coach Turner during the team's morning practice in hopes that Kyler would see, and she could make him suffer just a little bit at not knowing.

As Lilah arrived at the field, she spotted Coach Turner instantly on the sidelines. He was quite hard to miss. He still looked every bit like the player that he was in his glory days.

"Damn," Gavin hissed, disrupting the concentration of a few players.

Kyler was annoyed at their lack of focus, but upon looking up, found what they were so distracted by.

In the golden early morning sunlight, walking along the track outlining the field, was the one person who could make or break his day. The way the light shined on her shoulder length chestnut hair, made it appear redder than he was used to seeing in the florescent lights of the library. She didn't dress like most of the girls he knew either. She wore a long-sleeved pink dress shirt, buttoned all the way to the neck, adorned with some frilly and girly bowtie, which was then paired with a skirt that flared just a pinch. It was short enough to highlight her legs, but still long enough to pass the school's fingertip test. Though she was in the distance, with each step she took, Kyler was certain that he could hear every click of her tiny heels.

"She's so hot for a nerd," Sean acknowledged. "Too bad evil runs through every bone in her body."

"Whatever," Gavin scoffed. "Nothing about her is nerdy." He completely ignored the evil part.

As if to back up his master, "She always has her head buried in a book. That's a nerd," Louis pointed out.

"I wonder what she's doing here, and talking to Coach," Sean speculated.

"Do I need to break out the nail polish and tea sets, or are we going to run the next play," Kyler asked with more than a hint of annoyance.

"Right, I forgot, you only have eyes for Sarah," Sean teased.

That was the furthest thing from the truth, but Kyler let it slide, especially if it meant that everyone could get back to playing and stop drooling over Lilah. He didn't care if they did, just not during practice.

* * *

"When I said first thing in the morning, this isn't what I had in mind," Coach Turner began.

"I needed to get here early anyway," Lilah lied. "So, I figured why not."

"You do realize that you're throwing my boys off their game..."

Lilah finally looked to the mass of blue and black on the field. She watched as the ball flew from Kyler's hand, missing whoever he was throwing to by a good three feet.

"I'll be honest," Lilah began very bluntly. Coach Turner recognized the same fire that he had seen a couple weeks ago in Principal Willis' office. "It was my intention to make Kyler squirm a little from this conversation."

Coach Turner gave a deep and hearty laugh. "I'd say you're doing a decent job then." He soon turned serious, not liking his time to be wasted. "Mr. Hughes told me that Kyler has gradually handed in a few of his missing assignments over the last few days. While he hasn't graded them, he said the quality looked to be quite good," he began.

"Yesterday was a little exhausting, but he should almost be caught up with the first two to three weeks of assignments."

"And he did all the work, not–"

Lilah interrupted Coach Turner before he could insinuate what she knew he was going to. "I couldn't care less if Kyler plays or not. I have never, and will never, do someone's work for them." She took a deep breath and continued. "As much as I'd love to tell you that he's every bit the slacker that I imagined, I can't. He actually put time and effort into his assignments and trying to learn the material."

"That's good to hear. In the past his grades have been some of the best on the team, but I guess that whole senior year not caring attitude gets the best of everyone," Turner speculated, but swallowed heavily as he saw the look of shock and disgust on Lilah's face. Of course, he shouldn't have said that to someone like Lilah McCallister. He cleared his throat. "Well, thank you for helping him out up until this point."

Lilah knew what that meant. She remembered the conversation in Principal Willis' office; however, ultimately it was on Kyler's terms, and Kyler insisted that he wouldn't need her services after Thursday. It didn't matter, she could still put tutoring down as an extracurricular.

Lilah stopped and turned back moments after she took a few steps toward the track. "Oh, Coach Turner?"

He grunted in acknowledgement.

"Could you do me a favor and not tell him that I said any of that," she asked nervously. When she received a skeptical look, "His ego is big enough, I don't think it could handle it."

Turner laughed, so loud that as the players set up for the next play, they definitely heard him. "Have a good day, Miss McCallister."

* * *

"West! Stop hovering and get in my office before you're late!"

Kyler quickly said his goodbyes to Miles, Gavin, and Dawson, who were just as anxious as he was about what was happening when it came to the game that night.

Coach Turner closed the office door and got straight to the point, not even allowing Kyler to take a seat.

"I know you saw your friend pay a visit this–"

"She's not my friend," Kyler interrupted, feeling the need to clarify.

Coach Turner grunted, but continued. "Anyway, you'll be on the field tonight," he said very nonchalantly.

Bells, whistles, fireworks, bombs, all those things exploded when Kyler heard that statement. He had to be sure he heard correctly. "Really? Are you serious?"

"Get to first period. The last thing you need is detention," Turner huffed.

Just as Kyler turned to leave, a never-ending smile plastered across his face, "What made you change your mind? What did she say?"

"So now you're one of those gossipy cheerleaders? Mind your own business and get out of here," Coach insisted, though his tone wasn't as sharp as his choice of wording.

Kyler was ecstatic when he left the locker room. As long as he kept up with the assignments and the quality was above seventy percent, he'd be good. As bad as it was to admit it, if it weren't for Lilah, he probably wouldn't be playing.

"What," an annoyed voice answered on the second ring.

"Well, someone got up on the wrong side of the bed," Kyler teased.

"Shouldn't you be in class," Krista speculated.

"Yeah, yeah. I'm headed there now. I just wanted to ask, what time do you go in to work?"

"Ten. Thankfully the news shows that traffic into the city is pretty mild today," she began.

"Yeah, that's great, but I don't have much time."

Krista huffed, already knowing her brother needed something. Although once he asked for the requested favor, she was a bit taken aback.

"That's…weird…"

"Come on. I can't leave the premises. I'll explain later," he begged.

"Fine. For a week, when I cook, you don't complain about the doing the dishes," Krista bartered.

"That's crap. You're going to use every dish in the kitchen!"

Krista stopped him. "No complaints."

"Fine," Kyler groaned as he ended the call.

* * *

Lilah was getting out the teal spiral and mechanical pencil to begin taking notes for calculus when she happened to notice the bright light inside her bag. She had just said goodbye to one of her friends, the other was in calculus with her, and she very rarely got messages from her parents throughout the day. The tardy bell had yet to ring so she curiously grabbed the device, shocked by what she saw on the screen.

Kyler: Can you meet me at the beginning of lunch?

To say that she was confused was putting it mildly. As of this morning, she was done with Kyler West. Not only that, but what he was suggesting was a strange request.

Lilah: Why?

Kyler: The bell is about to ring. Can you?

Lilah didn't think, only responded.

Lilah: Fine!

Kyler: Awesome. Not in the lunch room. Fountain past the gardens.

Lilah threw her phone in her bag just as the bell rang, and like clockwork, the teacher began running through the roster.

Of course, Kyler wouldn't want to meet anywhere near his friends. The gardens were just past the outdoor eating area of bistro sets and picnic tables.

There was a fountain in the middle with the school's mascot. It was a bear standing on its hind legs with water shooting from its claws.

Generally, the only groups that hung around outside for lunch were the ones who didn't want to be in school in the first place or the nature club members.

Overall, most everyone stayed inside during lunch. At least meeting Kyler at the fountain meant that his friends, nor Lilah's, could give them a hard time; although, somehow Lilah thought that Kyler might catch the worst of it, what with needing a tutor and all.

* * *

He wasn't nervous. He had no reason to be nervous. At least that's what he told himself. He looked down at the kraft box tied up with red and gold ribbons. It was the nice thing to do. Even his mother would have told him that much. He thought about running the idea by her first, but as a general surgeon, he was sure she had more pressing matters that morning.

Lilah always had some pep in her step, always preferring to get to where she needed to be sooner rather than later. When the senior lunch bell rang, she made an exception. She wouldn't say that she was nervous, more like confused, extremely confused.

Kyler watched as she exited the doors near the patio area. She was hard to miss, something about the way she dressed and the way she carried herself. The worst part was, she knew that, and she acted like that made her better than everyone else.

He took a deep breath and shook his head. He had to be crazy.

"Hey," Lilah acknowledged once she was within talking distance.

She quickly noticed the box next to Kyler along the side of the fountain. She clasped her hands in front of her and shifted her weight, unsure if she needed to sit down for whatever he needed to say. He answered her without answering when he stood.

"Here," he said plainly, handing her the box.

She took it, looking at it for a second, and then bringing her eyes up to meet his. "What is it?"

"It's a cupcake."

Her face clenched and her eyes dropped back down to the box. She had never received any gifts from the opposite sex, unless of course she could count her father. Even then, he usually hired someone to buy birthday and Christmas gifts for her and her siblings. This was strange because it was for neither occasion.

When her nose crinkled a little too much for his liking, "Do you not like cupcakes?"

"I just don't eat them," Lilah admitted.

"What?!"

Lilah glared at him. He was looking at her like she was a monster. "My mother doesn't keep any sweets in the house. I guess I've gotten accustomed to the food she has prepared, and I generally don't eat sweets," she admitted, as though it were completely normal for a seventeen-year-old to not eat cupcakes.

"Prepared," Kyler asked, drawing out the word.

He watched as red crept to her cheeks and he couldn't help but feel a little bad for her.

"Someone prepares most of–"

He cut her off. "Your family has a private chef."

"You don't have to say it like that," she spat.

He didn't mean to offend her but the whole notion was a little outrageous. Then he remembered where they lived, and when it came to Raymere Grove, the McCallister's might as well own the town. They probably could if they wanted.

"If you don't want it, just throw it away," he carelessly told her.

"No," she gasped. "I want it...but...I don't understand."

Kyler had lost track of what he was supposed to say. He was taken off-guard by the fact that she didn't eat sweets and had a chef.

"Right. It's a thank you."

Lilah looked at him in shock and softly repeated the words to herself.

"Yeah, like, thanks for tutoring me this week. Also, thanks for whatever you said to Coach. He's letting me play tonight."

The faintest drop of excitement ran through Lilah. She didn't know squat about football. Her father never had time to waste on *three hours' worth of commercials* as he called it. All she did know was that it was a big deal for most of Raymere's citizens. She just didn't understand what about it made the players at the school seemingly gods in everyone's eyes. It's not like any of them would find a cure for a rare disease in their lifetime.

Trying not to be bitter after receiving a gift, "That's great." Sensing a growing awkwardness, Lilah figured that she needed to be leaving. "Well, thanks for this," she said, delicately holding up the box. "You didn't have to."

Just as she turned to leave, Kyler stopped her.

"Actually, that's not it," he sheepishly admitted.

Lilah turned back to meet him. A guilty look was plastered across his face. He rubbed the back of his neck in frustration, failing to make eye contact with her.

"I was wondering if you could help me through the season, like originally planned."

Lilah thought she might faint. Never in a million years did she see that one coming. She opened her mouth to speak but couldn't find the words.

"It wouldn't have to be every day now that I'm kind of caught up. Maybe just two or three times a week," he continued.

She couldn't believe it. "You're serious?"

He groaned and rolled his eyes. This felt like the low point of his senior year, practically begging Lilah McCallister to be his tutor. "Yes. I was in Hughes' class this morning, and...You explain everything really well. I guess I hadn't realized that until I truly paid attention." Admitting that felt like swallowing vomit.

Something about her changed. He watched as her cheeks lit up a rosy pink and she bit down on her lip in contemplation. For the briefest of seconds, he thought it was cute. He shook the idea immediately, but had to ask himself one question. Had he just complimented her? Most girls wouldn't take that statement as meaning a whole lot, but maybe in Lilah's world it did.

"I'll think about it," she finally said.

She didn't want to appear eager. She wasn't. She was the one giving up her time for no reason at all, aside from the fact that Principal Willis had asked and that she'd get a few letters out of it all. That was it.

"Sounds fair."

Lilah then turned to leave again. She didn't expect Kyler to leave with her. He wouldn't want to be seen with her, nor she with him. They were in completely different social circles, and it would forever stay that way.

"Hey," he called out, stopping her one last time.

She didn't fully turn, only enough to make eye contact with him. With the distance between them, he couldn't have much left to say.

"Are you and your friends coming to the game?"

If he expected any change in Lilah, he got his answer soon enough with the sinister, snarky, snobbish laugh that fell from her lips.

"Not a chance!"

* * *

"Whoa," Alice gasped as she leaned over the table to investigate the box. "I haven't had a Petal Pastries cupcake in forever. What made your dad send that today?"

"I don't know. I guess he feels bad. He's been working a lot more than usual lately," Lilah partially lied.

Lilah stared down at the contents in the box. It was almost too beautiful to eat. It was obviously a chocolate cupcake. Lilah couldn't remember the last time she had chocolate cake. It was topped with a red rose made of buttercream. Lilah didn't know that's what it was made of, but apparently Alice did. Then, just to add something more to it, there were bits of gold sprinkles all over.

"Well! Are you going to stare at it or eat it?!"

Lilah momentarily glanced up, hoping that Kyler wasn't watching. He wasn't. He and his friends were preoccupied with Sarah, Britt, and Abby. The cheer trio from hell.

Lilah was surprised and reached for a napkin as soon as she bit into the monstrosity.

"What kind of filling," Alice quickly asked.

"Your obsession over a cupcake is bordering on manic," Jolee pointed out.

"Strawberry," Lilah mumbled through a mouthful of deliciousness.

Why in the world did her mother ever decide to give this up? It was so moist. Sweet but not too sweet. It was the most enchanting and intoxicating surprise in her mouth. She hadn't realized until then how much she missed dessert.

＊ ＊ ＊

"What's so funny," Sarah asked with a nudge.

Kyler quickly diverted his attention from Lilah's table. It seemed with Sarah's little bit of contact she had scooted closer, leaving Kyler feeling claustrophobic between her and Miles. It didn't help that her perfume was overpowering to the point that he could no longer enjoy his spaghetti, not that school spaghetti had anything on his sister's anyway. Seriously though, he could deal with fruity, even floral, but whatever she had on smelled like walking through the perfume section of a department store. It was too much.

"Nothing."

CHAPTER 7

The weekend seemed to drag on for Lilah. Jolee was going to a play in the city with her parents; whereas Alice preferred to sleep in and play video games. The same went for Rover. Lilah asked him numerous times to go to the park, but apparently he had timed raids with his group of online friends. Whatever that meant.

Lilah's parents were a different story. Her father had a routine for the most part. Saturday he stayed in his office working while on Sunday he gave himself a break and went golfing. Her mother on the other hand went to brunch with the girls and shopping. She had asked Lilah to come, but after emphasizing that Rover would be left alone and she'd have to take him to a friend's, Lilah got the hint and declined the offer. Asking her to hang out made her mother feel good, but Lilah could tell that her mother didn't really want her around. That didn't stop Jenna from bringing home bags of much unneeded designer clothing for Lilah.

Lilah sorted through some of the pieces. Her mother insisted that at her age she needed to start showing off her assets. Lilah didn't like the idea and found that the new batch of clothes that her mother bought for her were a little revealing and possible flags when it came to school dress code.

At some point Lilah did check social media and saw that the Raymere Bears had won Friday night's football game 31 to 17. She looked at the two pictures in the article. Despite a helmet, Kyler's face on the field looked the happiest that she had ever seen. Even though it was just a silly game, she supposed that he deserved the win.

✳ ✳ ✳

Kyler quickly hit the showers after eighth period. He'd have to get work done as soon as possible after school, as he had to be somewhere earlier than he expected that evening. Therefore, he had asked Lilah to meet at the school library, as opposed to their later meetings at the public library.

As he made his way through the bookshelves of the school library, he heard another voice with Lilah's and he couldn't help but eavesdrop.

"If you weren't so cold, he'd probably ask you out," Alice insisted.

"I'm not cold, and I told you, I don't have time for silly boys," Lilah huffed.

Kyler had to hang back now; curiosity had gotten the best of him.

"You've said that all through high school. You do realize that you're going to graduate and go off to college, never having even kissed a guy."

"There's nothing wrong with that," Lilah said quietly. "Plus, it's not like you and Jolee are doing much better."

"Are you kidding me," Alice gasped. "Jolee made out with a senior her sophomore year!"

Lilah tried to hold back a laugh. "Shh, we're in a library," she pointed out. "Also, that's because the Juliet got food poisoning and Jolee was the understudy. Apparently, it was so bad; that's why she turned to technical theater."

Alice groaned. "All I'm saying is, it looked like Simon was trying to flirt with you this morning, and you were really dismissive about it. I thought you liked him."

Lilah sighed. She did like Simon. He was nice and smart, but she didn't know if she liked him in any of the ways she had read about.

"You need to be going. I'm sure Kyler will be here any second."

Alice leaned farther into the table, a wicked smile appearing. Lilah knew exactly what she was thinking.

"No, absolutely not," she whispered, trying to appear as outraged at the idea as possible.

"Fine." Alice pushed her chair back and rose from the table. "Just try to be a little more friendly the next time Simon is clearly flirting with you." She proceeded to sticking out her tongue like a child before turning to leave.

Kyler would be the first to admit that he probably should have made himself known sooner. Those few minutes of concealment by the bookshelves had given him a lot of information. Obviously, Lilah would be into Simon. He looked like a model going under-cover as a nerd. The only difference was that he was insanely smart as well.

What really stirred Kyler, even though it shouldn't have, was the idea, the fact, that Lilah had never even kissed a guy. If he thought about it, he could mildly understand why, but even he had to admit that she was doing well in the looks department. Stupid guys dated horrible women all the time for no reason other than being hot.

Kyler sat his bag down and began rummaging through it for his tattered copy of *Hamlet*, as well as his notebook and two new assignments from Mr. Hughes.

"Hey," Lilah finally said, breaking the silence.

"How was your weekend?"

She was taken aback by the question.

"Fine, I guess." She felt like she suddenly needed to say more, to make conversation, as Kyler got all his things put into place. "Congratulations on the win Friday." It felt strange saying that.

Upon hearing those words, Kyler looked up, mak-ing eye contact with Lilah. Her bright green eyes looked back at him with a nervousness he wasn't used to seeing in her.

"Thanks. You and your friends should come to a game."

He expected her to change the subject, but she didn't. She broke eye contact with him and doodled with her pen in the corner of her almost finished assignment from Hughes.

"I probably wouldn't understand it."

Kyler was shocked. Last week she laughed in his face like it was the most absurd idea she had ever heard, but now?

"You could bring Antonio. I'm sure he–"

Lilah slammed her pen down and stared daggers at Kyler.

"I'm going to tell you this," she began angrily. "I swear you better not tease me about it."

Kyler laughed, holding his hands up in surrender. Though he'd never tell her, and even the idea in and of itself creeped him out, she looked cute when she was angry.

She put it out there bluntly and simply. "Antonio is my dad's driver."

Kyler's face turned to stone as the laughter faded. She had a chef and a driver?

When Kyler didn't respond, Lilah grew embarrassed. "So, just drop it with the Antonio boyfriend comments," she quietly insisted. Before he could say anything, she changed the subject. "I've already started on one of the new worksheets for Hughes' class. It was pretty easy. I think we should try doing those first and, then if we have time, continue on with your makeup assignments. If I recall, you only have three left."

Kyler nodded, making a mental note to stop teasing her about Antonio. From there on, the only talk was about *Hamlet*, the play that never seemed to end.

* * *

Lilah and Kyler met three days that week, Monday, Wednesday, and Thursday. Lilah would have preferred to meet on Friday to cover the assignments and readings issued for the weekend, but she was well-aware that those would always be game days. Neither of the two had dared mention meeting on the weekend.

Both had to admit, though they wouldn't, not to each other, not to another soul, the tutoring wasn't so bad. Occasionally they made small talk, but they kept it very minimal and only surface level deep. They were not friends by any means.

"Hey," Kyler began, a lingering question behind the one word. Lilah looked up and waited, zipping up her bag after putting up her highlighters. "I have a five-page paper coming up for criminal justice, and–"

"What," Lilah gasped jokingly. "You mean you have to do more than watch movies in there?"

Kyler nudged her as they made their way from the public library. "Very funny. Actually–"

"You need my help," Lilah interrupted once again.

"If you'd let me finish," Kyler grumbled. "I can handle a paper. I don't need you for everything," he said, not meaning for his words to sound as harsh as they probably did once he said them. He quickly looked to Lilah beside him. If she took offense, she didn't show it this time. "I was just wondering if you'd have time to look over my citations. It's confusing and tedious, figuring out all the different sources and how to cite them."

"Sure."

"I haven't started on it, but I should have something for you to look at by the end of next week."

Lilah thought he was being very optimistic with his time frame, but she refrained from pointing that out.

The sun was in the final stages of setting, the steps cascading down from the library barely lit in gold and orange. Once they reached the final one, Kyler turned to say what Lilah assumed was nothing more than goodbye.

"Do you need a ride?"

The way he said it was different than the first time. He didn't seem annoyed or bothered at having to go out of his way.

"I'm sure you have somewhere you need to be," Lilah speculated.

"Not today."

For the briefest of moments, a chill ran through Lilah, taking away all thoughts and ability to speak.

"So," Kyler pressed, awakening her.

She recovered, fumbling for words. "Actually, I have a ride...Antonio."

Kyler did a poor job at hiding the smirk on his face.

Lilah rolled her eyes and headed to the black car just across the street. "Goodbye, Kyler."

"Goodbye, Lilah," he chuckled back.

A part of him began to turn and head toward the library parking lot on the side of the building, but something else kept him locked in place, forcing him to remain until she was fully across the street and he saw an older gentleman step from the car to open the door for her. It wasn't until the car was well into the distance that Kyler made his way to his truck.

* * *

Lilah didn't see Kyler the next day. The only time she could recall seeing him throughout the day was lunch, and it was a well-known fact that for some reason the football team received a special lunch outside of the cafeteria when they had away games, which apparently they were having this particular day.

"You look sad, or disappointed," Jolee pointed out.

"No. Just tired, I guess." It was a lie. Lilah didn't feel tired.

"Oh, I haven't told you guys. They decided on a fall musical for the end of November."

"What," Alice barely managed through a larger than life bite of hamburger.

"*Little Shop of Horrors.* It wasn't my top pick, but the runner up was *Beauty and the Beast.*" She made a gagging noise shortly after revealing that last bit. Needless to say, romance wasn't something that Jolee thought of as intriguing.

Lilah found that more than once she glanced into the distance at the empty table where the football players usually ate. Not giving much thought, she took out her phone and beneath the table hovered over her message thread with Kyler.

Lilah: Good luck tonight.

Something soared in Kyler upon reading the message. He couldn't quite figure her out. There were moments when she was really nice, and he thought that he might actually like that.

Kyler: Miss seeing me at lunch?

Lilah tried to hide her embarrassment. If Alice or Jolee thought something was up, she'd never hear the end of it, not that anything was going on with Kyler. She just didn't want them getting that impression, which they most definitely would. Alice had already vaguely hinted at it.

Lilah: Hardly. For once it's peaceful without all the testosterone leaking throughout the room.

She was certain that Alice would have scolded her for her response, but it's not like Kyler was flirting with her, not like Simon, which, in the last few days, had happened twice already.

Kyler: I guess that means you're not coming to the game?

Lilah: I don't go to home games, what makes you think I'd go an hour away?

Kyler: To support me.

Lilah: Hence the text in the first place.

Kyler: Thank you. Have a good weekend.

And that is what Lilah hated about texting. She scrolled back through the message wondering if she had offended him. Gradually he was becoming more confusing.

"Hello, Lilah," Alice nearly screamed.

Lilah finally looked up from her phone.

"Is everything okay," Jolee asked, clear concern crossing her face.

"Yeah, it's fine."

"Well then, can you," Alice asked. Though the confused look on Lilah's face made her repeat a much earlier question. "We wanted to go for lunch and ice cream downtown tomorrow, then maybe a movie. Are you in?"

Lilah thought for a moment and disappointment hit. "I can't. I'm sorry. I signed up to do volunteer hours for the honor society tomorrow."

"That sucks," Jolee groaned. "What do you have to do?"

"Just hang out at the hospital gift shop. They might make me do other odds and ends if they think it's something a teenager won't mess up."

The lunch bell rang shortly after and the girls went their separate ways until Monday.

CHAPTER 8

Exhaustion.

Kyler was utterly exhausted by Saturday morning when he got to the hospital for his shift at seven. By the time the bus got back from the consolation dinner, if fast food could be called as such, it was already after eleven. He barely got six hours of sleep, which wouldn't have been the end of the world, but he took one or two good hits the night before and his body was feeling it.

"I've got your cart all set up," Hal informed him as soon as he punched in. "I see you're doing twelve hours today."

"Yeah," Kyler yawned.

Hal patted Kyler on the shoulder, which was quite difficult considering that he was barely over five feet. "I'm sure your mother is grateful for the help."

Kyler didn't know about that. His mother begged him to enjoy his senior year, to focus on football and academics. She didn't want him to have to work; however, after certain things were brought to light, there was no way that he was going to spend all his free time hanging out with his friends.

"Why don't you take the café?"

Kyler eyed Hal suspiciously. Hal must have sensed that he was struggling with the morning. The café at seven in the morning was usually the easiest place to clean, as it didn't receive much traffic overnight.

Normally he would have argued with Hal, but he was the head janitor, whatever he said was the final word, and right now, Kyler wasn't complaining with starting off slow.

✻ ✻ ✻

"We're just waiting on your partner to show up," the volunteer coordinator informed Lilah as she scribbled something down on her clipboard. "Are you comfortable with working the register or should I do another example?"

"No. I think I've got it."

Lilah jerked her head up as soon as she heard footsteps from the entrance and her heart stopped. There was no way that she was making it through the day.

"Mr. Campbell, right on time," the woman exclaimed, checking his name from some list. "Alright, so, I've already informed Miss McCallister on how to operate the register. She'll pass that information along. Saturdays are usually our busiest days for visitors, so if either of you feel overwhelmed, call the general help number listed on the phone and someone will be here momentarily. We'll also send an adult volunteer in sometime around noon to give you a lunch. Any other questions?"

"I'm good," Simon said rather casually.

Lilah, however, felt very overwhelmed already. She had a hard enough time talking to Simon in school around other students, but now she was going to be alone with him for eight hours.

As soon as the woman left, Lilah realized that she should have asked if the gift shop had an adjustable thermostat. Suddenly the normally cold hospital felt exceedingly warm.

"I guess we're both here until four," Simon began.

"Looks like it."

Lilah hated the arrangement of the smaller stuffed animals and busied herself with tidying them into rows while Simon took a seat behind the register. Once she was done with the rows, she then rearranged them so that they were color coded. After that, she went on to the candy rack. Thankfully it was a complete mess and would take a great deal of time to get in order.

"Do you have any other big plans for the weekend," Simon asked, interrupting her thought process of stacking.

"No." Lilah felt horrible that she wasn't giving him more, but she absolutely did not know what to say.

"I might go hiking outside of Raymere. Do you hike?"

"No."

"Not much for conversation either I see," Simon chuckled.

"I'll probably catch up on some reading." There. Lilah felt as though she could let out a breath. She was able to form an actual sentence.

"Well, if you'd like to try out hiking, let me know."

"I'm not much for sports, or the outdoors," Lilah admitted.

"Oh, that's cool. Would you be up for something else?"

Lilah was a bit surprised by his boldness. "Maybe. I'd have to see."

Simon leaned forward over the counter, full of confidence. "How about lunch, say in three to four hours, hospital café," he asked with the cutest boyish grin.

Lilah laughed. "Yeah, okay. I can do that."

Slowly her nerves faded and the time that once seemed stuck on the minute hand soon passed faster than she would have liked.

* * *

Kyler felt the blood drain from his body as soon as he and Hal walked into the café.

What was she doing here?

He looked at the person next to her making her laugh. Simon Campbell. He had to assume her friend was right after all. Simon looked very much into both Lilah and the conversation.

"Alright, I'll bite," Hal announced through a mouthful of his sandwich.

"What are you talking about?" Kyler was eating as fast as possible. Not only had he missed breakfast, but seeing Lilah made him remember that he had brought along his work for his criminal justice paper that he was hoping to get some time on during his lunch break.

Hal gestured to a table near the center of the café. "The cute couple. You know them?"

Kyler clenched his teeth. "Just some kids from school."

"Ah, I see," Hal sang out.

Kyler glared at him. "What do you see?"

"You've been in a foul mood ever since we walked in here and you saw them. It's the girl isn't it?"

"I don't know what you're getting at," Kyler scoffed, turning his attention away from Lilah and Simon.

"So, there's nothing going on with her?"

Kyler appeared offended, nearly choking on his sports drink. "No way. She's just my tutor. Definitely not my type."

"So beautiful isn't your type?"

Kyler laughed. "Lots of girls are beautiful."

"She's wearing a volunteer badge. Caring isn't your type?"

Kyler laughed even harder. Caring would not have been a word that he or anyone would have used to describe Lilah. At least in the past that wasn't true. Now he wasn't so sure, but he wasn't going to tell Hal that. "She doesn't care. She's just here for honor society volunteer hours. They have to have so many a month."

"So, she's your tutor and in the honor society. Smart isn't your type?"

Kyler tossed his trash in a nearby can. "Are you going to keep doing that?"

"Maybe," Hal teased.

"I still have thirty-five minutes left," Kyler began, changing the subject. "I have some schoolwork I need to get started on. I'll be in the courtyard if you need me before then."

Hal gave a deep and hearty laugh, a raspy undertone coming through with each breath, having been a former smoker. "Alright, but this conversation isn't over."

* * *

Simon must have noticed Kyler exit the café into the courtyard just as soon as Lilah had.

"I wonder what he's doing here." He then scoffed. "Clearly he's not in the honor society."

Lilah broke her attention from the glass encasing the courtyard and shot a glare at Simon which he didn't notice. It sounded exactly like a comment she would have made, but something about it rubbed her the wrong way.

"Ready to get back," he asked, dismissing any further discussion about Kyler.

"Umm, yeah. Actually, why don't you go ahead? I have to go to the restroom and make a quick call to check in with my parents," Lilah lied.

Simon shrugged but thankfully took their trash away and left the café. Lilah, on the other hand, headed to the doors leading out to the courtyard.

* * *

Kyler took a deep and frustrated breath as soon as he felt someone sit on the opposite end of the bench. Before she managed to greet him, he somehow already knew it was her.

"Hey," Lilah began meekly, quite unlike her.

Kyler tried not to pay her much attention. "Hi."

She fumbled with one of her perfectly painted nails until she felt it beginning to chip.

"What do you want," Kyler huffed. He wasn't in a mood to deal with Lilah. He also didn't want to explain his situation. His own friends didn't know everything, why should she?

"I just saw you and I thought I'd come say hi," Lilah responded with a hint of growing agitation.

"Yeah? Well you've already done that. You should probably get back to volunteering."

Kyler flipped a page in a book beside him on the bench. He wasn't accustomed to being so cold and Lilah hadn't done anything to deserve it, but this seemed easier than flatly telling her to go away and mind her own business.

"I see you're working on your paper," she began.

She glanced over at the pictures throughout his book, recognizing his chosen person of interest. Kyler still hadn't even looked up at her, and for a moment she had to wonder if she had somehow upset him. She even went out of her way to text him before his game the previous day.

What was she thinking? Two weeks ago, she dreaded the idea of working with this guy, and now she was sitting here wondering if he was mad at her?

"Look, I'm a little busy," Kyler told her, attempting to brush her off once more.

Lilah reached over and slammed his book shut.

"I was writing a quote from–"

She had already snapped. As she rose from the bench, her hands on her hips, "What is your problem?!"

Without thinking, "You're annoying me. Just go get your stupid credit and leave me alone."

As soon as he said those words, he swore he saw a flash of hurt in Lilah's enraged eyes.

Her small frame stood over him, barely shielding him from the sun. A breeze blew lightly around him, and he was certain that despite all the brightly colored flowers in the area, it was her that he could smell with each breath he inhaled. He hated it. He hated whatever she had put on that morning. He hated how sweet, soft, and subtle it was. It was a barely there scent that made him want to breathe in as deeply as he could so that he could get just a bit more of it. He hated that with a passion.

"You are a complete jerk right now," she screamed, her voice rising with each word. "No, not even right now. You're just a jerk, period." She turned to leave, but quickly spun around and started jabbing at the notebook on Kyler's lap where he had been attempting his rough draft. "And just so you know," she began, a jab with each word. "Gary Ridgway's name

89

doesn't have an *e*! Even your stupid book could tell you that much. Considering he's your whole paper, you'd think you could spell his name right."

She then stormed off; however, came to a swift stop at the doors. Kyler couldn't help but make eye contact with her. There was nothing there. Her features were as cold as ice and her eyes didn't have the same glimmer in them that he had seen when she was at lunch with Simon. He couldn't imagine that she'd possibly have anything left to say, but then she surprised him.

Through gritted teeth, "By the way, you were on page 137."

Then, just like that, she was gone.

* * *

"It's fine. You don't have to say anything," Hal said, finally breaking the silence as they made their way to the elevators.

"Nothing to say," Kyler managed to reply.

Hal pressed the button to go up and their wait began. "Well, with your attitude today, no wonder she's with the other fellow." He watched Kyler from the corner of his eye. If Kyler didn't want to talk, he'd find a way of breaking him.

"Well, good for her then. They're perfect for each other," Kyler grumbled.

"You know something, I've always hated that word. *Perfect.* No such thing. Seems like an undefinable word to me."

Kyler rolled his eyes. He was all too used to Hal's old wisdom. "Last time I checked, it's in the dictionary. Not that I care about either of them, but they're perfect for each other," he repeated, his voice dripping with a little more disdain than before. "Both are insanely rich, and smart, and–"

"Let me stop you right there, boy. It takes more than money to make you rich, and more than books to make you smart. You'll go a lot further if you just remember that," Hal interrupted.

At that moment, more than just the bell on the elevator went off.

CHAPTER 9

"I wasn't sure if you were coming," Kyler said once Lilah entered their usual area in the school library.

She was late. The last bell had rung more than twenty minutes ago. Usually Kyler was running late from eighth period practice and his shower, but today it was Lilah. The calculating look on her face told him it was intentional, and he was aware that he probably deserved it.

"I was busy. I got your texts."

He had text her three times that Monday, once even at lunch, but she was nearly certain that she could feel his eyes burning into her from across the crowded lunch room, and she had dared not to check it until after she was out of his sight.

"Yeah, but you didn't respond," he pointed out.

Lilah tossed her bag down and withdrew her notebook and a multiple-choice assignment packet.

"So, this is the last week for *Hamlet*. You should have all your assignments in. I overheard that Mr. Hughes is going to announce tomorrow that–"

"I'm sorry, okay," Kyler interrupted.

At least that had gotten her to stop speaking, and she finally brought her attention to him, and not all the work on the table separating them.

For the first time, her eyes were disarming. They were so big, and so green; the light streaming from the window behind Kyler somehow made them appear that much brighter, and for a second, he felt almost hypnotized.

Lilah crossed her arms and leaned into the table. "Yeah? For what?"

Kyler should have assumed that she wouldn't make it easy. She wasn't the type of girl to just laugh it off and tell him that it wasn't a problem. "I'm sorry for Saturday." He meant for his words to come out more sincerely, but realized how forced they were.

Lilah shrugged. "You're not sorry. That's just how you are."

"Look, I'm trying to apologize..."

"You don't need to. You can be a jerk all you want. I get it. That's how you are," Lilah said unemotionally as she twirled a pen at him. "I agreed to do this, and I intend to see it through. At no point was there any mention of the two of us being friends," she concluded. She then changed the subject back, completely dismissing his apology. "Now, as I was saying, there's a rumor that Mr. Hughes is going to move the huge *Hamlet* test from Friday to next Monday, possibly Tuesday. That would really work out in your favor considering that the teachers have to have all their grades put in by Sunday at noon."

Kyler was skeptical. "How sure are you?"

"Nearly very."

Kyler laughed. He noted the way Lilah watched him, but he still couldn't figure her out. Something about her just made him want to be sharp and almost cruel, but gradually there was something else that she was bringing out, and it was very unsettling.

It wasn't until the lights in the very back of the library shut off that Lilah bothered at glancing at her phone. It was 4:50. The school library would be closing for the day. They had managed to finish any and all missing and late assignments, as well as start on the multiple-choice packet that wasn't due until the end of the week. There was no need for them to continue to the public library.

"Oh, I have a favor to ask," Kyler cautiously began, knowing that, at the moment, he was in no position to be asking for such. Lilah didn't really respond, only made a barely audible noise that he took as a means to continue. "Friday is another away game, but it's a little farther."

Lilah wasn't stupid. "So, the football team will be missing their afternoon classes?"

"Yeah, and I have–"

"Hughes' English class in the afternoon."

He stopped packing his bag and narrowed his eyes in her direction. She looked up and innocently met his.

"You were wondering if you could borrow my notes," she continued, before he could find a way to ask.

"Yes," he sighed, hoping for the best but anticipating the worst.

Kyler was surprised when she gave a single word response back and nothing else.

"Fine."

Kyler had one more other thing he wanted to run by Lilah, but figured that in person was probably not the way to do it. He didn't care for her to laugh in his face, and he was still debating about Dawson's suggestion from lunch earlier that day. The best way to bring it up was like any normal teenager, through text.

* * *

"You know mom isn't out with girlfriends," Rover bluntly announced as he flopped on the sofa after supper.

Lilah swatted at his feet. "You know shoes aren't allowed on the furniture."

"Who cares. It's not like there's an adult here to correct me," he joked. Deep down, no matter how big and bad he acted, the truth was, he was only eleven, going on twelve. His sisters, particularly Lilah, scared the living daylights out of him. With that, he removed his feet from the couch.

"How do you know," Lilah asked, now curious. She had suspicions, but it was one of those things she'd rather not know.

Very nonchalantly, "I went through her phone."

"Rover!"

A fit of laughter ensued on his part. "Come on, I love mom and all, but face it, we got her looks, not her brains. Her password is 1-2-3-4."

"First of all, that comment was a little rude. Secondly...wow...I have so many questions. Why were you in her phone?"

"She controls the parental locks on the television from there," he answered.

Lilah was a little stunned. She knew the damage that Rover could cause if he got his hands in the right places, but he was getting a little bold for an eleven-year-old.

"Anyway," he sang out, after realizing his sister was a little speechless. "I figured I'd look through her texts, considering she's always on the phone tapping away."

Lilah felt sick. She didn't want to know, but some part of her already did. The worst part was that her little brother had come across that, given, it was his own fault for snooping, but she couldn't imagine the hurt and pain that realization must have been for him. "And," she pressed on after Rover neglected to continue.

"There's this guy named Rob."

"That's it?"

"Well, no. I mean, it's not like I found anything worse than what you can find online," he began, growing a bit embarrassed.

"Oh, god! Rover," Lilah screeched. "No, just no. You cannot go through people's personal stuff like that!"

"So, you don't care that mom is probably having an affair?"

"Stop it," Lilah hissed. She didn't want to hear that, especially from her little brother; although, if it were true, he seemed to be taking it quite well.

It was at that moment that a welcomed distraction eased the tension in the form of a text alert from Lilah's phone. It was on the couch next to Rover as she had been getting the television set up for a movie.

He picked it up and glanced at it, a coy and sinister grin creeping across his thin boyish lips.

"How about you deal with this," he said as he waved the phone around. "And we postpone the movie for another night."

Lilah glared at him. She was much better and had a greater deal of experience with what he was trying to do. "You just want to go play your video games."

He shrugged. "Maybe, but I'm sure you'd hate to keep Kyler waiting."

Lilah's eyes widened and a lump in her throat formed, preventing words from coming at that moment.

Rover tossed the phone back on the couch. "I'll be in my room if you should need me."

Lilah did not want to imagine what he'd be like as a teenager. She gave up on the movie they were supposed to watch together and went for her phone. She couldn't hide the fact that it felt like she had eaten something bad not too long ago. Her stomach flipped once more when she opened her messages.

Kyler: I forgot to ask. Do you have plans Saturday?

A million questions bombarded Lilah's thoughts. Why was he asking now, at seven on a Monday night? Did he want to meet to study? To get Friday's notes? Was it a different reason entirely?

Lilah nearly dropped the phone as she forced herself to stop thinking, a single question via text sending her into a near panic attack.

Lilah: Why? Do you need Friday's notes?

Kyler: Haha, no, but thanks for thinking of me. Actually, I was going to see if you and your friends wanted to go to a party.

Lilah stared at the screen and reread the message over and over. She was not the type of person that most people would invite to a party, especially one filled with a bunch of jocks, which she assumed it would be, as that was pretty much the entirety of Kyler's circle. Another text soon came through.

Kyler: Dawson told me to invite you and your friends.

Lilah exhaled. That made much more sense. She had been invited to one of Dawson's parties long ago, before she earned the reputation as the biggest snob in school. She never went to it of course, but she knew how his parties were. His parents were fairly wealthy and of good standing in the community. He didn't have the sort of parties like she had seen in the teen movies, full of drugs and alcohol. For the most part, people went for his insane pool and game room. The general rule was that everyone leave by dusk. Supposedly it was on the mild side when it came to a high school party.

Lilah: We'll think about it.

Kyler: Cool. It starts around 2pm.

Kyler thought about leaving it at that, but it was the perfect way to feed his curiosity, and at least through text he didn't have to be scrutinized under her skeptical gaze.

Kyler: Feel free to bring Simon too.

Lilah: What?

When Kyler took longer than thirty seconds to clarify, Lilah shot off another message.

Lilah: Why would I bring Simon?

It was a bad idea mentioning that. He realized after it was too late. Thankfully, hidden behind a screen, it was far easier to come up with a response, even if it meant that his best friend was going to take the hit for it.

Kyler: I don't know. Miles mentioned that he thought you two were together or something. I just wanted to make sure that you knew you could bring him along as well.

Lilah: Well, when you see Miles, be sure to correct him before he continues to spread any other rumors.

He was pretty sure that she was livid, stomping around in a pair of dainty designer shoes. However, something about her text was strangely reassuring.

CHAPTER 10

Kyler removed his shirt and dusted off an old pair of stained up jeans before entering the house. The smell of bacon hit him instantly and he felt his stomach respond with an array of growls.

"You're up early for having such a late trip back," Krista said without turning around. She had heard the mower turn off through the sizzling of bacon.

"I wanted to get a few things done for mom before Dawson's little party."

Knowing that breakfast would be ready soon, he ran upstairs and quickly put on a change of clothes. There was no point in showering; he still had a great deal of stuff he wanted to take care of outside and he'd only have to shower again before leaving the house.

It was just Krista and himself on this particular Saturday morning. He had been awake when his mother left for the hospital, but it was still too dark to get outside and do anything, so he had remained in bed until the sunlight slowly began to creep through his blinds.

Krista placed an overly full plate and glass of juice in front of Kyler. "I'm surprised that you're not at the hospital today."

"Hal figured I'd be useless after the game and ride back. I think he's just like mom, thinking I need to enjoy being a kid," Kyler scoffed.

"They aren't wrong. Trust me. College was hard, but after college is the worst, especially when you realize your degree and all that time meant nothing," Krista said, picking at scrambled eggs loaded with cheese.

Kyler knew his sister was struggling as well. She had graduated from college roughly four months prior. Her hope was to get a job as a developer; however, all she had managed was sales for McCallister Industries. It was a good company and she had a lot of room for advancement, but her impatience was a whole different story.

She didn't make enough to warrant getting an apartment in the city, and living with roommates didn't appeal to her; therefore, she continued to live with Kyler and their mother, Helen, and just make the commute.

"Mom has been through a lot. I wish I would have known everything earlier, but at least now I can help out, hopefully make things a little easier for her," Kyler admitted, dismissing his sister's thoughts that he should enjoy childhood.

"You just turned eighteen, you don't have to–"

"Can you just drop it? I'm going to Dawson's this afternoon; that's enough for me right now," Kyler interrupted, sparing himself a lecture.

Krista left it alone. She watched her brother grow up a lot since their father's death more than six years ago, but it wasn't until recently, when he discovered the issues of finances that he really tried to step up and contribute more. Suddenly, friends and video games didn't seem to be the center of his life.

Krista didn't see her brother anymore until around lunch time. There was no telling what he was doing. She thought she heard something on the roof and remembered that her mom had made the smallest comment about the gutters. It was insignificant at the time, but there was no doubt that Kyler had probably made a mental note.

"I've got you a sandwich in the fridge if you want," Krista pointed out, shutting off the vacuum once her brother entered.

Kyler wiped sweat and dust from his forehead. "Thanks. I'm starving."

"Oh, you should probably check your phone," she informed him.

Kyler looked around, not remembering where he last placed it. Ultimately Krista had to point to an end table for him.

"I wasn't being nosey," she felt the need to establish. "I just heard texts going off over an hour ago and figured..." She let her words drift off as she watched Kyler read through the phone, flashes of annoyance and frustration in his wild blue eyes.

"It's nothing. Just some of the guys," he finally told her.

When he looked up, Krista held a smirk on her face as she leaned on the handle of the vacuum.

He groaned and made his way to the refrigerator. "You looked at it, didn't you?"

"I just saw the name Sarah pop up," she calmly admitted.

Kyler dismissed that text as soon as he saw it. Of course, Sarah had to know if he would be hanging out at Dawson's house that afternoon.

"She's just a cheerleader."

Krista gagged a little. Obviously, her brother, star quarterback, would be into a cheerleader.

"So, cupcake girl is a cheerleader. How cute," Krista scoffed. She quickly regretted it. Just because cheerleaders were jerks to her back when they first moved to Raymere Grove didn't mean they were all like that. Not to mention, she couldn't remember the last time her brother talked about a girl; judging his choice was rude on her part. She was just about to apologize when Kyler turned toward her and pressed his backside into the kitchen island.

"No," was all he said through a mouthful of what appeared to be half his sandwich.

"Wait, I'm confused." Krista then began rolling up the cord to the vacuum. It was a constant chore with the four-legged creature who desperately seemed to need a haircut. Come to think of it, she should probably look for the dog...

"Sarah is just a cheerleader. We all hang out together."

"Yeah, I'm not talking about Sarah anymore," Krista teased.

If Krista thought she was getting anything else out of her brother, she was sorely mistaken when he excused himself and rushed up the stairs. She'd be on her own until he and their mom came home for supper, which both assured they would. She realized that she should probably start her afternoon off with finding the dog.

* * *

"What time will you be home," Steven asked before Lilah could get to the bottom of the staircase.

"Honestly, she's almost eighteen. She needs to get out and have some fun," Jenna interjected, before Lilah could answer.

Lilah saw the way her mother looked at her. She didn't approve of her choice of outfit. She had tried to get Lilah to wear a skirt too short and a top too low. They were items that she had bought for Lilah during one of her binges; they were also items that would remain in the far corner of the closet with the tags still on.

She had opted for a pair of low-rise skinny jeans and a snug Rolling Stones shirt with sleeves down to her elbows. It might have seemed boring to her mother, but she thought it was just the right amount of cute and sexy, if there was such a thing. It was that thought alone not even thirty minutes ago that made her want to change her mind about going. Parties were not her thing, and while she dressed in a pristine fashion for school, she had no idea why she was putting so much thought and effort into a party she didn't want to go to in the first place. However, after she had told Alice about it, she knew without a doubt they'd all be going.

"Don't worry, dad," Lilah reassured him. "Dawson's parents want people off their property by nightfall."

"I'm well-aware of his parents. He and his family aren't the problem. It's everyone else who might be there."

Jenna tugged at her husband's arm. "Don't do this. Lilah doesn't have many friends as it is."

Lilah didn't know why her mother attempted to whisper that only feet from her. Perhaps she wanted Lilah to hear. If so, that was cold, even for her.

"Look, I'm going with Alice and Jolee. Jolee just text me that her mom is parked on the street outside of our gate. I also talked to Antonio. Should I want to leave earlier, and they don't, he said he'll be on standby. Unless of course you have something come up," Lilah sighed, suddenly feeling like a small child.

Reluctantly her father stepped aside, and she was out the door before either parent could lecture her about anything else.

CHAPTER 11

Throughout the insanely large game room, which had garnered a pretty decent crowd by 2:30, Kyler could easily hear Sarah's high-pitched shriek nearby.

"Are you serious? This has to be a joke," she squealed to Britt and Abby on either side of her.

Sean, who was only a few feet from her, talking with Cash and Louis, looked up to what had sent Sarah into a fit. He then proceeded to hollering at Dawson, who was setting up for another FIFA match on one of the big screens.

"Come on, man. Hot or not, did you really have to invite your nerd friends?"

Sarah and her friends gathered in closer. "Uh, hot? I know you're not talking about one of *them*!"

Kyler's attention immediately went to the entrance. He'd be lying if he said he hadn't scanned the room for her, but only once or twice. He couldn't believe she came, and it was just her and the two girls he always saw her with. He shouldn't have expected differently. Lilah had set him straight about any suspicions of Simon earlier in the week.

As she walked farther into the room, hesitant at first, Kyler couldn't help but watch her every move. She looked so different. He couldn't recall ever seeing her in anything other than some business-like skirt. Something about the way her jeans clung to her frame caused his gut to clench. He hated how small her shirt looked; with even the slightest movement, he was sure that he could see skin between the hem of the shirt and the top of her jeans.

He was jolted from his trance by another comment from Sean as well as the overly sweet stench that he recognized as Sarah's perfume. She must have bathed in it on that particular day.

"Next time you're going to have a chess club meeting, tell us."

Kyler quickly interrupted, knowing he'd have a lot of explaining to do. "He didn't invite them. I did."

The gasp from Sarah was so outrageous, and had he not been aggravated by Sean's stupid remarks, he probably would have choked from laugher at her ridiculousness.

"What," Sean hissed, stepping closer in Kyler's direction.

"I said," he began, enunciating every word as though Sean had a problem understanding. "Dawson didn't invite them. I did," he repeated.

"Why in the world would you do that?"

Kyler wasn't sure what made him do it, and honestly, he was surprised the truth hadn't come out in the locker room talk, but he decided to let everyone know. At least this way it was on his terms.

"McCallister is my tutor for Hughes' class."

There was a bit of silence at first, along with a couple gasps from Sarah and her friends. Kyler's friends thought nothing of it as they had known from the first day.

"So that's why you get special treatment? That's why you get to skip out on practices," Sean began, a jealousy quickly growing.

Dawson stepped in before Kyler could say something to further irk Sean. "Look, this is my house. She's been helping Kyler, which in turn helps the team. I told him to invite them. If you have a problem, teammate or not, you know where the exit is."

Sean didn't move at first. He locked eyes with Kyler. Searching.

Kyler only felt uneasy once a satisfying smirk appeared on Sean's lips. It was an expression that was far too calculating. Wheels were definitely spinning, and Kyler didn't like it one bit.

* * *

"This place is awesome," Alice quietly screamed.

Lilah had to give it to Dawson's parents, they definitely had a game room alright. Three big screens, with wrap around couches surrounding each of them separately, seemed to be the drawing card for most of the guys. There were some kind of video game sporting competitions going on. There were two pool tables, mildly in use, foosball, pinball machines, lit up squares embedded into the floor for dancing, and the list went on. Large double glass doors opened to a beautiful outdoor area with the pool as the focal point; however, the late September air had started to grow cool, and very few took the liberty of enjoying the pleasures of swimming.

Jolee nudged Alice to a far-off corner, which only led to a greater sense of awe. Four long party tables were set up with an array of every snack imaginable, from sweet and salty, to cold and hot, to healthy and greasy, even to foreign and domestic.

"This looks like something your mom would do," Jolee pointed out.

"Yeah, if I liked even ten percent of the amount of people here," Lilah replied, all the while continuing to check out her surroundings.

She stopped evaluating the place once her eyes landed on Kyler. He was talking with Miles and seemed to be enjoying himself. She rarely saw such a genuine smile on his face. With her attention also on Miles, she hoped that Kyler remembered to set Miles straight concerning any rumors about Simon and herself.

As she watched Kyler from afar, it was then that she really looked at him. He was taller than most of his friends, easily six foot something, but she already knew he was tall just from standing next to him. His hair was more styled than when she usually saw him, given, she saw him fresh from a shower after practice. However, it looked like he had put effort into his appearance today. He had on a fashionable pair of dark jeans, not at all like the skinny or cut up ones that several of the guys had on. He paired it with a short sleeved grey Henley with just a button or two undone. It truly accentuated his arms, so much so that Lilah thought he could have used a bigger size.

"Please tell me that you're not drooling over one of them already," Jolee sighed, breaking Lilah from her trance.

"Absolutely not. Just watching them in their native habitat," Lilah laughed, hoping that Jolee hadn't seen that she had paid Kyler a bit more attention than she should have.

Lilah was surprised that after an hour she wasn't bored to death, but then again, she was enjoying simply spending time with her friends. They had found an empty bistro table just outside the doors so that Alice had a nice place to sample nearly every food available.

From time to time Lilah looked around for Kyler. She assumed that since he had invited her, he'd at least have the decency to say something to her, but it was as though he didn't even notice her presence. She told herself that it was probably for the best.

"I am so stuffed," Alice groaned, although she took another bite of some sort of flaky pastry.

"I'm tired of sitting. Is it cool if we leave you and walk around inside," Jolee asked.

Alice nodded and continued eating, this time more slowly. Full or not, she intended to sample everything.

"At least she's enjoying herself," Jolee said once they were back inside.

The volume, as well as crowd size, had grown since they stepped outside.

"And you're not," Lilah asked.

Jolee shrugged her shoulders at first. "I'm just not friends with anyone here, and right now, you and I are a cross between invisible and the plague."

Lilah laughed at Jolee's ever dramatic phrasing, despite its truth. It stung just a little. Even with her confidence and not caring too much about what people thought, she had not been able to speak to the person that was her whole reason for coming. She shook the thought. He wasn't the *reason* she came, but he had been her invite. Every time she had seen him though, he was engrossed with some other football player. Well, there was that one time he was talking with Sarah, but it's not like she paid too much attention to that. Either way, she felt like an outsider, and it was becoming clearer that maybe the whole ordeal was a mistake.

Jolee excused herself to go to the restroom while Lilah hung around one of the pool tables. About half of the balls remained, but there were no signs of a game in progress. Bored with waiting, Lilah occupied her time with the dull act of rolling the cue ball around the table, never allowing it to leave her grasp and for some reason not allowing it to bump into any of the other balls; that was, until an unrecognizable voice sent chills down her spine.

"Want to play," someone breathed into her ear, far closer than her comfort level allowed.

Lilah turned, almost to bump into Sean, towering over her. She backed into the table in hopes of creating a little bit of space between them. While he was about Kyler's height, his size was much larger and bulkier. Lilah didn't know what he did on the team, but she assumed he was one of those in charge of trampling everyone in his path.

"No," she answered, bluntly and coldly. She let the ball leave her grasp and she stepped to the side, looking behind Sean toward the restroom doors.

"Come on, it'll be fun. I promise to go easy," he laughed.

Lilah narrowed her eyes and did a brief evaluation of Sean. Nothing about him appeared to be trustworthy, but she didn't know what he was getting at. Generally, the only time she had any interaction with him was when he was sneering at her in class for answering correctly. Something was off about him today.

"Actually," he continued. "If you don't know how to play, I could–"

"I know how to play," Lilah spat. She might not have a game room like Dawson, but there was a pool table in her home.

Sean clapped his hands and reached for the rack. "Eight-ball good for you," he asked as he began placement of the balls.

*　*　*

"Okay, okay," Gavin said as he motioned with his arms. "And then, you'll never believe what happened. Are you ready?"

He was a horrible storyteller and Kyler and Miles had a difficult time following along. For Kyler, it soon became less about Gavin's ability and more about the scene across the room.

"Dude," he insisted with a nudge when he realized Kyler's attention was elsewhere. "You really have to listen to this part."

Kyler was somewhere else entirely. While Gavin didn't seem to notice, as his best friend, Miles picked up on it immediately.

Miles interrupted Gavin once he saw what had captured Kyler's attention. "What the hell is that about?"

"I don't know," Kyler growled, taking one foot in the direction of the pool tables, only to be jerked backward.

"And worse, what do you think you're doing?"

"He's clearly annoying her!"

Miles' brows shot up questioningly while Gavin proceeded to look around in confusion. "Since when are you her protector?"

Kyler scoffed. "All Sean is doing is trying to get a rise out of me," he responded, dismissing the question.

"Obviously it's working. Now my only question is, why would you care if he's talking to Lilah?"

Kyler clenched his teeth and stared at Miles for a moment. He had this playful and knowing grin on his face that Kyler didn't like.

"Whatever you're thinking, you're wrong," he insisted, leaving before Miles could say another word.

"And yet, he's still going over there." At this point Miles was talking to himself, as Gavin was already on Kyler's swift steps toward the pool tables.

* * *

Sean's persistency greatly annoyed Lilah, so much so that she soon gave in to his request for a friendly game, completely aware as to what he must be thinking.

He handed her a cue stick and laid out some rules, or lack thereof. "So, you know how eight-ball works?"

Lilah didn't want to appear overly confident or cocky, but internally rolled her eyes. She probably knew more than him. "Stripes or solids, eight is the last one in," she shrugged, putting it as simply as possible.

He grinned. "We'll keep it easy. You don't even have to call your shots."

Upon evaluating Sean, Lilah wondered if that statement had more to do with the fact that he probably wasn't as good as he claimed.

Both Jolee and Alice were nearby now, quietly waiting, not saying a word. They knew better. They also disliked Sean just as much as Lilah.

Lilah's confidence faltered a bit when from the corner of her eye she saw Kyler finally approach her, along with a couple of his friends.

"What's going on," he asked, feigning a calm and carefree demeanor.

Lilah wasn't sure whether he was talking to Sean or herself. His eyes were very much locked on hers and they didn't appear to be pleased. It was Sean that took the second of silence as his duty to answer.

"We're just going to play a round."

Lilah diverted her attention from Kyler to Sean. There was something calculating in his voice.

Just as he leaned down to break, he rose. Lilah knew it. This wasn't a simple game of pool. The twinkle in his eyes and smirk on his face meant that it was absolutely more.

"You know what, how about we make a little wager?"

Lilah swallowed heavily. Money. Of course. "How much?"

"No, no, no," he laughed. "We're not bringing your daddy's money into this."

That, Lilah was not expecting.

"How about," Sean began, leaning on his stick and pretending to think, although Lilah was beyond certain he had long ago had something in mind. "A kiss."

Lilah choked on her own spit and gave a deep cough. "Excuse me," she managed.

Sean only chuckled. "Yeah. If I win, I get a kiss, and not some innocent one on the cheek."

Something in Kyler snapped. There was no way that Lilah would play this ridiculous game. He was just about to step in between the two when Lilah's next words caused his blood to drain, weakening him from head to toe.

"Fine," she said firmly. Behind her she heard Jolee let out a faint groan. "And if I win–"

Her statement was briefly interrupted with laughter from Sean and his two ridiculous besties, Louis and Cash.

She began again, more loudly. "If I win, you will never again speak to me, good, bad, or anything in between. I don't want your breath anywhere near the space I'm occupying."

Kyler's vision shot to Lilah and he couldn't turn away. Her words were cold and bitter. Even when she was upset with him, she hadn't spoken so harshly. The strange thing, she could have asked for or made Sean do anything she wanted, if she won of course, and yet, all she wanted was to have nothing to do with him ever again. He swore that a chill ran through the room just from her words.

He didn't allow himself to be affected and quickly brought himself back to the reality of the situation. The reality was, she stood a fifty percent chance of losing, probably even more so. He didn't want to judge, but she didn't look like the kind of person who would be good at any sports, pool included.

His insides twisted as he heard the rattling of the balls being broken and a solid going into one of the pockets.

Kyler made his way off to the side to Lilah's two friends. Neither had said anything to sway her insane decision to go through with a game he desperately wanted to come to a stop. Maybe it wouldn't have been so bad if Sean hadn't brought that stupid wager into the picture, but now that he had, and it seemed like Lilah was a willing participant, he lost it.

One of the girls was devouring a cone of ice cream, while the other looked nearly as unapproachable as Lilah. He wasn't sure if he could make a good decision, but he went with the unapproachable one.

"Jessie, right," he began as a poor introduction.

Jolee barely turned her head in his direction, although he could feel the daggers shooting from her eyes. "Sure, *Tyler.*"

Great, he had already gotten off to a bad start. "I'm sorry, I just don't–"

"I get it. If we're not out there shaking our pom-poms, you have a difficult time remembering our names."

Ouch.

"Jolee!" He remembered. He knew it was a stranger name than Jessie.

"What," she hissed, now turning to him.

"Look," he began, stepping closer and lowering his voice. "Can you call her over and talk some sense into her?"

Jolee's eyes narrowed. "Why would I do that?"

Kyler's jaw nearly dropped. "Do you really want that scum taking advantage of her?"

A villainous laugh fell from her lips and her eyes became unreadable, partly because of all the darkness they were lined with.

"Lilah seems to be doing fine," she calmly said, reverting back to her uncaring stance.

That did little to ease any tension Kyler was experiencing. "Can you just call her over?"

Jolee, now annoyed, stepped in front of him and crossed her arms. "Why?" She eyed him up and down and before he could answer, "If you want to talk to her so badly, why don't you?"

Kyler was quick in his response. "Because apparently no one else has a problem with this and I don't want–"

She stepped closer, now invading his space. "Why do you have a problem then?"

He couldn't answer. Words failed him. Breathing failed him. What was he doing? What was he thinking? Why did he have such a problem? There wasn't any answer he could give that would satisfy Jolee, both of them knew that.

Jolee continued to watch him suspiciously, but finally she gave in. "Lilah," she called out, just as Sean sank his second solid after his break. Lilah turned and Jolee waved her hand, beckoning her.

Lilah made her way over, and though she found it difficult, ignored Kyler's presence. "What?"

"He wanted to say something, but apparently he was too embarrassed in front of his friends."

Kyler's face clenched and he narrowed his eyes at Jolee.

Lilah turned toward him. "What do you want?" He knew she was still riled up a bit from Sean, but Jolee's comment couldn't have helped.

"I just think that this is stupid, and you should–"

"The game has already started," she interrupted.

Finishing off the last bite of her waffle cone, Alice now joined in. "You do realize if you lose," she started, scrunching her face before continuing. "Sean will be your fir–" Her statement was interrupted by her own shrieks of pain as Lilah jabbed her in the foot with her stick.

"I'm well-aware of the circumstances," Lilah growled.

Kyler knew what Alice was about to say and his thoughts went back to when he overheard their conversation in the library.

Alice shook her foot in hopes of easing the pain and grumbled a bit. "Fine, I get it."

"Are you going to shoot or what," Sean called from behind her.

Lilah directed her attention to Kyler. She couldn't let him throw her off her game, but something made her want to stare in his eyes for just a moment longer, searching. The only problem was, she wasn't sure what she was searching for when it came to him.

Sean's voice rang out once again, this time in a teasing and mocking tone. "Is there a problem, West?"

Kyler let out a breath and tried to remain calm, but how he hated Sean.

Lilah had to get back into her zone, and she shook whatever momentary spell Kyler had placed upon her and turned back toward the table. It was her turn.

She didn't want to be cocky right at the start. She'd allow Sean to have a bit of confidence. It would only make the end result that much more satisfying.

Kyler positioned himself in the vicinity of Lilah's two friends, along with Gavin and Miles, who looked quite uneasy as well, but still intensely focused on the game.

"Isn't this against some feminist belief of yours," Kyler huffed, not being able to stand how calm Lilah's friends were.

"Not if she's going to wipe the floor with him."

Kyler didn't see that happening. Lilah only had one of her balls in to Sean's two, and now it was his turn. He got another one in and then missed at a second.

Lilah had her second go of it and missed. She didn't even miss a little or miss to the point that a ball was almost near a pocket. She missed hitting any ball on the table.

Kyler rubbed the back of his neck in frustration.

While Jolee didn't care for any of the football players, Kyler wasn't the worst. She didn't know what his motive was, and while she was a little bitter at him for inviting Lilah and then ignoring her, there was a sense of warmth that she got at his concern for Lilah's wellbeing. It was a very small warmth, and she hoped that he cared about what happened to Lilah and this wasn't some sick game to him.

"You need to relax," she said quietly. "Lilah isn't stupid."

"Somehow I don't think being valedictorian is going to help her win."

Jolee held a satisfying grin on her face, and Kyler narrowed his eyes. He was missing something. "No, but being patient and incredible at geometry will."

"What?" He was beyond confused.

"I don't get it either," she shrugged. "Lilah tried to teach me before. That's what she always insisted. 'It's just like geometry.' It wasn't that easy for me," she laughed, which was rare. Kyler didn't think she could ever laugh, unless you call that evil cackle from earlier a laugh. She continued on. "Her parents have a table and, let's face it, she stays inside, buried in a book most of the time. She had to find something to do for mental breaks. While she won't be going professional, she easily has this."

Sean sank another ball and made his way closer to Lilah than Kyler would have liked. He watched her tense, knowing that she was bothered by Sean's presence as well.

"Get ready to pucker up, sweetheart," he whispered, or so he thought. Kyler, as well as Jolee, Alice, and a quiet Gavin and Miles all heard the disgusting statement.

Livid, Kyler turned to Jolee. "He only has two balls left, not counting the eight, and she has five. So, at what point..."

He lost his words when Lilah turned back, a small smile hidden in her eyes just for her friends. When she briefly glanced at him, he thought that maybe there was something there for him as well.

Suddenly her expression turned serious.

"9, corner pocket. 14, side pocket." She tapped her stick to the pockets she just called out.

"Here we go," Alice groaned.

As soon as the two balls went into the exact places that Lilah called, Kyler fought to contain his smile as he watched the blood drain from Sean's face. Per Sean's rules, they hadn't been calling their shots.

The next shot took Lilah a little longer as she appeared to be evaluating it from all angles. Her surroundings were a now a blur. All that mattered was winning. She couldn't wait to shut Sean up.

After a great deal of thought, she called and sank the next one. Then another, and then the last of her group.

"And finally," she said, her voice harboring a hint of boredom. "8-ball, corner pocket."

Alice let out a small squeal and jumped up and down, the pain in her foot now nonexistent. Kyler hung back as she and Jolee made their way to Lilah.

"There, are you relieved now," Miles asked with a knowing smirk.

"She beat Sean, so yeah."

Miles scoffed. "Whatever, man. You would have gone ballistic if he would have won and she would have gone through with–"

"Drop it," Kyler growled. He continued to watch Lilah for a just a little longer, but ultimately, she had her friends. She didn't need him.

For a moment Lilah expected Sean to make some rude remark or at the very least accuse her of cheating, but apparently his fragile ego couldn't handle it.

Immediately, he threw his cue stick on the table and stormed off, followed closely by Cash and Louis.

"That was awesome," Alice laughed, throwing a hand up for a high-five.

"Yeah," Jolee chimed in. "Way to show that idiot."

Lilah giggled slightly. The look on Sean's face was worth it. It would be something she'd never forget. She looked behind her friends and attempted not to act surprised, but they noticed right away how her smile faltered.

"I think he needed some air," was all Jolee said, referring to Kyler.

Lilah shook her head as though she didn't care, and quickly changed the topic.

CHAPTER 12

Though socializing was a bit difficult, the girls found that they actually had a pretty good time. It wasn't until late in the afternoon, early evening, that they decided to leave.

Lilah didn't want to come outright and say it, but before they left, she wanted to find Kyler. She was unsure why herself. Maybe she'd start with thanking him for the invite.

"Are you sure that you don't want us to wait for you," Jolee asked for the fourth time as Lilah walked with them to the exit.

"I'll be fine," Lilah laughed. "Antonio will be picking me up at the park. It's basically right across the street."

She told her friends goodbye and made her way in the other direction toward the double doors leading out to the pool, patio, and lawn. The last time she had seen Kyler he was headed outside, but even though it contained a much smaller crowd, she still didn't see him anywhere.

She pulled out her phone and clicked on the message tab with his name. It was at that point that movement in her hands stopped. Anything she thought about saying suddenly seemed stupid.

Before she could come up with something, her thoughts were interrupted.

"He's not out here," a dainty yet venomous voice spoke from behind.

Lilah quickly turned, only to have the oxygen sucked from her. There before her, hands on her hips, in an outfit suitable for a Barbie doll stood Sarah, eyeing her from head to toe. Lilah subtly glanced around, half expecting Britt or Abby to jump out from hiding, as they were generally glued to their leader.

Not that it was any of her business, but Lilah responded with, "I just came out to get some air."

There was that annoying and high-pitched chipmunk laugh of Sarah's. "You must think I'm stupid."

Lilah truly wanted to reply with what she was thinking, but opted to play dumb. "I don't know what you're talking about."

"He told everyone that you're tutoring him," Sarah barked out.

Lilah was stunned. She didn't think Kyler wanted anyone knowing that. From the very beginning he seemed adamant about it.

Sarah took a step closer, a look of revulsion plastered on her face. "Just be sure that you remember that's all you are."

Growing agitated, "And what is that supposed to mean?"

"It means," Sarah huffed. "You're just helping him with his homework, because we all need him this season. Don't start thinking he's your friend, or heaven forbid, anything else."

Lilah kept a straight face, but somewhere deep inside those words caused her to feel a little sick. Maybe she was starting to think that she and Kyler could be friends, or...No. Sarah was right, and those words shouldn't bother her.

"Well, thankfully I'm not a delusional ditz and I know the bizarre social constructs of high school." Her voice had grown cold; however, the dumbfounded look on Sarah's face told her that her words had flown over her head.

"Is that your way of calling me stupid," Sarah spat.

Lilah put on the fakest smile she could and very sweetly, "Of course not."

Apparently that only fueled Sarah's rage, and she stomped right into Lilah's face, nearly losing a flip-flop along the way.

"Listen, and listen good. What Kyler and I have is not going to be interrupted, especially by you."

There was so much about that statement that caused her blood to boil. First of all, she was definitely aware that Sarah, as well as all the other cheerleaders, hung all over the players. It wouldn't be your typical high school if they didn't. However, Kyler had never given her the impression that he was actually with any of them. While Lilah wasn't very good at picking up on signals when it came to guys, and Alice constantly pointed that out with Simon, she could have sworn that there were super rare moments where it felt like Kyler might have been flirting. Either he was complete scum, or she really sucked at reading the opposite sex and those forms of social behaviors.

What really struck her about Sarah's words was that very last part.

"What do you mean *especially* me?"

Sarah scoffed. "Perfect little rich snob, Miss Know-it-all. You think you're so smart, so pretty, you can get whatever you want with your daddy's money," Sarah began ranting.

Lilah's anger grew. Her looks were genetic, and her grades she worked for.

"One thing you can't and won't get, Kyler. So. Back. Off."

Sarah stomped in front of her as though she were going to push her. Lilah knew it was just a scare tactic. Sarah would be stupid if she attempted to put one finger on Lilah. At the end of the day, assault was assault.

Regardless how much Lilah did not want to cower down, there was no point getting into it any further with Sarah. She didn't do drama, and drama followed Sarah.

"Glad you got that off your chest," Lilah managed through gritted teeth.

Lilah proceeded to walk past Sarah. She no longer cared if she saw Kyler anymore. She'd wait until the next day and text him a quick thank you and that would be that.

"Wouldn't want to end up just like your mother," Sarah mentioned just before Lilah was out of earshot.

At that, Lilah spun on her flats. "What's that sup-posed to mean?!"

"Nothing." The smirk on Sarah's face told Lilah it was a whole lot more than nothing. "It's just that the girls and I were out the other night and happened to see your mom having dinner with Doctor Greene. He's married by the way," Sarah whispered, although no one was around. She made an insincere face of pity before bursting into a giggle fit.

"Maybe you should worry about your own family before you stick your nose in mine," Lilah retorted.

She knew nothing about Sarah's family, but she couldn't think of anything clever to say after that blow. She hoped it wasn't true. Maybe it wasn't. Her brother had mentioned a Rob. Doctor Greene's first name was definitely not Rob. How many guys were there in her mother's life?

"Face it. Your mother is a homewrecker, and it looks like the apple doesn't fall far from the tree," Sa-rah teased as she made her way back inside.

Lilah wanted nothing more than to pull her long blonde curls and throw her into the pool, but she was frozen. Only once Sarah was back inside could Lilah breathe. She had no desire to enter that place again, and with Alice and Jolee gone, all she wanted was to get away.

Past the lawn, down a slope, through trees lining the fenced in property, there was a garden gate, right across the street from one of the entries to Raymere Park.

Lilah quickly sent Antonio a text saying that it would be another hour or so and she headed across the lawn to the gate. Right now, she just wanted to be alone, and the park seemed like the perfect place to get some air.

* * *

Kyler cornered Sarah and her friends just as soon as he could get away from Miles. He had seen a good portion through the glass, and all he knew now was that Lilah was gone.

"What did you say to her," he growled, more possessively than he intended. He was sure Sarah picked up on that, as her smiled instantly faded.

"Say to who?"

"Lilah."

"Oh. She just wanted to know where the bathroom was," she said innocently, though Kyler knew it was anything but.

"Sarah, I'm serious."

She could tell from his eyes alone that he was not happy with her. "I don't know, Kyler. She's a little brat who probably didn't get her way. I have no idea what's wrong with her, but it was nothing I said. I don't see why you care..." She dragged her words out as though there was a lingering question beneath them. If there was, Kyler gave her no answer.

"Wow," Britt gasped. "I can't believe he just left."

Sarah crossed her arms and scrunched up her face, annoyed as she watched Kyler make his way across the room and out the doors leading to the patio.

"Do you think something is going on between them," Abby speculated.

Sarah pretended to choke. "Of course not. He's just using her to help him pass so that he can stay on the team. He'd be stupid if he thought of anything more with her."

"I know," Britt chimed in.

"She is really pretty though. I mean I guess I could see–"

Sarah cut Abby off instantly. "You better not finish that!"

"What is wrong with you," Britt added, feigning disgust.

"Well," Abby hesitantly continued. "If he were into her–"

"Just shut up," Sarah snapped. "She's a snob that has no friends other than those two losers, a science nerd and some goth. And she's ugly," Sarah added for good measure.

CHAPTER 13

Lilah ultimately decided on a bench near a willow tree shortly after entering the park. Surprisingly, it was pretty quiet. It would give her time to think. She clearly needed that, as her head was a complete mess.

She had no idea what was happening to her family. They were perfect. Everyone said as much. After hearing what her brother told her, and now Sarah, she couldn't imagine that there might have been signs that she was too blind to see. Worse yet, what if she was too stuck on herself, in her own world, that she had seen everything unfold right before her eyes, but she didn't care, didn't pay enough attention.

Then there was Kyler. That was a different jumbled mess of confusion. They weren't exactly friends, but he did invite her to the party, and since their spat at the hospital, which by the way, had never really gotten cleared up, they seemed to be on pretty good terms. While she knew that whatever Sarah was insinuating wasn't true, maybe, just for a second, she had thought that there could one day be something.

Lilah shook her head and laughed aloud. There was no one around to judge her. She closed her eyes and allowed her head to fall back. "You really are delusional," she whispered to herself. "There's absolutely nothing there."

Although when she said those words, she thought about that time in the library, and found herself touching the top of her hand. The tingles he left weren't there anymore, but she could remember how they felt over and over again. Unfortunately for her, it was something that hadn't gone away.

"What's not there," a voice a few steps away on the path spoke.

Lilah's eyes flew open and she jolted her head up fast enough to cause whiplash. Her eyes had to be deceiving her. It had to be anyone other than *him*.

After adjusting her posture, "What are you doing here?"

"Fine, avoid my question," Kyler joked.

Lilah refrained from pointing out that he too avoided her question. He now stood right in front of her and she had a hard time looking up at him with the sunlight that had started to begin its descent.

"Mind if I sit?"

Lilah scooted over as far as she could to one side of the bench, although it was completely unnecessary. It could easily have fit three people comfortably.

An uncomfortable silence ensued.

When Kyler stormed off, he hadn't thought about what he'd say or do if he found Lilah. Though there was an air of melancholy surrounding her, she looked alright.

No, she looked like emotionally she was alright. Physically she looked beautiful, but he wouldn't tell her that. It would be weird coming from him.

She looked adorable in her outfit, so simple and casual. He loved it. Although, he had been right when he first saw her. As he scanned over her body, he saw that from sitting, her shirt had risen a great deal in the back, and he was painfully aware that if she were to stand, little hints of skin would peek out between her shirt and jeans. He had done a good job ignoring it when she was playing pool, but now he was so close to her that it was difficult.

"I've been sitting a while," Lilah began, with the smallest bit of hesitation in her voice. "Do you feel like walking?"

"Yeah, sounds great."

Kyler rose along with Lilah. Though she tried to pull her jeans up and shirt down, it was all in vain and only drew his attention more to specific areas of her body. He didn't want to see her like that, to think of her like that. Why couldn't she be in some prep school outfit like she wore to school? That image no longer helped either, as now he thought about the cute skirts she wore and how her heels made her legs stand out. He wasn't aware that his internal groan was expressed vocally.

"Are you okay," Lilah asked, slowing her pace and falling into step at Kyler's side so that she could look up at him.

"Fine."

"Shouldn't you be getting back to the party," Lilah asked, still not understanding what he was doing in the park of all places.

"They'll be fine without me," he laughed.

"I doubt that." She didn't mean to sound bitter, but understood that's how it came out. She also noticed that despite the two of them being alone right now, he had hardly said a word to her at a gathering that he invited her to.

Kyler glanced at Lilah briefly and saw the stern and focused look on her face. "Are you mad at me?"

Lilah scoffed and shook her head. She hadn't been mad at Kyler. Maybe she was earlier. When she came to the park it wasn't the case, but now that she had time to think...

"Yes."

Kyler was genuinely surprised, and his steps faltered. "Why?"

Lilah stopped and stepped in front of him so that they were no longer side by side and now facing each other. Looking at him was difficult in the setting sunlight. The light wasn't the problem. The problem was what it did to his features.

His seemingly normal blue eyes lit up like iridescent pools of the most serene waters. If she stared into them for too long, she'd become blind or hypnotized. Then there was his hair, his incredible hair. He didn't style it much for school, or maybe it was one of those things she hadn't noticed until today. If there was such a thing as a combination between messy, spiky, suave, and neat, he had nailed it perfectly.

Though she would have said that the color was like a light brown, with the sunlight, she noticed little strands of gold in its unique color, making it appear just a bit lighter than the freshly washed look she had grown to know.

"I think it's a little rude to invite someone to a party and then ignore them."

He could no longer make eye contact with her. "I didn't ignore you."

Lilah let out a sarcastic laugh. "You didn't speak to me until Sean did, and I don't even want to know what that was about."

"You had your friends."

"So?"

He shrugged. "It's a little weird. I don't know them and–"

"That's how you get to know someone, by speaking." Lilah nearly choked on her words, and cursed herself for being such a hypocrite. She hadn't done a very good job at taking her own advice.

Kyler stepped around her and continued walking. "I don't understand why you had to make such a showing with Sean anyway."

"I didn't make a showing! It was a simple game. I don't see why–"

"The two of you had to make it a stupid bet, that's why," he answered before she had the chance to finish her statement.

"So," Lilah pressed on. Kyler was exhibiting signs of the same frustration as before and she was too curious to let it go.

"So? So what if you would have lost?"

Lilah hadn't really thought about it. She definitely wouldn't have gone through with her end of the deal, but she wasn't going to tell Kyler that. Also, she had never intended on losing.

When she didn't answer, "Would you have really kissed him?" Kyler held his breath waiting for her to respond. He didn't picture her doing something like that, but then again, he never pictured her showing up at the party to begin with.

"I don't know. Does it matter," she asked back, noting that her heart rate felt faster as the conversation progressed. She wanted it to stop but no thought nor deep breath could help with whatever feeling was racing through her.

Kyler wanted to bash his head against a tree as soon as she asked the question and he silently answered it to only himself. *Yes! Of course it mattered. Sean didn't deserve that privilege.* How he wanted those thoughts to stop. He didn't want to think of anyone kissing Lilah, himself included.

"Sean is a jerk. You could do better," was what he finally said.

"Thanks? But I'm not interested in Sean. It was just a game, and a silly bet. The only reason I went through with it is because I had no intention of losing," Lilah teased, hoping to lighten a heavy air that was falling all around them.

"He was only messing with you because of me," Kyler admitted.

"Care to explain?"

The path dropped down on one side and Kyler hopped to walk below while Lilah teetered on the stones along the side, giving her about a three-foot or more height advantage over Kyler, depending on the slope of the wall.

"We don't get along," he began.

"Why?"

She made him nervous, stepping one foot in front of the other across the rocky ledge, so carefree. "Just be careful," he grumbled. He tried his best not to reach out every time she looked a little wobbly. She was completely out of character and it took him a moment to get used to her not being the same uptight brat that he had grown to know.

Lilah rolled her eyes and ignored his warning. "Are you going to explain?"

"I don't know why he doesn't like me. He thinks I have it so easy, that I have this perfect life just handed to me. I guess he's just jealous, especially when it comes to the attention at school." He shrugged. He knew why he disliked Sean. He was a rude and unlikeable person, but he had no idea why Sean ever tore into him in the first place.

"You do get a lot of attention," Lilah admitted.

Kyler glanced up at her and found that she wasn't looking at him, only staring at her feet slowly making their way across the stones.

"Well, so do you."

Lilah chuckled. She was aware as to her reputation. It wasn't as favorable as Kyler's, but she didn't feel the need to mention what he already knew.

Changing the subject, "Honestly, why didn't you say anything to me at Dawson's?"

The fact that she was constantly around her friends had little to do with it. Something about when she walked in made him feel nervous and uneasy. For the first time in a long time, he was actually afraid to walk up and talk to a girl.

It was at that moment that a realization hit him. He shouldn't have followed her to the park. He shouldn't be walking with her, alone, at sunset. He needed to find an excuse to leave.

Lilah continued to press for an answer. "Why?"

"You can be a little intimidating," he finally responded.

"Wow." She thought for a moment. "I guess you're right. I've been told more than once that I'm a bit on the unapproachable side."

Kyler didn't know what had gotten into him when he asked, but he did it anyway. "Did you want me to approach you?"

Lilah stopped in mid-step and turned on the rocks to face Kyler. For once, he was the one looking up at her.

As soon as she looked into his eyes, her stomach flipped. She wasn't sure if it was flutters or knots, but it was stronger than she had ever felt, and it sent a dizzying feeling shooting through her.

"No," she ultimately answered, knowing it was a lie.

She attempted to continue on and that's when her balance failed her. The slick bottoms of her flats didn't connect well with the smooth stones lining the path, and though she attempted to veer toward the path on the left, that was only a few inches down, she found herself falling to the lower one, the one Kyler was walking on. Instantly, she prepared herself for the embarrassment.

Only, when she opened her eyes, her predicament was far worse than landing in the dirt on the path.

Her whole body became engulfed in a warmth she had never known. Panic ran through her as her eyes shot open, only to meet a strong and hard chest inches from her. She didn't dare look down. She could feel his hands, one on her back and one along her hip.

Kyler gradually loosened his grip, realizing that Lilah was still suspended against him, and allowed her to slip downward so that her feet were on firm ground.

The warmth from her skin seared through the palms of his hands. Why couldn't she have been wearing a sweater down to her knees? Though he was terrified of making any sort of movement, he couldn't help but let his thumb slowly massage its way along her hipbone. He never thought he'd have her this close and he had to touch her as much as she'd allow. Currently she hadn't said a word, hadn't objected, hadn't pulled away, which only caused the pounding in his chest to quicken at the thought of what he might do if she didn't.

It wasn't until their eyes finally met that something happened, something deeper. Without saying anything, each was certain that the other had to feel it.

Holding Lilah firmly into place, Kyler brought one hand upward and pushed a lock of chestnut hair behind her ear, only for it to sway back and forth across her shoulder with the breeze. She closed her eyes briefly and let out a small breath, and in that short bit of time, he wanted to remember every detail about her face, even something as silly as the way her bangs danced across her forehead.

He slid his fingers along her face until they were softly wrapped around the back of her neck, only for his thumb to remain, lightly grazing her cheek.

Lilah felt helpless. She couldn't pull away and a part of her didn't want to. She could no longer think. All she could do was feel, and Kyler's touch felt amazing, like nothing she had ever expected from a boy, and though she knew how clouded her mind was, she wanted more.

"Lilah," he whispered, all but begging her to look up at him. He needed to see her eyes again. He needed to know that she wanted this as much as he did.

As if awakening from a dream, Lilah blinked up at him, her doll-like emerald eyes full of a mixture of wonder and fear.

Just as Kyler was about to pull Lilah forward, he felt her step closer into him and his heart began to race. As if she was unsure what to do with her hands, she placed them against his chest. Her eyes widened as she allowed them to trace upward, skimming along the ridges concealed by the fabric of his shirt.

Kyler couldn't take the anticipation any longer, and with the heat radiating from her skin, he figured that the same went for her. He tipped her head slightly until he could easily meet her.

Their lips met softly and hesitantly. It was a simple kiss, one to test the waters, as both were not only unsure of the person before them, but they were unsure overall about what was happening.

Kyler was the one to pull back, not quickly, and not immediately, and he still didn't dare let Lilah slip from his arms.

Lilah wasn't sure what she was doing, or even if what she did was close to being right. All she did know was that she didn't want it to end, not yet. Nervously, she ran her hand upward along Kyler's chest until she clasped him around the shoulder. Applying the gentlest amount of pressure, she silently begged for him to continue.

This time when their lips met, there was a deeper hunger and desire, as though it had been something they wanted since the first day in that library.

Lilah felt herself stumbling backwards and realized that Kyler was delicately walking her into the path's stone wall. It was for the best, as the cold stones on her back eased the fire burning inside her as well as steadied her from blissfully falling into space.

Without thinking, Kyler deepened the kiss. For a moment, Lilah's whole body tensed against him, and just as he thought about pulling away at having pushed too far for her first kiss, she let out a delightful moan and softly dug her nails into his shoulders.

There was an electricity running between them, one that increased and heightened every normal human feeling.

Lilah's phone must have rung several times before Kyler was able to pull away from her, the sound finally registering to his ears.

"Your phone," he managed while trying to catch his breath.

Lilah barely looked at the screen before answering with shaky hands.

"Miss McCallister, I'm outside of the park. I don't see you," Antonio's voice came through. Though it wasn't on speaker, Kyler was still pressed against Lilah, steadying himself on the wall behind her, and caught every word.

Antonio's voice brought Lilah back to reality, and every portion of the day before now flashed through her mind.

Trying to control her breathing, "I'll be right there." After ending the call, Lilah directed her words to Kyler, who had now managed to put the slightest amount of distance between them. "I have to go," she said, turning to hoist herself on the stones to the path above.

"If you want, I can take you home," were the first words that flew out of his mouth. Something about what had just happened made him want to have a few more moments with her.

"No. My ride is waiting."

He tried helping her up, but she coldly brushed him off and managed herself. When she was on the path above him, all she could allow was a quick good-bye, leaving him stunned and confused. With that, she quickly rushed away, never turning back.

Kyler didn't go back to Dawson's, but he didn't go home right away either. Instead, he found himself wandering through the park, his head and heart a complete mess.

If anyone would have mentioned kissing Lilah McCallister a few weeks ago he would have thought they were insane, but in that one moment that passed between them, he had no choice. Even now, after she had completely run away from him, all he could think about was her taste, how soft her lips felt, how her body melted into his.

He wanted to pull his hair out just thinking about her. There was no way that he could be falling for Lilah McCallister. Is that even what was happening? Was he falling for her? He honestly didn't know; however, he did know that after more than half an hour, he couldn't ignore the pounding and aching in his chest.

CHAPTER 14

Lilah managed to make it through the rest of the weekend by avoidance. Alice and Jolee knew that if she were to get wrapped up in a book or her studies, they'd never get in touch with her, so after a couple texts, they had given up; however, judging from the messages, they would be all over her come Monday. Oddly, Kyler had not text her, and she had made it a point to do the same to him.

"Don't even try saying that nothing happened," Alice began.

"I can't believe you two spied on me," Lilah teased, as they made their way from a picnic table toward the school upon hearing the first bell.

"We just wanted to make sure you were okay," Jolee chimed in.

"Ugh. Then we saw Sarah. We were like two seconds away from heading out there, fists swinging," Alice playfully growled.

Jolee rolled her eyes. "No, we weren't."

They grew quiet. Lilah knew there was more; there had to be more. However, upon hearing Sarah's name, she felt sick to her stomach. Sarah's words continued to echo in her head. That, combined with the kiss, made her feel like such a disgusting person.

She was even more upset with Kyler. She wasn't going to give him the satisfaction of knowing that he was her first kiss, and as amazing as it was, it now seemed tainted. How could he kiss her if he and Sarah were dating?!

Alice's words woke her from her thoughts. "Now we're just curious about what happened with Kyler."

"What do you mean?" Lilah had no choice but to play dumb. They hadn't been there; they had no idea. This was something she'd like to keep a secret, especially should a wandering ear hear and send it back to Sarah. She wasn't afraid of her, but she didn't need the drama that followed Sarah.

"He looked really upset after talking to Sarah and we assumed he followed you..."

Jolee, not caring about boys and Lilah's love life, or lack thereof, turned down a separate hallway. "Sorry guys! See you at lunch." She then waved goodbye.

For the first time since school started, Lilah hated that she had calculus with Alice. It meant that there was no dismissing or letting up about Saturday.

"You have to tell me something. You're super jittery, like you've drank a pot of coffee," Alice quietly asked as they took their seats next to each other.

Lilah wanted her to stop talking about it. She had fought for more than twenty-four hours to get Kyler's kiss and the feeling of his hands and body out of her mind, and Alice bringing up his name wasn't helping.

"Oh. My. Gosh," she hissed, glaring at Lilah as if she could see right through her.

Lilah looked around to see if there was something that she was missing, but no, Alice was looking right into her soul.

"You kissed him," she exclaimed a little louder than she wanted, which only drew the attention of a few students passing through the aisles. When Lilah could not keep her cheeks from turning blood red, "You did! Tell me everything? How did this happen?"

Thankfully, Lilah was partially saved in the form of a substitute teacher.

"Alright class, settle down," he began in a monotone voice which showed his complete lack of care for the job. "Your teacher is out today, obviously. She left some notes that I'll be writing on the board for you to copy. I guess just try to keep up."

"Excuse me," a dainty voice came from the back. Lilah turned to see Sophie flailing her hand in the air. "You didn't take attendance."

The sub, who hadn't even bothered to introduce himself, stared her down for a minute and then quickly glanced about the room. "All the desks are full." He then turned to the whiteboard and picked up one of the markers.

Lilah knew that it was too good to be true as soon as Alice slid a piece of paper on top of her desk. It was going to be a long class period.

* * *

"What's up," Miles asked once they took their seats at the lunch table. He had a variety of tones

when he said those words, but this was most definitely his more serious one as if to say, *I know
something is wrong, spill.*

As soon as the question was asked, Kyler went to
one encounter that plagued his thoughts. He thought
working a twelve-hour shift at the hospital on Sunday would help wash it away, but the solitude only
left him to overthink the matter.

He glared at Miles as soon as he heard him
chuckle with a mouthful of burger.

"I'm not a therapist, so if you don't want to talk,
you don't have to," he began after swallowing. "But I
was right there."

"What are you talking about?"

"Your little tutor," Miles now whispered. He had no
intention of airing his best friend's business.

"What do you want me to say," Kyler grumbled. He
allowed his gaze to glance to where Lilah was sitting,
and he wished that he wouldn't have. Just looking at
her caused his insides to twist.

"What happened between the two of you?"

It wasn't a big deal. It's not like he needed to have
a sleepover and paint his nails with Miles to get it off
his chest.

With a shrug, "We kissed."

"That bad?"

Kyler couldn't describe it in the way he wanted.
The last thing he needed was his best friend teasing
him about being some romantic sissy. He also didn't
want to point out that it was one of his more real
kisses as well.

His first kiss hadn't been all that great. He was fourteen and his twelve-year-old neighbor had the biggest crush on him. When she and her family moved and they all said their goodbyes, she took it to be the end to an overly dramatic movie, probably one in which half of the couple dies. It ended up being Kyler's first kiss.

Since then, well, football took priority over girls. It's not that he didn't notice girls; he most certainly did, but something about high school, and the girls in high school, always seemed to contain a lot of drama.

"It was good," he finally corrected.

"Then what's the problem?

Kyler scoffed. "She's not the kind of girl I'm into." He felt bad about saying those words, but he didn't bother rectifying them.

Miles laughed. "And Sarah is?"

"Absolutely not!"

"If you want me to be honest," Miles began, now back to a hushed voice. "Would you catch hell from every guy on the team for pursuing the little ice princess? Definitely. Do their opinions matter when it comes to that? Hell no. Personally, I don't care who you date or don't date, as long as your passes are better than this morning," he concluded with a nudge.

Kyler groaned.

"Hurry up and get it out before Gavin and Dawson get here," he quickly spoke, nodding in the direction of the lunch line for pizza.

"I think I might have scared her. She just took off after it happened."

"I thought you said it was good," Miles cautiously asked, his mind now beginning to wonder.

"Yeah, but...I don't know. I probably shouldn't have shoved my tongue down her throat the first time kissing her." Kyler refrained from letting it slip that he knew he was Lilah's first kiss.

"Whoa," Miles gasped. The tomato from his burger fell to his tray, but he was so shocked by what Kyler admitted to that he didn't even notice. "I thought you meant kiss, like a kiss, as in singular. Maybe spur of the moment, you were in the same breathing space, I don't know...But you made out with her? Wow. Now I do have to ask, what's the deal?"

"There is no deal," Kyler growled, quickly ending the conversation as Gavin and Dawson approached. Miles shot him a look that meant he still had a great amount of explaining to do.

* * *

Lilah sat in the library and waited for Kyler. Like always, she knew that he wouldn't be there immediately after the final bell, as his eighth period was athletics; however, she was shocked when she received a text from him.

Kyler: Doing afternoon practice today.

Lilah: Test in Hughes' tomorrow. You can have my notes.

Kyler: You don't need them?

Lilah was thankful that Hughes announced on Friday that the test had been postponed until Tuesday. She wouldn't tell Kyler, but all she did was prepare for the test on Sunday.

A part of her was disheartened to learn that she would not be studying with Kyler that afternoon. She thought he might ask to meet at the public library later that evening, but when he didn't, there was also a small amount of relief that came along with that. Up until now, she hadn't spoken with him since the kiss, and she hadn't figured out what she would say when they should eventually meet in person.

She didn't bother messaging him back to ask how to get the notes to him. Instead, she boldly headed to the field. If he had told his teammates that she was his tutor, why should it matter?

Lilah completely ignored the mass of bodies on the grass grunting and running into each other like they had no sense, and made her way to the gruff man yelling commands from the side.

Coach Turner appeared very irritated. As red as his face was, Lilah figured it might be from the heat, but changed her mind as a cool breeze blew past her. It was a breeze that left her with the same feeling only two days prior when...

"Excuse me," she coughed, tapping Coach Turner on the shoulder. If he were any taller, she'd be on her tiptoes.

"What?!" He appeared taken aback when he turned to face the dainty little girl behind him. He cleared his voice and gained his composure. "Miss McCallister, sorry about that."

"That's alright," Lilah said, now slipping her bag from her shoulders.

Coach Turner eyed her suspiciously as she rummaged around, finally withdrawing a purple spiral. She stood and proudly presented it to him.

Lilah read the confusion on his face. "If you could see to it that Kyler gets that?"

"Oh! Yeah, yeah. Of course. Everything still okay between you two? Is he staying focused?"

Lilah took in a shaky breath and felt her skin heating. The coach meant his studies, she knew that, but she couldn't tell her mind and body to cool it with how it registered when he asked about Kyler's focus. All she could think about was the focused attention he had on her for those few moments on Saturday, and the sickness and disgust at being some *home-wrecker*, kissing another girl's boyfriend, regardless how horrible said girl was, returned.

CHAPTER 15

Kyler dug through his bag and withdrew the purple notebook that his coach had given him.

He had seen Lilah at practice, and while she caused him to lose focus at first, something else about her presence gave him the energy and adrenaline that his body desperately needed after a long and stressful weekend. Though he was ready to crash and call it a night, she had gone through the trouble of getting her notebook to him, so the least he could do was spend some time studying and pray that he passed the test.

It was going well at first. She took amazingly concise notes and had some of the prettiest handwriting he'd ever seen.

Everything would have continued perfectly, had he not come across a folded piece of paper that obviously didn't belong in the notebook. It looked like it had been crumpled at first, then folded, and it had probably fallen into the pages somewhere along the way. He should have ignored it, but his curiosity as to its contents was too overwhelming.

He moved from his desk to his bed and tirelessly plopped down. Before he even had the paper completely unfolded, he already knew it was some form of note. There were two distinct pieces of handwriting, one in pink, and one in black. Kyler easily recognized the one in black as belonging to Lilah.

Maybe he wouldn't have read it had it not been for that first sentence; however, that one line drew him in.

I can't believe you kissed him!

Stop it and take notes.

Shut up! That was your first kiss! How was it?

Fine.

Lilah!!! Tell me. This guy is boring and writes slow.

We kissed. It was an accident. What more do you want?

Kyler froze when he read that and felt his insides churn. An accident? He couldn't believe that's what she thought about it. Her slipping and falling was an accident, but it's not like she accidentally fell on his lips. Hadn't there been some kind of moment between them, drawing them together? He shook his head at the mushy thoughts running through his mind and kept reading.

So your first kissed sucked?

Pretty much. Now will you drop it?

I could have sworn that you were going to say you saw fireworks and were madly in love with Kyler West.

Sorry to disappoint.

Not even a little crush?

Not in this lifetime.

Strangely, those words were worse than any blows he had taken on the field. He couldn't explain why he suddenly felt queasy and dizzy, but he did. A million different thoughts ran through his head.

Aside from a couple texts about meeting for tutoring, he had no contact with Lilah since the kiss. She left coldly. Maybe she did regret it. Maybe, rather than confront him with how she really felt, she intentionally placed that paper in her notebook, knowing that he'd find it.

He thought about putting it back, but instead ripped it to shreds and tossed it into the trashcan near the bed. He wanted it gone forever.

Fueled with frustration, surprisingly he was able to study. At least how well he did on that test was in his control.

Forget Lilah McCallister.

Forget that stupid kiss.

Forget is what they both did.

CHAPTER 16

"Why do you think we're being called to a family meeting," Rover huffed as he landed on the sofa.

Lilah didn't bother looking up from her book. "No idea."

"I heard Jamie isn't coming home until Thanksgiving break."

"Good."

Jamie was the eldest of the siblings, needless to say, she and Lilah did not get along. Jamie was pretty much the Sarah in high school, and Lilah knew it. Her first two years of high school were her sister's last.

Jamie thought herself to be a model, even if it was only to her social media following. As far as school, she was in the process of getting a degree in some sort of fashion. That's about all Lilah knew. Their dad was not pleased about it.

"Did you max out any credit cards? That would warrant this," Rover continued.

Lilah finally put her book down and shot him a look. "Where would I go to max out a credit card?"

"I don't know, a bookstore," he laughed.

Lilah rolled her eyes and was just about to get back to her reading when her parents, Steven and

Jenna, ominously strolled in. Just the looks on their faces suggested that something was seriously wrong.

While their mother sat down a distance away from them in an accent chair near the windows, their father remained standing.

Rover quickly spoke up. "Did someone die?"

Lilah groaned at her brother's candor.

"No, son," Steven spoke in a commanding voice. "We're here to talk to you about the status of our relationship," he continued in a formal way.

Lilah felt sick to her stomach. What were they doing? Were her parents complete idiots when it came to actual parenting? What they were saying just couldn't be happening.

"So you're still going to live here," a confused Rover asked after a great deal of explanation, mostly from Steven.

"Yes. While we haven't started with formal divorce proceedings, we are separated, and though we'll live under the same roof for the time being, we are living separate lives," Steven continued.

"That doesn't make sense," Lilah screamed.

"Sweetie," Jenna chimed in. "I know this is a lot, but this has been going on for some time. We figured that we needed to tell the two of you before–"

"Before what, mother," Lilah spat as she rose from her seat. She didn't intend on listening to much more. "Before Rover found some Rob guy in your phone? Before my classmates saw you out to dinner with Doctor Greene, who, by the way, is married as well? Before that? Is that what you're talking about? If so, too late!"

Lilah stormed out of the living room and up the stairs to her bedroom, tears quickly finding their way down her face, blurring her vision. Once she reached her haven, she slammed the door and locked it. She then flung herself on her bed, buried her head in a pillow, and allowed the tears to come. It had been so long since she had truly cried.

Her head was so confused. She had the perfect family, everyone said so, and now her parents were destroying it.

* * *

From the distance, Kyler noticed that something seemed off with Lilah. Over the last two weeks, since the *incident*, he and Lilah had fallen into a comfortable level of acquaintanceship. If he was honest, she still sent his stomach into a tailspin anytime they held eye contact for longer than they should; however, she never mentioned the kiss, so he never mentioned it. After all, the note pretty much said all he needed to know.

He had to wonder if her friends noticed. They seemed to be chatting like normal, but when there was laughter, Lilah's smile was forced and insincere. He'd know. It was a rarity to even see.

"Hey, Ky," Sarah said, interrupting his thoughts of Lilah.

He quickly looked away from her table. He wasn't sure what the deal between Lilah and Sarah was, but he didn't want to find out. High school girls could be evil and vicious. The last thing he wanted was to get in the middle of that.

"What's up," he casually responded, so as not to be rude. He didn't intend for that to be an invitation for her to sit down.

"Since you don't have a game tomorrow, what are your plans?"

Kyler hadn't given much thought to it. He had to work tonight, but he had been given the weekend off, Friday included. He should have tried to work since it was their bye week, but was excited to get a full weekend off from it all. He had hoped to relax and perhaps do a few odds and ends around the house to help his mother and sister out; however, his mother had Saturday free and wanted to go into the city. He had heard her mention the zoo. While it seemed childish, he had a greater appreciation for those kinds of days since his father had gone.

"I'm not sure. My mom probably has a list of junk for me," he answered, placing the blame on his mom. Sarah was annoying but he didn't want to be rude and sharp with her if he didn't have to. Sadly, she had difficulty getting the message.

"Do you think you could go to a movie tomorrow? After school? Or maybe later in the evening?"

Kyler gave her his attention now. He didn't mind girls being forward, but sometimes it gave off the wrong impression, especially in Sarah's case. It immediately made him think of Lilah and how shy and hesitant she became the few times in the past when they had gotten off topic, how easily she blushed, how nervous she was in the park.

He mentally scolded himself. One of the hottest girls in the school was basically asking him out and all he could do was find fault with her, all because of some girl who wanted nothing to do with him.

"I don't think so."

Sarah's jaw dropped. Obviously, she wasn't accustomed to rejection. "Well, that's still tomorrow." She shrugged and thought how to recover. "Why don't you think about it and let me know?"

Kyler took a deep breath and went back to his previous thought. She absolutely didn't take rejection. "Yeah. Sure," he replied to shut her up, though his words held no weight or meaning.

It seemed enough to please Sarah and she patted him on the shoulder and excused herself to go back to her friends.

He watched as she left. Every guy on the team either had a crush on her or, at the very least, wanted to hook up with her, but something about Sarah just didn't do it for him. Looking at her body, she was gorgeous, like a manufactured Barbie, but he cringed when he had to talk to her. That was a good enough reason to not date her, right?

Kyler: Public library today? 5-6:30 or so?

When Lilah read the text, just out of a strange habit, she looked up to where she knew she'd find Kyler. He was laughing at something with his regular group of friends. She smiled just looking at him, remembering how his laugh sounded. It was melting. She shook the thought away. Who cared about Kyler's laugh? He just happened to get lucky being born with it. She did notice that, surprisingly, Sarah wasn't cuddled up next to him like earlier. Not that she cared about that either, but it was worth noting.

Kyler was disappointed when all he received back was a one-word confirmation.

Lilah, Jolee, and Alice split off in different directions after lunch, as they did every day. With different interests, they had very few classes together.

Lilah nearly screamed bloody murder when she felt a tug, yanking her into the cubby of a classroom that had no class for the upcoming period. She knew because she remembered, and the strangest sense of déjà vu flooded over her.

"What is wrong with you," she snapped.

Kyler held the door open to the darkened room and Lilah looked at him like he had lost his mind.

"Tech apps is off for this period. While I was waiting, I decided to try the door." He played with the handle to show her that it was indeed unlocked. "Can we go inside to talk for a second?"

Lilah glared at him. "Absolutely not."

He let the door close. "Fine. Here is good too."

He crossed his arms and leaned into the door behind him. Lilah couldn't help directing her attention to his chest. She had never noticed how strong and manly his arms looked, but of course they would, he obviously worked out more than he studied. She vomited a little after associating words like strong and manly with Kyler. She didn't want to picture him like that.

"Are you sure? You're not embarrassed that someone might see you talking to me?"

Kyler remembered what that friend of hers had said at the party and rolled his eyes. "On the contrary, people might think I have magical powers if I can get the most stuck-up girl in school to talk to me."

Lilah huffed and spun on her heel to storm off, but Kyler softly placed his hand on her shoulder, causing a warmth to spread all the way down to her toes, disabling any further movement other than turning back to face him.

"Sorry."

"Don't look so broken. It would take more than that to hurt my feelings," Lilah sighed impatiently. She didn't want to be late, and Kyler was dangerously close to making that happen.

Kyler watched her carefully. Something was definitely different about her. Even her words, as cruel as she intended for them to be, came across as lacking.

"Do you want to talk?" He clenched as soon as he said the words. He sounded like some weird counselor or therapist.

Lilah now crossed her arms and evaluated Kyler, wondering what he had up his sleeve. Before she could say anything, he rather nervously continued on.

"You look a little off today. I just wanted to see if everything was okay."

Now Lilah truly froze. She thought that she had done a pretty good job of getting through the morning so far, even Jolee and Alice didn't comment on her behavior. How could Kyler possibly think such a thing?

"I'm fine."

He took a step closer, studying her. "You don't seem fine." He swallowed heavily, not believing how bold and forward he was being with her.

Lilah forced herself to push certain thoughts away, thoughts of her parents, thoughts of how good Kyler smelled. It took every ounce of energy in her to maintain her demeanor.

"You don't know me. Don't go making assumptions like you do," Lilah told him as coldly as she could.

Before he could get any closer, before he could touch her again, she tore off to her next period class, the tardy bell ringing, silencing her panicked breaths from the situation she had just left.

CHAPTER 17

Lilah still felt guilty when she woke Friday morning, but after lunch, there was no way that she could spend nearly two hours with Kyler. He was caught up with his assignments for the most part, even passing English with a solid B at the moment. So he could miss a few of their sessions. While he complained relentlessly, he seemed to be doing much better with *Pride and Prejudice* than he did with *Hamlet*, although, if Lilah had to hear one more comment about Kiera Knightly, she was going to lose it.

School was just another day. She tried to put on her best fake smile when she was around her friends; if they noticed anything, they didn't say it. She'd get through her family drama in time. There was no sense in dragging outsiders into it as well. She found that she was even more self-conscious when it came to lunch. She tried her hardest not to make any eye contact with Kyler, but from time to time it was like she could feel his eyes on her, and twice she broke down and looked up, only for him to immediately look away.

She could assume that he was irate at her for canceling, but he'd have all weekend to get over it.

By the end of the day, Lilah felt like she could finally breathe. She had no plans for the weekend other than staying in her room and reading. With the cool temperatures coming in, maybe she'd even take Rover to the park. Little did she know, when she walked through the entry, her mother had other plans, plans that didn't involve her or her brother.

"Where have you been," Jenna screamed before Lilah could even close the door.

"School," Lilah replied bitterly. Over the last forty-eight hours she had suddenly grown quite sharp with her parents.

"I have been texting you!"

"My phone must have been on silent in my–"

Her mother interrupted her. "I'm dropping Rover off for a weekend sleepover at a friend's house. Go pack a bag," Jenna insisted.

"What do you mean go pack a bag? Wait, where's dad and Antonio?" Until then, Lilah hadn't given it much thought. When Jolee insisted that Lilah ride home with her so she could tell her about her upcoming weekend trip to her grandmother's, Lilah didn't bother calling Antonio. It would have been nice to know that he wasn't even an option should she have needed.

Lilah watched as her mother fumbled for words. "The two of you haven't been spending near enough time with your friends. I thought you might like to get out this weekend."

Lilah narrowed her eyes. "No thanks."

She could see right away that her mother wasn't pleased with her words, but she also knew that her mother caring about whether or not she saw her friends was a load of lies.

"Lilah," Jenna sighed. "It's not an option. You need to go stay with one of your friends this weekend."

"Why?!"

"I don't have to explain myself to–"

"Let me guess, so you can have the house to yourself? So you can shack up with one of your *friends*," Lilah spat, now furious with her mother.

She wasn't stupid. Her mother's week-old pink nails were now red, and she wasn't capable of attaining the remarkable waves through what appeared to be newly bleached hair on her own.

"I am your mother. Don't speak to me like that. What has gotten into you?"

"Me," Lilah screamed. "What has gotten into you and dad? You two are the mental ones!"

"I don't have time for this little outburst of yours. Go pack a weekend bag–"

"So, you're kicking me out," Lilah interrupted.

Jenna skeptically watched her daughter, feeling like whatever her response was, Lilah had a hidden agenda. Sometimes she hated how smart her children were.

"No," she slowly answered, now more calmly. "I think that you need to get out and spend time with your friends."

Lilah quickly had a response. "Why can't I have my friends over then?"

"Don't push me," Jenna growled, growing angrier with her daughter, as well as the quickly passing time.

"And if I have nowhere to go?"

"Don't be dramatic. I'm sure one of them finds you tolerable enough to deal with you."

Lilah grit her teeth and didn't allow her mother's words to have an effect on her. "When can I come back?" It felt like the strangest thing in the world to ask that. Her mother had never behaved like this before.

"Your father will be back from his business trip sometime Sunday morning. So, Sunday morning."

Lilah heard a slight bit of uncertainty and nervousness in her mother's words. Rather than argue, Lilah decided to sit back and think things through. She didn't hate her mother by any means, but she was extremely upset by what she was trying to do. There's no way that their father would be on board with her sending his children from their home while she used it as...Lilah didn't even want to think about what plans her mother had for that weekend.

As soon as she got to her room, she grabbed a pink backpack and small matching duffel bag from her closet and began packing. Her main categories were always sleepwear, comfort wear, and generally an assortment of nicer attire, skirts, dresses and such. As she folded each item, she found that she leaned more toward the side of comfort this time. While Raymere Grove had its fair share of places where she wouldn't be caught dead in a pair of jeans, she didn't imagine she'd be venturing to any of those for the weekend.

Thinking about the weekend, knowing Jolee wasn't an option, Lilah sent Alice a text. She kept it simple, only asking if she could spend the night. Alice would want more details than a text allowed. Lilah only became uncertain and a bit frantic when more than thirty minutes went by in silence from Alice. Unfortunately, her mother's screams shattered that.

✳ ✳ ✳

Kyler parked his truck in the parking lot of the Raymere Public Library with twenty minutes before its early Friday closing time of seven. He didn't know how much work he'd be able to get done over the weekend, but he'd rather have the materials just in case.

"Picking up an online reservation," he responded when the woman at the desk asked.

"Last name?"

"West."

She clicked around on the keyboard before, "Oh, yes. I just pulled those. One moment."

Kyler gave her some time to collect the books from the unorganized cart behind her and begin scanning them out. He leaned into the counter and observed the rest of the library. It was dead on a Friday night. There was an elderly couple in the computer station, and a woman with an armful of cookbooks in the nonfiction part. What caught Kyler's attention most

169

was someone past a set of glass windows leading into the children's reading room.

It was the brown hair with just the right hint of red that caught his attention. Though he was tired from the lumber he had unloaded that afternoon, as well as the warm shower that soothed his muscles, something about seeing her in such close proximity was like the jolt of caffeine that he desperately needed; however, he was still very much irritated at her for bailing on him the day before.

The woman at the counter broke his train of thought. "Here you are then. These are due back in two weeks."

Kyler crammed the books in an empty drawstring bag he had stuffed in the back of his jeans. He slipped it over his shoulders and began to make his way out, but before he reached the exit, he turned and headed to the children's room. The library would be closing soon anyway. If she became sharp and nasty, he wouldn't have to deal with her for long, but he really wished that she wouldn't be.

By the time he finally walked in, she was curled up in one of the beanbags, quickly reading through a book. No wonder she excelled in English, as well as every other subject. She had probably memorized *Hamlet* before he ever got through the first act.

Lilah hadn't noticed Kyler quietly making his way across the room. She was well into *Charlotte's Web*. It had always been a childhood favorite of hers, but reading it today proved difficult through the blurred vision and sniffles that refused to go away.

Startled from nearby movement, Lilah pulled the book down and looked to the beanbag next to her. Her tear infested vision had to be betraying her. It had to be some sort of sick mirage. There was no way that Kyler West was sitting next to her in the children's reading room of the public library on a Friday night.

Kyler tried to hide his shock. He wasn't sure if he should look away or continue to stare at her like she was some three-headed alien. He tried composing himself the best he could. He knew something had been off with Lilah the day prior, but never in his life did he think he'd see her crying.

"It's allergies," Lilah immediately responded. She tried dabbing at her eyes delicately enough so that she wouldn't have mascara smeared all over.

Kyler wanted nothing more than to call her out on the lie, but she genuinely looked to be in a state of undoing. He had only seen her vulnerable once, but he immediately pushed that thought away. What he saw in front of him was something completely different.

"What's wrong," he asked, only for her to shake her head and refuse to meet his eyes.

Her nose was buried in the book, but she was no longer reading, only using it to put up a wall between herself and perhaps the one person she refused to believe knew anything more about her than her name.

Kyler grabbed the top of the book, softly closed it and place it next to Lilah's feet. He didn't say anything, only sat back, made himself comfortable and waited for her to talk. It was something his mother always did with his sister, particularly when she was going through a breakup. Not so strangely, he was near certain that wasn't Lilah's problem.

Lilah stared at the laces on her sneakers, terrified to look up, terrified to speak, terrified of the person next to her seeing her like this. With all her might she stopped her emotions from coming through. She blinked several times and dabbed at any remaining wet spots beneath her eyes. After taking in a few deep breaths, it seemed to work. She could fall apart later.

While Kyler waited for Lilah to compose herself, he took notice to the bags she had with her and became even more concerned. He was just about to check the time when the woman from the desk popped inside and gave them a ten-minute warning.

Kyler knew that Lilah didn't drive and he had so many questions that would take longer than ten minutes to answer, which is how he found himself asking, "Have you had supper yet?"

Lilah narrowed her eyes and finally looked up at him. The answer was obvious to him, but so far, she had barely said anything to him. He thought a question would at least break the ice a bit, obviously he was wrong.

"I'm going to head to Flip's Grill for a burger, if you wanted to come along," he finally asked, trying to suppress a smile as her eyes widened at the suggestion.

Lilah swallowed heavily. She wanted to ask Kyler if he had lost his mind. Flip's Grill, named after the funniest person in town, Philip Rogers, was busy on even the slowest of days. Friday nights through the weekend were crazy.

Rather than decline or accept, "Aren't you afraid we'll run into some of your friends? I'd hate for you to be seen with–"

"Stop," Kyler huffed. "It's not like you go out of your way to speak to me in public." While he didn't want to argue with her, at least it seemed to be a distraction from whatever else was bothering her. "Just so you know, I planned on using the drive-thru. I'm starving and don't feel like waiting on a table and then my order, and if you decide to come with me, I'm pretty sure you don't want to be seen in a crowded restaurant right now, regardless of who you're with," he pointed out.

Lilah didn't want to appear too eager, and while she still hadn't figured out her situation for the evening, she wasn't for a second under the assumption that she could simply hide in the bathroom until the library closed.

"I don't eat burgers."

Kyler laughed and reached for her bags. "Then you can get a salad or whatever."

Lilah tried grabbing her bags just as Kyler stood with them, but he waved her off and whispered something about having them. He was only being nice because he saw her crying; that's what she told herself.

She wouldn't tell Kyler, but Lilah had to admit, as soon as they drove into the parking lot of Flip's Grill, she had a craving for the greasy goodness that Alice drooled over. Since her mother's diets, she mostly ate bland vegetables, salads, and any meat was generally baked and dry enough to choke on. Therefore, when Kyler asked her what she wanted, there was a brief spark of happiness that flickered through her as she told him a cheeseburger. It took him by surprise as well.

Lilah clammed up as soon as Kyler pulled in to one of the parking areas of Raymere Park. From the corner of her eye, he looked as calm as could be, which only further proved to her that anything about that moment in the park was a joke and meant nothing.

"Don't forget your drink," he said as he grabbed his own along with the large paper bag.

The ten-minute ride had been miserable. The smell of the food nearly killed them. Lilah hadn't been in the mood to talk, so she didn't bother to ask Kyler where they were headed, and he didn't see the point in telling her.

While there was still a bit of daylight for the late evening, the fading sun combined with the clouds had been enough to cause the lamplights to come on.

Lilah continued to follow closely behind Kyler, to hopefully prevent any conversation, as he made his way to an area of picnic tables and lamplights that looked like giant candles.

Lilah stood, waiting, feeling awkward about the whole situation, while Kyler sorted through the bag.

He read over the labels and placed two burgers and fries in front of him, and a burger and smaller box of fries across the table.

He looked up at Lilah. "You okay?"

"Yeah, fine," she nervously answered as she took a seat where he had sat out her food.

Kyler couldn't hide his laughter when Lilah took a bite and let out the smallest of moans, like it was the best thing she had ever eaten. Even in the dim light he could see the pink tint of her cheeks intensify.

"It's really good," she mumbled through a full mouth, which she never did. Something about eating a greasy burger in the park made her feel more comfortable, and she was able to forget about her manners.

"When was the last time you had a burger?"

Lilah had to think. Technically she had one about two weeks ago, but if she told Kyler about that, she'd never hear the end of it. The thing she ate was nothing like what she had in her hands.

"I guess when our grade went on the end of year trip to the theme park, so sophomore year."

Kyler shook his head. "I don't know how you do it."

"Well, I don't or can't cook, and I don't go out much. So, I only eat what's prepared when I get home."

She grew quiet when she mentioned home, and he watched as whatever little glimmer of light that had started to come back faded away.

It probably wasn't the right time to ask, but he got the impression that there wasn't going to be a right time. "What's with the bags?"

"Nothing," Lilah immediately responded, a little too quickly for his liking.

A cool October wind passed by that sent chills through Kyler. He saw Lilah try to hide her shivers, not once complaining. He was just about to ask her if she was cold but realized how stupid and unnecessary the question was.

He wrapped the remainder of his burger back up in hopes it would stay warm. "I'll be right back."

Before Lilah could swallow, much less say anything, he had jogged off. She took that small window of solitude to finally breathe, partly from trying to eat what seemed too large for an average burger, and partly from being around Kyler.

"What are you doing," she whispered to herself. She glanced around and listened for footsteps. The last thing she wanted was Kyler popping up on her again while she was talking to herself. She shook her head. "This isn't a date. Absolutely not a date. Just because he paid doesn't mean...Ugh...What is wrong with you?"

She put the last few bites down. Her body could not handle anymore. Even though Kyler was probably twice her size, she couldn't understand how he could eat two as well as the fries.

She looked off to the side when she heard fast approaching footsteps. Kyler had something dark in one of his hands. Lilah couldn't figure out what it was until it was flung in her face.

He didn't want to make a big deal of it, so he casually tossed the hoodie to Lilah, knowing that his mother would be scolding him right now for his delivery.

"What's this," Lilah asked, recognizing what it was, but taking a second to process.

"You looked cold," Kyler said with a shrug and got back to finishing his second burger.

Lilah squirmed from side to side. It was such a kind gesture, even though he threw it at her like a football. She tried to calm whatever was going on in her stomach, from the burger no doubt, as she put her arms through the overly large sleeves. That's when she caught a whiff of it and wrinkled her nose.

"It's clean," Kyler grumbled.

"I didn't say anything!"

"You didn't have to. You made a face."

Lilah looked away, trying to hide the redness coming to her face. "It's not like that," she mumbled.

Kyler barely heard her, but dropped it. It wasn't a conversation worth pursuing, not when there was something bigger going on with her.

Lilah honestly didn't mean to make a face, nor did she mean to offend Kyler, especially after he had done one of the nicer things any boy had ever done for her. The truth was, his hoodie didn't smell bad at all, not an ounce of sweat, although she was beginning to wonder if that would have had a negative or positive effect on her now. Instead, it smelled just like whatever he showered in or sprayed on. It was a scent that made her feel like a silly girl with a ridiculous crush, and that wasn't her.

She was snapped back to reality when Kyler repeated, "Are you going to finish that?"

Now her face scrunched up in slight disgust. "No...Why?"

He didn't answer her, only shoved the remaining few bites of her burger in his mouth.

"What," he asked, genuinely shocked, when he saw the way she was looking at him. "It's no different than me..." He stopped before he could finish that sentence and cleared his throat. He then guzzled the rest of his soda to account for the reason there was now an uncomfortable silence.

"Thanks for the meal," Lilah said.

She realized that whatever they were doing was now coming to an end. It was getting darker and cooler and Kyler, who kept glancing at the time on his phone, appeared to need to get somewhere.

He looked up at her, his face serious, and those gorgeous blue eyes masked a million questions running through his mind.

"What's going on with you?"

So far Lilah had felt so much better since leaving the library. Sure, there was still that tiny voice she kept buried deep within, warning her that she had yet to figure out where to go for the night. "Nothing."

"Stop! I can see you. I can look at you and tell that something is wrong. Then there's the bags. What's up with that," he began, his words now very insistent.

Lilah rose. "It's probably time to leave."

Kyler quickly shoved the remaining trash into the paper bag and tossed it in a nearby trash can as he rushed to keep up with Lilah.

"Hey," he said, gently pulling on her elbow and forcing her to turn around to face him.

He regretted it immediately. Tears streamed down her face and she refused to make eye contact with him.

"If you won't tell me what's wrong, will you just answer some yes or no questions?"

Lilah reluctantly nodded.

"Are you running away?"

She met his eyes briefly and scoffed at the suggestion. Apparently, it was absurd enough to cause her tears to slow.

"Okay, did you get kicked out?" When she didn't answer, his stomach flipped. "What did you do to–"

"That's not a yes or no question," Lilah screamed, now turning from him.

He had never seen her so upset and dramatic. Though her back was facing him, he could see that she was trying her best to dab away her tears with the sleeves of his hoodie; however, he found that he didn't mind.

He was surprised that she spoke on her own free will, without him asking another question.

"I was asked to go stay at a friend's this weekend."

He didn't understand why that was a problem and was just about to speak up when he realized that she really didn't have many friends.

Everyone in school knew her. Rich girl. Her dad owned McCallister Industries. Genius. She'd probably end up going to Harvard. Beautiful. If she cared more about her looks than studying, no doubt she'd be on a billboard somewhere. Yet, with everything going for her, she was as cold as ice and had very few people in her corner. Maybe with everything she had going for her, people failed to see that she was severely lacking in some areas. It took that very moment for Kyler to realize it.

She turned to him, her eyes now dry, but he could tell she was trying her best to keep more from surfacing. "Jolee is out of state for the weekend. I was waiting at the library to hear back from Alice. It turns out her parents let her drive to a conference in the city. I tried calling my dad, thinking maybe he could get me a hotel room, but he didn't answer, besides if he knew that..." She let her words drift off. She absolutely should not be telling Kyler about her parents' marital problems.

"You have nowhere to go..."

"I know what you're thinking. How pathetic."

Kyler stepped forward. He wasn't sure what he was thinking, or what was coming over him, but all he wanted was to have her in his arms. Just to hold her, to make her feel wanted. Instead he blurted out the most ridiculous statement he could have made. "That's not what I think at all. Why don't you stay the night with me?" He quickly corrected himself after Lilah's eyeballs nearly dropped from their sockets. "I mean, at my house. Why don't you stay at my house?"

He repeated the words to himself in his head after saying them. Perhaps he should have ran the statement through his head prior to vocalizing it. What in the world was he thinking?

Lilah felt like the burger was about to make a second debut. She couldn't have heard him right; however, the eerie and awkward silence suggested differently.

Kyler shifted his weight uncomfortably and waited for her response.

Lilah's head was a jumbled mess, but if she looked past it all, the only lingering question she had was where she planned on going.

"It's not a big deal, you can crash on the couch for a night," Kyler finally spoke. He could tell that a million different thoughts were running through Lilah's head, ones that he knew she'd never share.

Lilah swallowed heavily. "I don't think that's a good idea."

"Why?" Kyler closed his mouth. He didn't want to come off as persistent, and Lilah was right. It wasn't a good idea.

"It's a nice offer, I just…" She couldn't find a good excuse. That was wrong. There was absolutely one very good excuse, but she didn't plan on treading into that territory, not tonight. "I just don't know you that well."

Hoping to lighten the mood, Kyler did the best thing he knew and made a joke of it. "You think I might murder you in your sleep."

The smile on his face eased the tension and Lilah took a deep breath. "I'm worth more to you alive than dead."

There was a little sparkle in her eyes and Kyler longed to keep it there. He couldn't stand to see her cry.

"Well, what do you say? If it makes you feel any better, my sister cooks awesome breakfasts on the weekend," he began, this time attempting not to come on so strong.

Lilah had a hard time looking at him, something about the light, or lack thereof, and his gorgeous features. He looked so sincere and innocent, and against her better judgement, she found that she wanted to accept his offer. She told herself it was only because it was getting late and she was running out of options, but the loud beating of her heart told her that wasn't the whole truth.

"On one condition," Lilah pointed out just as they reached his truck.

It was almost like he could read her mind. "I'd prefer that no one at school find out either," he said with the cutest boyish smile that nearly made Lilah melt right there.

CHAPTER 18

"Is this the cheerleader," were the first words out of Krista's mouth when Kyler walked in with Lilah.

He watched as Lilah's expression turned into an icy cold hostility. Not only did his sister just assume that she was a cheerleader, which for some reason Kyler didn't think Lilah would find as a compliment, but the statement also suggested that there was clearly a cheerleader in the picture. While nothing had progressed since the kiss a couple weeks ago, Kyler still didn't want Lilah getting the wrong impression.

Thankfully a slobbery black and white mammoth cut the tension by nearly knocking Lilah over. She braced herself on the back of the couch and Kyler pulled the dog back, realizing that Lilah looked absolutely terrified.

"Sorry. Max really likes people."

"No, it's fine. He just took me by surprise," Lilah insisted, but Kyler had already started pulling the dog to a set of sliding glass doors.

He cautiously released Max. "Really? It looked like you were afraid of dogs."

"Of course not." Her voice rose a bit and a genuine smile came to her face as she knelt closer to the floor to be on the same level with the dog. "We're just not allowed to have them," she admitted.

Kyler watched her with Max and a rush of feelings came soaring through him. He hated how she kept doing that. He wished that she would have stayed that same girl that he thought he had known for years, that cold and distant know-it-all.

Krista finished drying a plate and placed it in the cabinet. Once she hung the dish towel in its place, she came around to the living room where Kyler and Lilah were playing with Max.

"Sarah, I presume."

Lilah stood just as Kyler began shouting. "Seriously?! What is wrong with you?"

"Actually, it's Lilah," she shyly corrected, feeling slightly uncomfortable staying in Kyler's home after remembering that wonderful piece of information.

"Lilah," Krista questioned, looking to her brother.

The awkwardness ensued. Great. Kyler had never mentioned her name to any of his family, and why should he. She was no one, other than a tutor, to him.

As if a lightbulb went off, Krista's demeanor softened. "The cupcake girl?"

Lilah quietly repeated the words to herself, her eyes narrowing in confusion.

Kyler huffed. He supposed it was payback for all the times he embarrassed his sister in front of her boyfriends. The only difference, he was a kid, he got a pass for that, and of course Lilah wasn't his girlfriend. It was still all very embarrassing.

"She's standing right here," Kyler grumbled.

Krista rolled her eyes. "My brother isn't the best with introductions," she began, now more eagerly and much more nicely than when she assumed Lilah was a cheerleader. "I'm Krista, his much older and wiser sister." She extended her hand and Lilah took it.

Attempting to ease the tension, "And the chef, right?"

A feminine laughter that easily resembled Kyler's masculine one came from Krista.

"I figured that's all he sees me as," she joked.

It wasn't until then that Krista noticed the pink bags near the entrance. Her eyes shot to Kyler and a sibling intuition kicked in. When Kyler became uncomfortable under her hardened gaze, she knew that he was hiding something.

He sensed that Krista was on the verge of asking to speak with him privately. Before she got the chance, he rushed over and reached for Lilah's bags.

"Krista, I'm going to show Lilah to my room, then I'll–"

"What," they both gasped.

Lilah could feel her face heating and reddening. When Krista didn't speak another word, only waited for further explanation, Lilah spoke up. "I thought I was just going to *crash on the couch*?"

Kyler sighed. "Hospitality and all," he grumbled. "I'll sleep on the couch."

Although Krista spoke not a single word, her eyes seared through him, saying all that needed to be said.

He was sure that once Lilah was out of earshot, she'd have some not so lovely things to say.

* * *

Lilah hovered at the doorway and watched Kyler plug his phone into a charger extending over his nightstand. His fingers slid rapidly over the screen as he checked over something and then he placed it down.

He glanced back to Lilah and chuckled. "You can come in."

Lilah took a few steps into the room. She felt drunk from the whole situation. No, that wasn't right. She didn't know what that felt like. She felt like she was in a dream. Never in any world did she ever see herself standing in Kyler West's bedroom, let alone staying the night at his house. She also couldn't believe the nature of his room.

Since she had never been in a teenage boy's room before, she expected what she had read in books or seen in movies, a complete disaster. Smelly socks. Soda cans. Paper plates growing mold. Walls covered in superhero posters.

Kyler's room looked like someone who was practical, clean, and grownup. The walls were free of holes where juvenile stuff might have hung in the past. There was no dirty laundry on the floor. Absolutely no cans or remnants of food were seen in any corner.

"Are you okay," he jokingly asked as she took in his room.

"Yeah. It's just so…I wasn't expecting…"

"You thought I'd be a slob," he laughed.

She turned red. He had been nice. Ever since the library he was near perfect; she really didn't want to go on and insult him with her preconceptions.

Kyler allowed her to look around. It was strange having a girl in his room that wasn't related to him. As she hesitantly made her way from one end to the other, to the window looking out below, Kyler quickly rummaged through his drawers, grabbing any clothes he'd need later after his shower.

"So, the bathroom is directly across the hall. Make yourself at home I guess?"

She spun around quickly. "This is weird isn't it?"

"A little," he admitted.

"I'm sorry," she began.

He wasn't used to seeing her apologetic, and he was about to let her continue, but he remembered how horrible she felt earlier, and he didn't want her feeling that way by thinking she was an imposition.

Before she could continue, "It's fine. Do you want to talk about it?"

"No," she answered, perhaps a little too quickly. She glanced away and toward the bed. Attempting to change the subject, "Do you have fresh linens some-where?"

"For what?"

She looked back at him. "So, I can change the sheets."

He shrugged. "They're pretty clean."

"Pretty clean," she repeated as a question, now scrunching up her face.

Kyler couldn't believe her. One minute she was crying because she had nowhere to stay, and now her biggest concern was how clean his sheets were. Did she seriously have someone come in and change her sheets every day like some hotel?

"I shower before bed, so yes, pretty clean." He crossed his arms and raised a brow, waiting for a snotty remark. When no words came, only a sigh, he added, "Unless you count Max."

"I'm sorry?"

He hadn't thought about that. "Yeah, Max likes to sleep on my bed with me. I'm not sure if he will with you, just close the door and make sure he isn't in the room when you go to bed."

Her eyes softened. "Do you close the door and leave him out?"

Kyler watched her carefully, concern blossoming across her entire face. "I usually sleep with the door open."

She took her hand and pressed on the mattress, gauging its firmness. Quite firm. "Then I'll keep it open. He might not understand what's going on and I'd hate to upset him."

Just like that, just when Kyler thought what a snobbish brat she was because of the sheets, she had to go and say something like that.

He had things to do, and suddenly he couldn't stand to be around her. "Do whatever you want," he mumbled, clenching the clothes in his fist as he left his room.

* * *

"She's not a stray puppy!"

"It's just for one night. Don't be so dramatic," Kyler reassured his sister.

Krista was balled up on the recliner, already in her pajamas, watching one of her cooking shows. Kyler knew she'd be asleep in her room by the time he got done with his work, so he had nothing to worry about when it came to her keeping him up.

"Does mom know?"

"I'm an adult and–"

"Her roof, her rules. I'm twenty-three and I'm pretty sure she'd flip if I had a boyfriend stay over," she scoffed.

Kyler seriously had to set her straight before she embarrassed him anymore in front of Lilah. "First of all, she's staying on a completely different floor. Secondly, cut it out with any mentioning of boyfriend and girlfriend."

"You are, aren't you," Krista pressed. She no longer appeared annoyed, as now she wanted saucy details that Kyler knew weren't there.

"She tutors me in English. We're barely friends. So, no." He turned and headed out the door to the garage, hoping to drop the conversation.

"So, a girl that's barely your friend–"

"Goodnight, Krista," he called out, quickly pulling the door behind him.

* * *

Lilah rolled her eyes from the end of the hallway near the stairs. Perhaps if she stayed close by for college, she imagined that would be a near identical chat that she and Rover would be having one day. Jamie had forgotten all about them when she went off to college, and Lilah didn't plan on doing that to Rover, especially now with their wreck of a family. Actually, Jamie was always that way, an older version of Sarah. When Lilah was a sophomore, Jamie was a senior, and of course head cheerleader. Lilah couldn't even remember a time that her sister spoke to her in school.

She put her thoughts of the past aside and came back to reality. It was barely after nine, but she already had a shower, dried her hair, and brushed her teeth. She had a couple books in her bag that she could read in bed before falling asleep. That would probably be for the best. After hearing that conversation, she thought it would be safer to steer clear of Krista for the remainder of the evening. Although she wasn't exactly sure why, she didn't care to see Kyler anymore either.

She had the door nearly closed when she remembered Max. A little bit of excitement ran through her as she thought about him coming and sleeping on the bed with her. She had always wanted a dog. Her parents insisted that they shed, even the ones that supposedly didn't shed. As she got older, she knew it was just an easy excuse, one less thing for them to worry about.

She was only about thirty pages into her book. Normally she could read a book a night depending, but something about being on Kyler's bed messed with her focus. It wasn't only the smell of his room and his pillows beneath her head, there was a constant tapping outside that wouldn't allow her to take in the words on the page. Feeling frustrated, she put the book down on the nightstand next to Kyler's phone. She scrunched her face. There was no way that she would leave her phone alone with a stranger.

Lilah pulled back the sheets, a slight anxiety running through her veins. She was going to spend the night in Kyler West's bed. When it was just that thought alone, it sounded exhilarating and exciting; however, in the end she assumed that he saw her as pathetic and alone, and tonight was nothing more than pity. She turned off the lamp light and was just about to crawl beneath the covers when she saw the light pouring through the blinds. She went to close them and that's what she saw what was going on below.

* * *

Kyler wanted to get it done by eleven, before his mother got home. She had been complaining about the broken railing and rotten boards on one particular end of the deck for over a month now. It was something on his list that he put off. She recently told him that she had met a contractor that did small side jobs, but he didn't want her wasting money on hiring someone for something so simple that he could learn. After looking online, and finally finding the boxes of tools that belonged to his dad, he decided to give it a go. It's not like he could mess it up more than it already was. Once he figured out the saw, everything came together a lot faster. He had used the drill for countless things, but ever since he was a kid the saw had terrified him. That was a long time ago though. He wasn't a kid anymore.

He stepped back to look at one of the sections that he finished. He put the level on the bannister. Not a hundred percent perfect, but pretty spot on, and it saved his mother from having to pay a contractor. He slid a few of the 2x4s farther down the deck toward some of the rotten ones still in place. He then reached for the crowbar and began the removal of two boards.

An eerie feeling came over him, causing him to stop and check his surroundings. An owl hooted in a faraway tree, but that was the only company he had for the night. He didn't even have his music from his phone; come to think of it, he didn't even have his phone. He didn't need it now. It would only serve as a distraction.

He glanced behind him to see if Lilah had turned the lights off yet. She had. That was good. It looked like she needed sleep. Something in the window, other than the lack of light, caught his attention. At first it frightened him, seeing someone standing there. Then he realized it was Lilah. She was watching him.

She gave a slight wave, to which he responded back with one, and then she disappeared.

Thankfully he didn't have to hide the smile that made its way to his face. Deep in his stomach he knew that he was in trouble. There was something more to Lilah than everything he assumed, and the more he got to know her, and the more time he spent around her, the more he wanted...her.

* * *

Lilah nervously bit her lip as she climbed into bed. That was weird. He saw her watching him, just staring at him. She wasn't sure how long she had been at the window, but she couldn't tear herself away. A little flutter ran through her. She had expected that he needed to be with friends or on a date, and yet, he was doing household repairs this late on a Friday night.

Didn't he have football? Wasn't there always a game Friday night? She made a mental note to ask him about that. If things became awkward, it would be a nice icebreaker.

Just as she got settled into bed, the smell of Kyler surrounding her, the ding from her phone caught her attention and she immediately reached for it. As soon as she grabbed it, she remembered that she hadn't put her phone on the nightstand. The alert had

193

started to fade, but the message was short enough that she saw all that she needed.

Sarah: Missed you tonight! See you soon!

Lilah slammed the phone back on the nightstand, perhaps a little more aggressively than she should have and buried her head in the pillow with an exasperated breath.

CHAPTER 19

Lilah generally woke more on the early side, but as she stumbled to her bag for her phone, she didn't expect for it to read 7:08. She rubbed her eyes and looked around. Her eyes popped open once she saw the black and white ball of fur roll into the middle of the bed and stretch out, taking up nearly the whole thing. He could have it. The noise outside wouldn't allow her to fall back asleep.

Excitement ran through her as she made her way to the windows, being sure to give Max a belly rub as she walked by the bed. Her eyes trailed back to the window, brushing over the nightstand, only to see an empty charger. An uncomfortable feeling scampered through her.

Kyler's phone was on the charger when she went to sleep. At some point he had to have come and gotten it while she was sleeping. She cringed at the idea that he saw her like that.

She pulled the blinds up, allowing more light to shine through the room. At that point she heard a thud and turned to see Max leaving. Apparently, he wasn't much for mornings.

"You have got to be kidding me," she sighed when she looked out.

Kyler must have been awake before the sun, as half of the rather large backyard was already mowed. Lilah groaned and made her way to one of her bags that contained her smaller makeup bag. He had to have been doing that to show off. There was no way that he was so perfect.

* * *

From his peripheral vision, Kyler saw his mother on the deck just as he was getting the last few swatches of grass. He turned the mower off and began rolling it to the garage. He was about to call out, but decided against it as he got closer to his mother.

She wasn't happy, and that was putting it mildly. She stood in her pajamas and robe, as the autumn air was quickly growing cooler by the day. One arm was on her hip while the other held her cup of coffee that she viciously sipped.

"Good morning," Kyler cautiously greeted.

"Good morning?! Kyler David West," she screeched furiously.

Kyler hated that she used his middle name, just as much as he hated the actual name itself. He feigned innocence, pretending he didn't know what she was so upset about, although he was more than certain, and it wasn't the slight dip in the banister.

"Why is there a girl in your room?"

He sighed. "Mom, I'm eighteen–"

Coffee sloshed from her cup. "Oh, no you don't," she continued to scream. "This is my house..."

Her words were lost on him. He had pretty much heard the same lecture from Krista the night before.

"The only reason I didn't wake the whole house up was because you were on the couch down in the living room and not in bed with her."

She finally stopped and Kyler took that as a sign that he needed to speak. His shirt, dripping in sweat, clung to him. He took it off and swatted at his jeans, attempting to get any damp grass off before he entered the house.

"It's a long story," he sighed. His mother didn't budge. He knew the exact words that she'd say if given the opportunity. *I've got all the time in the world.* Which they both knew wasn't true. "To keep it simple. She had nowhere to stay last night."

His mother laughed a bitter laugh, showing that she didn't believe a word he was saying. "Your sister said that her father is Steven McCallister. You're going to have to do better than the whole taking in a homeless stray story."

He tried that story once and his mother would never let him live it down. Their neighbor in the city was horrible and often put his beautiful white cat out on the balcony. Kyler couldn't stand how sad it always looked and one day managed to get it across to his side. He then covered it in mud in hopes that his parents would believe that it was a lost and abandoned cat; however, when the neighbor came by later that night, and the cat betrayed their secret, that was the last he ever saw of it.

"No. I'm saying that I think she's having some problems at home and she wasn't exactly welcomed there last night."

Helen eyed her son suspiciously, but found that she believed him more than not. "Did she tell you that?"

"She didn't say too much. She cried a lot, even though she tried not to," he told his mother, shifting uncomfortably as some of the memories of last night came back.

"And though there's nothing going on between the two of you, she slept over? She had no other—"

Kyler interrupted her. "She's popular and all, but for the most part she acts like she's better than everyone else. Kids know her, but they really don't want anything to do with her. She doesn't have many friends."

Helen rolled her eyes. Sadly, she believed her son. "Get in and shower. You smell." A small smile came to her face, flooding Kyler with relief. Just as he reached the sliding glass doors, "The deck looks amazing by the way."

When he turned back around, he saw a light in his mother's eyes that wasn't there too much anymore. It filled him with a great sense of pride and accomplishment.

* * *

Lilah stood in shock at the doorway from the bathroom to the hallway; the sweat from Kyler's chest now stuck to her forehead. She hadn't been expecting anyone to be in the hall, let alone to be entering the bathroom just as she was exiting. Above all, she most definitely wasn't expecting Kyler barefoot and shirtless, in nothing but a pair of grass stained jeans.

She didn't know where to look, and as difficult as it was, settled on his eyes, noting the sense of humor behind them, which matched perfectly to the smirk on his face.

His eyes shifted over her body, but did a deeper evaluation of her face. "Are you already wearing makeup?"

For the most part, Lilah always wore makeup. If she wasn't going anywhere on a Saturday, then maybe not. When she woke, she knew that she'd have to see Kyler at some point, and there was no way she wanted him seeing her so exposed.

"For me," he questioned her teasingly.

"Get over yourself," she huffed.

Taking her free hand, she shoved him, as he was blocking her way into the hall. She froze once her hand connected with his chest. It lingered there for just a second past awkward before she yanked it away, her eyes falling to the floor.

He watched her face redden, and was frustrated at how cute he found her to be. All he could think about was kissing her, but now wasn't the time, and over the past few weeks, he was coming to the conclusion that there might never be a right time.

He leaned in and sniffed. "What are you wearing?"

He was used to her light and flowery scent, but something was different now. She smelled...almost masculine

She huffed. "I assumed I was staying at Alice's and I forgot to pack my body wash."

Kyler's heart began to race at the thought. "So, you used mine?"

Lilah's face scrunched up. It did that so often and Kyler had to hold back his laughter.

"My sister actually has some underneath the sink. She put it in a safer place after I spilled it," he admitted, realizing that the more he spoke to her, the closer their bodies became.

Lilah tried to keep her composure with Kyler's debilitating effect on her. "Well, now I know." It was a stupid thing to say. She'd never again need that information. "Had I known earlier–"

Kyler interrupted her. "Would it have made a difference?"

Their eyes locked and something passed between them. It was both good and bad, both pleasure and torture. Kyler hated how cold and closed off she still seemed, and Lilah hated that he was such a flirt, just teasing her.

"I have to get dressed. If you could please move," Lilah softly insisted after attempting to move from left to right but realizing she'd bump into Kyler no matter what if he remained in his current place.

He stepped aside just enough. Strangely, he enjoyed making her uncomfortable, knocking her down from her high horse for just a moment. "Sure."

His eyes drifted over her body as she hurriedly made her way past. He was used to her businesslike schoolgirl look that he so often saw her in, but he had an everlasting image of her in jeans and a Rolling Stones t-shirt that was a little too small embedded into his memory. This one right now would be another.

He never thought he'd ever see Lilah McCallister in sweatpants and a simple t-shirt. Although he had to admit, the teal sweatpants hung lower on her hips than he could bear, and the shirt looked like something suited for a doll. Normally he wouldn't complain, but having her like that, so close, took everything in his power not to touch her.

When Lilah got across the hall to Kyler's door, she made the mistake of glancing back. Kyler was standing in the mirror splashing his face. For some torturous reason he hadn't shut the door yet. That's when a marking took her by surprise, capturing her attention.

Though it was far away, and she couldn't make out all the intricate details, she could tell it was a bird of some sort on his right side.

Kyler brought his face up, water dripping from it and saw Lilah's reflection in the mirror, an inquisitive look on her face as she leaned into the doorway of his bedroom. He was conscious as to what had captured her attention.

He turned, his face now stony and unreadable and closed the door to the bathroom. Lilah waited for a moment. The water to the shower soon came on and she felt as though she was finally able to breathe. Recently, being around Kyler made that very difficult. She then rushed into the bedroom and locked the door, her primary goal: changing as quickly as possible and getting away from Kyler.

CHAPTER 20

Lilah wasn't sure there would have been a right decision to make when she went downstairs, and Krista insisted that she sit and stay for breakfast. It smelled heavenly, and Lilah knew it would be rude to refuse, but being alone with Kyler's mother and sister was a little terrifying; however, she had nowhere else to be.

Krista continued banging around in the kitchen while Kyler's mother read over the newspaper and sipped on her coffee. Lilah sat uncomfortably, unsure how to proceed.

Helen folded up the paper and placed it to the side. Her eyes narrowed playfully as she took in a long sip of coffee, quietly evaluating Lilah from behind the mug.

"So, Lilah," Helen began, slowly drawing out her words. "How's school this year?"

Lilah tucked a bit of hair behind her ear. "I guess pretty good."

"Not if she's stuck tutoring Kyler," Krista yelled from the kitchen.

Lilah bit her lip, concealing a small smile.

That gave Helen a way in. "How exactly is it going with tutoring my son?"

Lilah felt so uncomfortable. She could tell that Kyler's mother was inspecting her. Waking up to some random girl in her house couldn't have been too pleasant.

"At first it was a little difficult, but it seems that he's genuinely trying now." That was the best way she could put it.

Krista and Helen gave each other looks that held some kind of message that Lilah wasn't privy to.

"Lilah, would you like coffee, tea, or orange juice," Krista asked as she placed butter and syrups on the table.

Lilah thought. That wasn't a lot of information. Black tea? Green tea? Herbal tea? What kind of coffee? Origin? Did the orange juice have pulp or not?

As if she could read Lilah's thoughts, "It's just plain Folgers, Earl Grey tea, or orange juice, no pulp per Kyler's request."

"Just coffee is fine."

"You sure," a deep voice came from behind her, sending chills along her neck. "It's not Starbucks."

Lilah glared at Kyler as he took a seat, unfortunately right next to her, which did no favors to her insides.

If she was being totally honest, she loved the smell of his body wash, both on her and on him. That was the grossest thing she could think of right before eating and she quickly took a sip of the coffee placed in front of her, hoping to get a good whiff of the bold and bitter scent to cover up any others that might be lingering around her.

Krista hit Kyler over the head with a potholder as she placed it on the table. "Stop being rude." She then went back to the kitchen and brought back a plate stacked with waffle after waffle, a bowl of scrambled eggs that looked to have more cheese than eggs, and another plate with enough bacon to give anyone a heart attack.

It was a breakfast Lilah definitely wasn't used to.

Kyler threw a waffle on Lilah's plate along with three on his, and before he could do the same with some bacon, "I can get it myself," Lilah hissed.

"Yeah, but you're not."

"What do you normally have for breakfast," Krista asked while refilling her coffee.

"We don't really eat breakfast like this, together. Generally, we just grab some fruit or a nutrition bar." Strangely, Lilah felt bad admitting that. She felt even worse as she sat there with Kyler and his family. Although she thought he was hiding something, it only made her see just how perfect his life really was.

It was in that moment that she realized something was missing. His father.

"Here," Kyler said, handing Lilah the butter and breaking up her thoughts.

"What's that for?"

He looked at her like she had just sprouted a second head. "For your waffle." When she didn't respond immediately, he took the knife and smeared a huge glob of yellow fat all over her waffle.

"Hey!"

"Trust me, okay," he insisted, now pouring a heaping amount of thick and sticky sugar on top of that.

Lilah could feel his sister and mother curiously watching them, and was thankful once Kyler removed himself from her personal space and went back to shoveling food in his mouth.

After she took her first bite, she knew she had been missing out over the years. Something as simple as waffles, bacon, and eggs, shouldn't have made her feel that way, but it did.

Kyler tried not to stare, but Lilah fascinated him. She seemed to have everything, yet she didn't even know how to properly eat a waffle, with pockets of butter and drenched in syrup. He looked away to hide the smirk on his face when she went back for a second. Despite how freaking awkward it was having her at the breakfast table with his mom and sister, something about it caused a rush of excitement and burst of energy to run through him.

Lilah sank back and finished her food while the rest of them had casual conversation. She already felt bad for imposing and she didn't want to take away what was obviously family time. From what she gathered, Helen worked a lot at the hospital as a general surgeon. It had to be a nice job and paid well, but she was in high demand in Raymere Grove, not to mention, if the hospitals in the city were at capacity, Raymere General was the next closest.

"That would be great," Krista shouted, clapping her hands together. Lilah had missed whatever conversation they were on to. "I left a few things at work.

I could drop you two off and meet back with you for lunch."

Lilah was more than confused.

Kyler was hesitant in saying anything, and he felt like he might have overeaten for once, as his mother spoke now only to Lilah. He dreaded what was coming and decided he was right; he didn't need that fifth waffle.

"What are your plans for the day?"

Lilah thought for a moment, but there wasn't much to think about. Jolee was out of state and Alice had just driven the night before for her mother's conference that was happening throughout the day now. "I'll probably go to the library." Thankfully she saw Krista now picking up dishes. In hopes that Kyler's mom wouldn't ask her another question, she quickly rose and grabbed her plate and cup and followed Krista's lead.

As soon as Kyler met his mother's devilishly calculating eyes, he shook his head and grabbed his plate as well.

"Lilah," Helen cooed.

Kyler couldn't believe it. He just knew that his mother was not going to mess up their little bit of free time together as a family.

"Why don't you come with us to the zoo?"

The plate slipped a bit from Lilah's hand on its way into the sink and made a loud clatter. "The zoo? In the city?"

Helen softly laughed. "Yes. I'm afraid I don't get much time off, and Kyler just loves the little animals," she added, ending her statement in a baby voice. This caused Kyler to turn bright red, and he sent her a look to let her know how inappropriate and embarrassing that was.

Lilah was fine. Spending the day at the library would be lonely, but she was used to that by now. "Thank you, but I really don't want to impose any further."

"Not at all! The more the merrier," Helen insisted.

Lilah hated that phrase. The more the merrier. That wasn't true at all, at least not for her.

She looked to Kyler to try to gauge his thoughts on the matter, but suddenly he appeared expressionless and wouldn't even look at her.

"I better not," she sighed. If she were honest, she was slightly disappointed at having to turn Helen down. She couldn't remember the last time she had been to the zoo. Anytime her mother took her to the city it was generally for shopping. "However, if I could get a ride to the library?"

Kyler rolled his eyes and finally spoke up. "Just come with us."

Lilah's eyes shot up to meet his from across the room. It felt like the air was being sucked out of her with the intense way that Kyler was looking at her. She could feel her face heating and more than anything she wanted to get away from the scrutiny of his mother and sister who appeared to be watching their every move.

✳ ✳ ✳

Lilah didn't bother trying to get in touch with her mother that morning, and her dad didn't answer her call. She shot Rover a text, but he was busy playing some online multiplayer thing. Lilah wondered if he ever even went to sleep the night before.

The car ride into the city wasn't the worst. Lilah did find that Kyler's mother was very inquisitive, but she eventually gave up after she realized that some of her questions affected Lilah, especially those when it came to family. Lilah was thankful to get a text from Alice. Whatever convention she was at was huge and had an unlimited breakfast buffet. Lilah desperately wanted to tell Alice about her breakfast but deleted the text before sending it. Alice would ask too many questions, knowing full well that bacon wasn't present in the McCallister household.

Kyler tried to keep busy on his phone, anything to distract him from the girl sitting next to him. He'd have to have a talk with his mother. He had never really brought a girl home, and when it came to Lilah, it was under completely different circumstances. His mother and sister just didn't get the hint.

He hadn't really talked with Lilah since the night before. She seemed quiet, but slightly happier, although he was pretty sure that someone like her would think going to the zoo was a pretty lame idea for an outing. He wished he could have had just a moment or two alone with her to ask how she was. Whenever his mother had brought up anything about her family, Lilah shied away from the questions. He knew something was wrong, and though he had no reason to care, he did.

Kyler: What are your plans for tonight?

He watched as Lilah froze, intently looking at the screen. Though childish, it was much easier than talking about it aloud in front of two very intrusive females.

Lilah: What do you mean?

Kyler: Are you going back home? You said you needed to be gone this weekend.

Lilah felt a sting of disappointment. She was stupid to think that Kyler would be asking for any other reason.

Lilah: Alice might be back from her mother's conference.

She thought for a moment and a wonderful idea came to her.

Lilah: Actually, they're in the city! Maybe I could get dropped off to where they are?

Kyler's insides knotted up. Lilah could see that he had read the text and he needed to respond quickly. Despite his mother and sister being around, and fully knowing that spending the day with Lilah was definitely not a date, he looked forward to it.

Kyler: All of your stuff is at my house.

Lilah: I didn't think about that. There's also no way that I could explain that to her, nor would I want to attempt to.

Kyler: What if she's not back tonight? Then what?

His pulse raced as he awaited her response. Maybe it was selfish to hope that Alice wouldn't return. There was also the tiny voice in his head screaming at the top of its lungs asking him if he had lost his mind. In what world would he want Lilah McCallister spending the weekend with him?

Lilah: I'll figure it out when the time comes.

Kyler dropped it. No matter how many times he told himself how stupid he was, he secretly wished that any plans she had would fall through.

CHAPTER 21

The zoo was slightly crowded, but that was a given for a Saturday. Kyler couldn't get over the fact at how amazed Lilah became with every exhibit. He and his mother came to the zoo at least twice a year, but from the looks of it, it was like Lilah had never been.

"Oh, Ky! Sweetie," his mother called out. "The elephant looks beautiful right now. Let me get a picture!" She dug her phone from her back pocket and shooed Kyler to stand in front of the exhibit.

Kyler was confused at first. His mother must have had a hundred pictures of him with the elephants. It wasn't until he saw her reach off to the side and grab Lilah that he understood. That was it. He really had to talk to her after this.

"Hmm…If you could move over just a little?" Just to annoy her, Kyler moved in the opposite direction from Lilah. "Kyler!" While it did his intended job, it also caused a faint giggle from Lilah that he found affected him more than he'd like to admit. "Just put your arm around–"

"Mom!" Kyler glared at her as she hid behind her phone, the smirk on her face clear as day.

She finally took the picture and Kyler stepped far away from Lilah. While she stood admiring the elephants, he pulled his mother to the side, making sure they were definitely out of earshot from Lilah.

"What are you doing," he growled.

Innocently, "I don't know what you mean. I just wanted a picture."

"One minute you're about to blow a gasket, and then ever since breakfast, you're trying to play matchmaker. There's nothing there and there won't ever be. I told you, she's my tutor and she's going through some family stuff right now. She just needed somewhere to stay this weekend," he emphasized.

"That may be true..." She allowed her words to slowly drift away

Knowing she wasn't done, "But?"

Helen shrugged. "I see the way you look at her."

"Gross. This conversation is getting weird."

"I don't understand why you're so shy. Just tell her–"

"Stop," Kyler whined, frustrated that his mom wasn't letting it go. Raising his voice, "I will never ever like her like that!"

Lilah tried not to let his words bother her, but they did. If she ever felt uncertain when it came to Kyler, that was a pretty strong and definite answer as to how he felt about her. It just sucked that she couldn't tell the butterflies in her stomach that whenever he looked at her in just the right way.

"I'm not used to so much walking," Helen sighed, taking a seat next to Lilah on a bench while Kyler went to the restroom.

"I'm sure you're on your feet a lot. You probably needed today to rest."

Helen laughed. "It's good to keep busy, and I like helping people. At least Kyler got that from me." When she noticed Lilah's reaction, she quickly corrected herself. "Although I guess I should replace people with animals."

Lilah wasn't following. "What do you mean?"

Helen realized that maybe Kyler was telling the truth, maybe Lilah was just his tutor and barely a friend. "Him wanting to be a veterinarian." She almost hesitated telling Lilah, but it wasn't some big secret. That's exactly what Kyler's plans for school were.

Lilah's face lit up. "Really?" Helen nodded. "Wow. That's..." Lilah watched her choice of words, feeling as though his mother would read into any little thing at this point. "Admirable." There. That was a good word. It, in no way, suggested anything that might be running through Helen's head right now. "I just assumed that he'd do football."

Helen shook her head. "No. He has more sense than that. He'll use football for a scholarship if he can, but he knows the chances and risks of going pro. It isn't something he's interested in."

That surprised Lilah. Up until recently, whenever she saw Kyler in school, that's all she saw. Star quarterback of the football team.

"Oh," Lilah gasped, remembering something. "Not to sound stupid, but why didn't he have a game last night?"

"It was their bye week." When Lilah looked at her with confusion, she absolutely knew that Lilah wasn't the kind of girl that Kyler was typically interested in. "It just means that it's their off week."

"Oh, okay," Lilah said with a sense of relief and understanding. She was thankful that she hadn't asked Kyler about it that morning. He would have thought she was an idiot.

* * *

The way back was a little easier and much less awkward after Kyler had talked to his mom.

"Lilah," Krista called from the driver's seat. "Are you staying for supper?"

It was only a little after three. Lilah still had half of the afternoon to decide what her plans were for the evening.

Kyler had leaned over earlier and was showing Lilah some of the pictures he took on his phone. Lilah immediately looked to him for an answer, but all he did was shrug.

"I really don't know yet."

"Well, I'm making a cottage pie–"

"Yes," Kyler softly exhaled, to which his sister shook her head and laughed. Directing his words to Lilah, "She's a really good cook and that dish is awesome."

"I'll see."

Lilah then focused back to the screen in Kyler's hands, and continued to watch him scroll.

"Wait," she gasped.

She grabbed his wrist to pull the phone closer and he tensed at her touch. If she noticed, she was too concerned with the picture to care.

She briefly looked up at him and smiled. "When did you take this?"

It felt like an intimate moment aside from the fact that his mother and sister were listening to every word between them. He had to brush it off. "Obviously, when we were at the gorilla exhibit."

Lilah playfully nudged him. For once she felt happy and relaxed. She didn't even allow herself to think that Kyler West had made that happen. "You know what I mean."

"I can send it to you if you want."

"Please," she said with a great deal of excitement.

The picture was of her leaning down toward the glass, the large gorilla on the other side raising his hand to try to touch hers, only the clear barrier separating their contact.

Kyler didn't continue to swipe to another photo, allowing Lilah to marvel at the one he had taken of her. The notification appeared just a split second before he felt the alert. Once he saw the name, he tried to clear it off, but Lilah's hand, that had been lingering on his wrist, immediately dropped to her side and she pulled her body back slightly, distancing herself from him.

Kyler tried to maintain his composure, but the girl had the worst timing.

Sarah: Are you coming tonight?

Normally he wouldn't have cared who saw his messages, but for some reason, he didn't want Lilah seeing that. He didn't know what Sarah said to her at Dawson's party, but he could easily tell that they weren't friends.

Feeling the need to clarify, "Some of the guys are getting together to go out tonight. Gavin told me they were going to play Frisbee in the park and then head to Flip's Grill after."

All Lilah did was nod her head. That's when a strange idea hit Kyler. Was it as simple as Lilah having an issue with Sarah over some stupid girly thing that he couldn't comprehend, or was Lilah jealous? If it had just been the two of them, he may have called her out on it; however, his sister's interruption proved that she and his mother were still very much listening in.

"So you're not staying for supper then?" Krista quickly turned around with a frown and puppy dog eyes, before turning back to the road.

Lilah saw that Kyler was tapping something out on his phone. A sick part of her desperately wanted to see what he was texting Sarah; however, her eyes widened when she felt her own phone vibrate on her lap.

Kyler: What do you think?

Lilah: I don't care what you and Sarah do.

Kyler couldn't believe that Lilah would actually say it like that. A sinister smile came to his face and even though it wasn't the best way, he was pretty sure that with her sitting right beside him, she'd at least give him some sort of reaction; however, once he hit send, he knew that he was starting to tread into a dangerous territory with her.

Kyler: I think you do.

He felt a blow to his chest when Lilah read the message and was able to keep a straight face, showing no emotion or even the slightest bit of discomfort. Was she that good at hiding her thoughts and feelings, or did she truly have none when it came to any interest in him?

Kyler realized that his sister was still watching him from her mirror, waiting for a response. "Hold on. I'll let you know in a minute."

Helen finally chimed in. "You rarely ever go out with your friends anymore. If you're not helping around the house, you're at work."

Lilah shot Kyler a look. Work? He had a job?

"Why don't you and Lilah go out with your friends tonight," Helen continued.

Lilah tried her best to recover from her own spit that she suddenly choked on.

"I get the impression that Lilah isn't the type of person to hang out with most of Kyler's people," Krista pointed out. Despite its accuracy, Lilah felt like it was a comment that she was supposed to take offense to; however, before she had the chance. "And that's a good thing."

Maybe she liked his sister after all.

CHAPTER 22

"I'm pretty sure I'll mess this up," Lilah repeated once again as she drained the potatoes.

Krista laughed. "I promise, you won't. Just put them back in the pot and I'll tell you what to add."

Lilah did as instructed. Krista assumed that she was bored and wanted to help out, but the truth was, Lilah had never really been in a kitchen and she was always up for learning new things. Most of her learning generally only came from books.

"Okay, I have the butter and milk measured out. Add that. Then look in the door of the fridge. There's a small block of goat cheese. Throw that in."

Lilah was good with following instructions and did just as Krista told her. "Now how do I mash them?"

Krista stopped stirring the meat mixture and reached under a cabinet for something with a cord attached. The little Lilah did know when it came to cooking, she was certain that the contraption that Krista just plugged in was not a masher.

Krista saw the confusion. "There are different ways. I want them smooth and creamy, so we're going to use a hand mixer."

Krista turned the machine on low and then handed it over to Lilah.

From the kitchen, the two heard Kyler yell from the sliding glass doors for Helen.

"She got called in," Krista yelled back. "Emergency procedure."

Upon hearing that, Kyler made his way into the house. Lilah glanced up briefly but not for long. She didn't need Kyler distracting her and for potatoes to end up all over the wall.

He was covered in a black goo, grease perhaps. He walked into the kitchen, only to be scolded by Krista about how he smelled. He then grabbed some paper towels in hopes of cleaning his hands a bit before washing all that grit and grime down the bathroom sink.

"Can I try some," he asked, hovering over Lilah's shoulder.

"No," Krista screeched from nearby. "Get out! You're gross. Lilah doesn't want you around."

Deciding to push his boundaries with Lilah once again, he took a step closer and whispered in her ear from behind. "Is that true," he asked in a low and deep voice, sending chills down Lilah's spine. "Do you really not want me around?"

Skittishly, Lilah turned, neglecting to turn the mixer off as she did so. Kyler screamed and stumbled backwards, doused in little remnants of mashed potato.

Krista quickly took the device from Lilah's hand and switched it off. For a second Lilah thought that she might be in for a scolding as well, but instead, Krista doubled over laughing.

"I'm glad someone thinks it's funny," Kyler grumbled. He pretended to be more annoyed than he actually was. After seeing Lilah's face light up with laughter shortly after his sister's, there was no way that he could be upset, not even for a second.

"Go shower and change," Krista managed as she tried to get some air.

"I'll get you back for that," Kyler warned, his attention completely on Lilah.

She rolled her eyes. "It was an accident."

"Either way."

Krista called out to Kyler as he was leaving the kitchen to head upstairs. "Did you ever decide on what your plans are?" She began pouring her meat and vegetable mixture into a large dish. "Not that it really matters. I probably made enough to feed half the team."

Kyler stood at the base of the staircase, thankfully his sister was busy with preparations and wasn't looking at him. He and Lilah locked eyes and he could tell that she was waiting for an answer as well, though he knew she'd never ask for it.

Very flatly, giving nothing away, "I'm staying in tonight."

Once he left, Lilah felt like she could breathe again. Did he know what he was starting to do to her? When had his sole presence caused her whole body to tense, become overheated, feel lightheaded and dizzy, as it did now?

She felt both excited and nervous when Kyler answered his sister; however, she felt guilt as well. Did he really want to go out with Sarah and his friends, and only decide to stay in because he felt sorry for her? She was fine. She had her books, and now Krista. Or did he actually want to stay at his home because she was there?

Lilah shook the thought and continued wiping the counter. Lately Kyler had been quite teasing and playful at times, but she couldn't tell if that's just how he was once he got to know someone, or if it meant anything. Then there was the kiss. They still hadn't talked about it, and since nothing had come from it, she had to assume it was just a one-time thing. Just another accident.

* * *

Supper was nice. It was different than Lilah expected. She hadn't realized what it was like to sit down and have a conversation during a meal. Generally, if her family ever did have a sit-down meal together, her dad was sending off business emails on his phone or even his laptop. Yes, he brought his laptop with him to the table. Lilah now assumed that anytime her mother was on the phone it probably involved texting another man. Overall, supper with Krista and Kyler was nice. Kyler was a little quiet, but most of the time the amount of food in his mouth didn't allow for lengthy conversation.

Lilah had made her way out onto the deck to the backyard, despite the fact that she had to bundle up. She didn't mind it. She had chosen Kyler's hoodie that he had allowed her to borrow the night before. It was much softer than any of hers, but not only that, it smelled wonderful, like being wrapped in a blanket of safety.

She sat on an older wooden bench covered with several outdoor pillows and opened her book to the spot marked off with a ratty sticky note. It was a silly romance, something that didn't normally appeal to her, but it had a cute cover when she saw it in the library and thought to give it a shot. Plus, she knew the genre was typically a fast and easy read. She had started reading it the night before and decided to finish it.

Several chapters later, a hand from behind caused Lilah to jump. Kyler flipped the book so that he could read the title. He scoffed immediately and made his way around the bench, taking a seat on the opposite end.

"*First Kiss Fiasco.* Sounds stupid."

Lilah huffed. Though she didn't close her book, she made sure to put the sticky on the page just in case. "Well, since you haven't read it–"

He interrupted her. "All first kisses are horrible. No need to write a story about it."

Lilah scrunched her eyebrows. Kyler was suddenly more annoying than usual.

"Well, I'm sure whoever the poor girl was feels the same way," Lilah retorted.

"Haha. I'm not so sure about that," he laughed, shaking his head.

Lilah eyed him suspiciously, a silent look telling him to continue, which he did.

"That's so sad," Lilah told him once he was finished with his story.

He chuckled. "For me or for her?"

Lilah couldn't help but smile. "Both, but you were probably her first crush. That had to be a sad day for her, saying goodbye."

Kyler rolled his eyes. He couldn't tell if Lilah was being serious and taking pity on the girl who was once his neighbor.

"I guess that's my story; that's all it is now. It's just one of those things that you remember, but not necessarily for good reasons, and it wasn't worth remembering anything more than the fact that it happened."

Lilah only now closed her book. "What do you mean?"

"I think it's the good things that we truly remember. At least for me it is."

"So you only remember your first kiss as something that happened."

"Pretty much," he laughed. "Maybe if it had been with someone I really liked, it would have been different, but it wasn't something that made my senses come alive. I don't remember how the air felt, what the lighting was like. I don't remember her hair, or the way her eyes looked up at me. I don't remember how I felt, the butterflies, the nerves, the hesitation." He paused, realizing that their conversation was quickly becoming dangerous.

"Well, I guess it is a lot to remember." Lilah could feel him looking at her now, but she just stared into the night sky. She swallowed heavily before asking, "Do you remember that much with anyone?"

Kyler couldn't answer that. She had to know that he couldn't. So instead, "Enough of me. I told you about mine. Now you tell me yours." He playfully nudged her shoulder, sensing the uncomfortable atmosphere between them.

"What? You want me to tell you some horror story about my first kiss?" She tried to laugh it off, but he detected the uncertainty in her voice.

"As long as it's the truth. Besides, I told you mine. It's only fair."

"I didn't ask for you to tell me," she pointed out, beginning to tense up.

"Come on, how bad was it," he teased.

"Nope."

"Did he have bad breath?" When Lilah didn't answer, "Was he shorter than you? I'd imagine that might be weird for some girls. Although..." He eyed her small frame for a moment. "You are pretty short, so I find it hard to believe that a guy would be shorter than you."

Lilah huffed and blew out a breath at the comment but still gave Kyler nothing.

"Was it really sloppy? Like a drooling dog? Or–"

Lilah slammed her book down between them, cutting Kyler off. "No!"

She screamed loud enough that the neighbors probably heard, but Kyler didn't breathe another word. He thought he might have finally broken her. When her fiery and confident eyes met his, he knew he had.

"Sorry to burst your bubble, but it wasn't the disaster that you'd like to imagine," she spat, more than visibly annoyed.

When she didn't continue, "Are you going to go on or just leave it at that, because I don't believe you. All first kisses are horrible."

Her demeanor softened. "Not mine." She thought for a moment. She really wanted to shove it in Kyler's face, especially after all his teasing. He'd never know it was him anyway. "Mine was wonderful. As sappy as it may sound, it was just like all those stupid romance books describe it. And I do remember everything," she pointed out.

She twisted her body on the bench to mirror his. When she met his eyes again, she saw that his brows were a little more furrowed, as though he was really thinking.

"Like what?"

Lilah swallowed the lump in her throat that may as well have been a brick. "I remember the air, the breeze, the sunlight," she began, trying to remember everything that he said he couldn't remember about his.

"So, it was outside," Kyler quickly asked.

Lilah crossed her arms and narrowed her gaze. "Do you want me to continue or not."

Kyler's face held the smallest of smirks as he threw his hands up in defeat. He could absolutely shut up to hear this.

Lilah closed her eyes. She could have made something up, but the tight knot in her stomach told her that the remembrance of their kiss was better than a dream of any other.

"I remember the way he smelled. Ugh, I loved the way he smelled. I remember the way he way he held me. He looked at me like I mattered, like I was the most important thing in his world."

Kyler remained quiet. Somehow her words and the way she described it seemed almost hypnotic.

"It was a mixture of innocent and passionate, and I'll never forget the way I felt, the butterflies, the nerves, the hesitation..." It wasn't until after she said it that she realized she probably shouldn't have ended on a repetition of his words. "I don't know what made that moment happen, but it was something I think I had wanted for a while."

Once Kyler was certain that she was done, he had to ask. Just one more question. "With him or just in general?"

Lilah smiled but found that she couldn't look Kyler in the eyes with the admission she was about to make. "Both, but definitely with him."

Kyler's insides twisted and he felt his palms growing warm and clammy. He had to have thought of a million different ways in that little window of time to tell her that he knew what she was talking about, that he knew exactly how she felt, but something made him refrain from doing so.

They sat quietly, looking into dark nothingness for what seemed like forever. Lilah sank back and rested her head against one of the outdoor cushions along the arm of the bench. In doing so, her bent leg grazed Kyler's, but neither seemed to mind.

When Kyler fell to assuming that there had grown an odd comfortableness between them, he decided to bring up the elephant that had been present since the night before.

"What's going on," he asked vaguely, although Lilah's deep breath told him that she knew what he meant without needing to be specific.

Lilah couldn't believe she was going to trust him. It was something she hadn't shared with her best friends, partly because she didn't want them worrying about her. "Promise not to tell anyone?"

"Of course."

He seemed sincere, and Lilah had to give him some credit, especially after what he had done for her the last two days.

"I think my parents are separating. I honestly don't know. Their arrangement is messed up right now," she sighed.

"What do you mean?"

"Well, apparently my mother is dating other men, but she's still legally married to my father, and we're all living under the same roof. I'm not sure for how long."

It was something Kyler didn't understand. His mother and father had a wonderful marriage, up until the end. He couldn't fathom infidelity on either part. Even after all these years, he didn't know if his mother had ever been on a date since his dad.

Lilah let out a sniffle. "My mom sent my brother to a friend for the weekend. I was supposed to do the same, but Jolee and Alice..." She let her words drift off there. She had told Kyler they were busy. She didn't want to harp on the fact that those were her only two options. "I know why," she continued, dismissing talk of her friends. "My dad is out on business, like he often is, and she wanted the mansion to herself." Her voice grew angrier. "She didn't want us around so that she could have her own little weekend entertainment with whoever *he* is."

Kyler couldn't believe what he was hearing. Everyone at school thought Lilah's life was perfection. If he wasn't sitting right there and listening to the sadness and anger in her voice, he would have never believed it. The McCallister's were the family that everyone wanted to be.

"Lilah," he softly began, but she stopped him.

"Please don't," she insisted. "I'm glad I was able to tell someone, but please don't look at me like I'm helpless or broken. Don't feel sorry for me."

Kyler couldn't look at her, if he did, that's probably exactly what his face would read, and he didn't want that for her. "Your friends don't know?"

"No, but I'm sure it's just a matter of time. My mother isn't exactly discreet, and Sarah already threw her suspicions in my face."

So that's why she and Sarah were having words at Dawson's party. Kyler didn't mention it because he didn't want to further bring up her name in their conversation, knowing that it had a negative effect on Lilah.

"Thank you for telling me," he quietly told her. Despite the nature of what she told him, something about her trusting him with it made him feel elated.

That's when he decided to tell her something he hadn't told a single soul in Raymere Grove. The truth about his father.

CHAPTER 23

"Oh, if ever there was a story of high school sweethearts, it was them," Kyler laughed. "It's a sickly mushy story that my mom loves to tell."

Lilah giggled. "I'd love to hear it one day."

One day. Maybe that meant that there would be another day like today.

"When it comes to that, I'll just make a long story short. She went to college and did the whole medicine thing, but had my sister and I very early in life. It wasn't until much later, after we were born that she went back and became a surgeon. She's been doing that for about ten years now, not quite. Anyway, after high school, my dad went into the military."

There was a pause, and in the darkness, Lilah watched as the light faded from Kyler's eyes, his facial features turning somber.

"That's usually where the story ends. Whenever people bring up my dad, I just mention that he was in the military and most of the time they get the hint and drop it," he sighed. "He didn't die in the military."

Lilah just let Kyler talk. She was afraid to say anything. Was his father dead? Did he abandon them? Were he and Helen just divorced?

Kyler played with his hands, cracking his knuckles a few times. He tried to relax by getting into the same position that Lilah was in. She scooted back a little to give his legs some room. A cold gust of wind hit them and that's when Kyler noticed that she was wearing his hoodie from the night before.

His eyes fell from hers when he continued. "I don't remember the time anymore," he admitted, almost feeling guilty. "Maybe I was eight or nine." He tried really hard to think about it. "Nine, almost ten." He only remembered now because he remembered the disaster that was his tenth birthday. "He came home one day, and he was different. It's like he was pissed off at the world, and he never went back to work. I guess I was too young for them to think to explain it to me then, but I later found out that he was discharged. I think it was something other than honorable, so I know he did something wrong, I just don't know what. It's what he did after."

Lilah prepared herself for the worst. Just by looking at Kyler she could tell that it wasn't a piece of his life that he told many people. "You don't have to if–"

"No." Kyler held a saddened smile as he looked up at her. "I want to." He took a deep breath, realizing it was a lot to throw on Lilah, but he wanted to show her that his life was more than the hotshot perfect quarterback. "He lost everything. Whatever he did was enough that the military gave him no compensation. After that he just gave up. As a kid, all I saw was that he just drank all day. Don't get me wrong, he still acted like he loved us. He was never abusive, but he was never sober either. If only that was the worst part."

Kyler felt the night air growing colder. When he looked at Lilah, it might as well be freezing the way she was bundled in his hoodie and huddled up. As painful as the story was, and as much as she needed to go inside, despite never saying so, he truly liked being exactly where they were.

"This was right around the time my mom had finished everything to become a surgeon; however, that also meant that she carried a lot of debt. Our family relied on his military benefits, and now they were gone." Lilah expected that to be the worst of it, but little did she know how bad it would get. "It turns out, while my mom was just getting started in her field, he was out gambling, gambling money that we didn't even have. My mom didn't find out the extent until shortly before he left us."

Lilah felt horrible for Kyler's family. She liked his mother and sister. They weren't what she was used to, but if she looked at her own family, maybe what she was used to wasn't how a family should be either.

"She blames herself. I know she does. I rarely ever saw them fight, but she was devastated about the finances. Who wouldn't fight about that?"

Lilah leaned forward and brought her knees to her chest, pulling Kyler's large hoodie over them. Kyler lounged back in nothing more than jeans and a t-shirt. She scanned down to where their legs had been touching. He didn't even have shoes on!

Lilah immediately stopped thinking about the cold and Kyler's bare feet when she looked up and saw the sparkling wetness in his eyes with the light streaming from the living room.

"I just get so mad. To this day I wonder if he ever thought about us. Didn't he want to see us grow up? To see what we would become? Didn't he know that we loved him?"

Lilah froze and it felt like a weight dropped in her stomach upon realizing what Kyler was saying.

Kyler shook his head and held back any tears from slipping out. "Anyway...Umm...Because of the way he died, the life insurance was gone. You don't get anything with suicide. My mom was in debt from school, in debt from his gambling, then she had my sister and I to support. My sister was about to go to college, and let me just point out that the little fund for her, completely gone. Then, about six months after his death, my mom moved us out of the tiny city apartment to here."

Lilah remembered. Kyler began school with her sometime during their eighth-grade year.

"I saw your curiosity pique when my mom mentioned work. Last year I found out that the financial problems were still lingering. Raymere Grove isn't exactly the most affordable place, but my mom refused to let us live in the city another minute. I guess I just wasn't aware what homes here cost, and then there are still the school bills and gambling debt. I couldn't let my mom, and now my sister, deal with that all alone."

Lilah understood now. "So, you got a job at the hospital?" She hadn't paid enough attention that day. She had wondered what he was doing there, but working never occurred to her.

Kyler shrugged. "Not my first choice, but it was easy to get hired. Beats working at one of the main hangouts where I'd have to see everyone from school."

"Do your friends know?" Lilah was surprised when Kyler shook his head. He had told her so much that he had never shared with those closest to him.

He clapped his hands, ending the conversation. "Anyway, despite the image you see at school, I guess I'm not the walking perfection most of them like to imagine either."

Lilah smiled as Kyler stood to leave, at least that's what she expected, but much to her surprise, he stood in front of her, his hand waiting for hers. She looked up to him with a mix of confusion and something else that he couldn't quite place.

"Come on," he began, pretending to be inconvenienced. "You're freezing. You can read inside, and I promise I won't make fun of your book."

Lilah pulled her legs from beneath the hoodie and spun to face him, slipping her cool hand in his warm one. How could he have such warm hands with the way it felt outside?

* * *

Kyler and Lilah stood in the doorway to his room, the air filled with slight awkwardness, both knowing that in the last twenty-four hours they had grown a lot closer, also realizing that they had shared secrets with the other that they didn't talk about freely.

"Do you need to get anything out of here," Lilah asked, stepping aside so that Kyler could enter, instead of casually leaning against the door jamb.

"I have a few things to take care of. I'll get a change of clothes and such when–"

Lilah interrupted him. "When I go to sleep?"

The grin on her face told Kyler that she wasn't extremely bothered by it. "Sorry about that," he mumbled, rubbing his neck. "I had forgotten my phone."

"As long as you didn't stand in the corner and watch me all night," Lilah laughed, thinking about a particularly horrendous vampire story that she wasn't able to finish.

"Are you kidding? Between you and Max I'm not sure who snores louder, or drools more." He was joking, but he wasn't about to tell her that he did indeed take his time getting his phone, the image of her asleep on his pillow one that he wanted to embed into his memory.

Lilah swatted at Kyler's chest. It was just as hard as she remembered. "I do not snore or drool!"

Kyler smirked and shrugged his shoulders, his silence causing Lilah's face to turn red. He could easily assume that she was mulling it over in her mind whether or not he was picking on her.

"I'll leave you alone," he began, swearing that just with those few words he saw a flash of something across her face that he hadn't seen before when it concerned him. Disappointment? "I'll get some of my things whenever you go take a shower."

"Thanks," was all that Lilah said in response. For some sick reason she didn't want the night to end. She had fun with Kyler throughout the day. Even the times where he was teasing her or annoying her, or even when they were bickering, it was still *nice*.

He took a step forward just as she began to turn from him and pulled her to face him. "Wait."

Lilah's breathing nearly stopped again with their closeness. Like a silly girl with a ridiculous crush, all she could think about was kissing him again.

He swallowed heavily and looked into the set of questioning eyes staring up at him. "What happened? With the guy?"

Lilah had to think for a split second as to what he was referring to. The kiss. Of course. "Nothing."

Kyler narrowed his eyes. She knew that he didn't believe her. "Nothing? Something that was so perfect...and nothing."

Lilah didn't want to talk about it and hated that he had to ask. She felt sick to her stomach with disappointment. "We just weren't suitable for each other."

Kyler took a step back, slightly aggravated. If she wasn't making up an insane excuse and telling the truth, why would she say that? "Suitable?"

"I'd rather not talk about it," Lilah admitted. The day had gone so well and now he was going to ruin it.

"Did you even try to work anything out," he pressed.

Lilah bit her lip, partly to stop from screaming at the top of her lungs. She just wanted him to stop. Why did he care anyway? He couldn't possibly know that it was him, so why did he need to know. "There was nothing to work out. We came from different worlds. He wasn't interested and I guess I wasn't either." That was the one time in her story that she lied.

Kyler was so close, too close, to correcting her, to telling her differently, but the stoic and emotionless look that her face held when she said those words told him that it was the truth, at least from her point of view. They had something between them, maybe not in the way he wanted, but he wasn't about to ruin whatever it was by saying something stupid at the wrong time.

He took a few more steps back, masking his disappointment. "Goodnight, Lilah."

Lilah sighed in annoyance and confused him when she walked forward, closing the gap. She didn't stop until her arms were around his torso. It took about two full seconds before he could respond. She was hugging him?

"Thank you. Today was fun. Also, whether you wanted to or not, thank you for staying here tonight."

So it didn't come across as too mushy, she added, "With me and your sister."

Kyler clenched at the mentioning of his sister. It had almost been the perfect moment. The perfect moment between friends.

When she pulled back, a look of embarrassment on her face, Kyler made himself clear. "I *wanted* to."

A look of surprise appeared on her face, but he couldn't handle anymore, and with that, he pulled the door shut behind him.

CHAPTER 24

Lilah couldn't believe how ridiculously well she slept in Kyler's bed for a second night. It was a thought she would never in her lifetime admit to having. For some reason when she went downstairs that morning, she already had expectations: Helen resting from a long shift at the hospital, Krista banging around in the kitchen, Kyler already outside working on something for his mother. However, as she made her way down the stairs, she only smelled the strong scent of black coffee and only heard light noises from the television, noises that sounded suspiciously like a cooking show.

When she finally got to the bottom of the staircase, she saw Krista, curled up with a blanket and a cup of coffee, and just like she thought, watching some culinary competition.

"Good morning," Krista called out cheerfully. After evaluating Lilah, "You look like you slept well."

Lilah tried to hide the embarrassment coming to her face. She did indeed sleep well, if only her dreams weren't constantly plagued by images of Kyler, and if only every time she breathed in, she didn't smell him on the pillows.

Lilah looked around. The house seemed void of anyone but Krista. Krista must have sensed Lilah's confusion, and before Lilah could ask she vomited all the information she had.

"My mom slept at the hospital. She has something going on this morning. Kyler was up at an ungodly hour. Apparently, they asked him sometime last night to work an early shift today."

"Oh," was all Lilah said, hoping to hide any disappointment.

Krista held a devilish grin that told Lilah there was something more. In a baby-like voice, "He left you a note on the entry table."

Lilah narrowed her eyes and allowed them to dart between Krista and the small table near the door that held an aged floral arrangement and a set of keys. Sure enough, there was a small piece of paper, torn from a notepad, folded into thirds, just as one would fold to put in an envelope.

Krista laughed. "He could have just text you, but I guess he didn't want to wake you." She pretended to think. "I didn't know my brother was such a romantic, writing handwritten love notes and whatnot."

Lilah flung her attention from the entry to Krista, appearing shocked and horrified. "You have the wrong idea, we're not–"

Krista busted into more laughter. "Relax, I know you two are just friends, for now," she added with a wink. "I also couldn't help but be a little curious. I mean, if he didn't want me to be nosey, he should have taped it up or something. Don't look so creeped out. It's just as silly as my brother." She rose and trudged to the kitchen refilling her coffee and grabbing a second cup from the cupboard.

Lilah didn't want to appear too eager, but as soon as Krista's back was turned, she rushed to the little table, her heart racing with anticipation. Kids their age didn't write letters to each other. Sure, in class they passed notes. It was safer than risking having your phone taken up. An actual letter, if that's what you could call what he left, was something completely unexpected.

I know you have to get back home today. I had to go into work, and I won't be back until three or so. If you need a ride, ask Krista. She's pretty useless on the weekends, unless she's baking.

If you don't have any plans for the day, there's an afternoon game coming on around the time I get home. Since I know you'll never come to any of mine, I thought we could watch that one. If not, I'll see you at school.

-Kyler

It definitely wasn't a love note, and Lilah hadn't expected it to be; however, he was asking her to spend time with him. He could have had any of his many friends over to watch a game, but instead he was asking her. Did that mean something? Or was she reading into something that was only real in her imagination?

"Well," Krista asked, phrasing it as a question, as she handed Lilah a cup of plain black coffee.

"Well, what?"

"I have an entire folder of game day snacks I've been dying to experiment with. So are you staying or not?"

Lilah didn't know. She thought about calling her mother. All she had been told was that she could come home Sunday morning. Would it really matter if she came home Sunday evening?

For once, she did what she wanted to do, and not what she thought she was supposed to do. "Yeah."

Lilah didn't expect the day to drag on as it did. Maybe it didn't. Maybe it was the strange anticipation of the afternoon to come that made time trail by so slowly.

She did enjoy getting to know Krista. As much as she would have expected her to be a chef, she learned that the hours of a chef could be crazy early or crazy late depending. She also discovered that Krista's cooking ability was only topped by her savvy ways with everything technology. Had she been more than a decade younger, she'd be the perfect match for Rover.

"Why are you only in sales then," Lilah found herself asking. She saw that she hit a nerve and thought about dismissing it altogether.

"It's just the company I work for. I got rejected as a developer, so I took what I could. However, one of the guys in my interview group, complete idiot, right out of college, he made it through." The knife she was holding appeared to obliterate the pile of herbs on the cutting board.

Lilah scoffed at the chauvinistic mentality. "I think I'd find a different company."

Krista stopped chopping, raised a brow, and cocked her hip to one side, her expression serious, and that's when Lilah knew.

"You're kidding me," she groaned, shaking her head.

"Don't get me wrong, McCallister Industries is a great place to work, but their hiring team leaves something to be desired." She took the butcher knife and swayed it back and forth in Lilah's face. "I swear, you better not go and tell your daddy. I want to get where I'm going in life the right way, even if it's the hard way."

Lilah agreed. Although she'd definitely talk to her father. She wouldn't beg him to just give Krista the job she wanted, but she'd insist that Krista get another interview.

* * *

After more than thirty minutes, Lilah finally gave up. What was she thinking? All she was going to do was sit on a couch and watch a football game. Kyler probably wouldn't notice what her makeup, hair, or outfit looked like. At first, she had put on the one dressy thing she packed in her bag. That was a mistake. It would be immensely overdoing it, something that Sarah would do.

She looked in the mirror and pulled her hair down from the fancy ponytail she spent a good ten minutes working on, hating herself that Sarah entered her mind. But how could she not? The two times she had seen Kyler's phone, flirtatious texts from Sarah popped up. Was aggravating him seriously her only hobby?

She then proceeded to wiping off her lip gloss. It was too shiny and drew too much attention to her lips. Normally that's what girls wanted, right? Somehow, she didn't. So far, she had gotten to be someone she wasn't while she was around Kyler, and that someone was herself.

She tossed all the little odds and ends in her makeup bag and decided that simple would be for the best. While waiting for Kyler, she began packing her things so that she could leave right after the game. She knew Kyler had an assignment to work on. The books that he picked up Friday at the library sat on his desk untouched.

"Rushing out," a low and soft voice asked from the doorway, startling Lilah.

She looked up and felt as though someone stole all the air in her lungs. Kyler's gaze drifted over her like she was on display for him.

"No," she finally answered. A part of her wondered what he was thinking as he looked her up and down. "I was just getting my stuff together. I should get home as soon as the game is over."

Kyler chuckled and headed toward his closet. "If you don't want to watch it, you don't have to. I honestly didn't expect–"

"I want to," Lilah interrupted, her words so fast that Kyler barely caught them.

His hand tightened on the hanger of the shirt he held. He didn't want to turn around to face her. She was too much. Too pretty. Too natural. Too normal. She wasn't at all like the girl he had seen in school over the years.

"Anyway, I'll leave you to...whatever," she began. "I'll see you downstairs."

Kyler let out a breath when she finally left the room, scolding himself for leaving that stupid note to begin with. What was he thinking? He wasn't. He never did when it came to her anymore. Perhaps if she had been standing in front of him when he thought it, he would have shut it down. He didn't expect for something so simple to give him the nerves it had.

He really needed to think about distancing himself from Lilah after this. It had been a colossal mistake to invite her to spend a night, the weekend, at his house. If he didn't pull in the reigns fast, it was going to be an even more monumental mistake thinking that he could stay just friends with her.

* * *

"I could have sworn I read that a touchdown was seven points," Lilah huffed while taking delicate bites of her wing.

Kyler chuckled, wondering when and where she saw that. "Not really. There's the extra point from the kick. Most of the time it's made, but not always."

"Okay." She nodded her head, extremely focused, now in learning mode, attempting to absorb the information. "Then what happened when I went to the bathroom? The three points," she asked.

Kyler turned from the television and toward her, bending his knee beneath him on the couch. "There are a few different ways to score." He held out his hand to count them off. "Touchdown, obviously. That's six points and then there's the extra point from kicking it between the posts. The next most common way is a field goal. It's three points, and usually done on fourth down when the team is..." He shrugged his shoulders thinking. "I guess around the thirty-five-yard line or closer, and they're not willing to go on fourth down and risk not scoring, so they try to get the three points. It's safer than going on fourth, depending where you are on the field and how bad the score is."

Lilah nodded. "Okay, I get it."

"Then you have two-point conversions and safeties. Both of those are two points."

Lilah groaned. "Well, what are those?"

"You'll hardly see them. The two-point conversion is usually done later in the game if the score is extremely close. Rather than take the extra point, the team that just scored a touchdown basically attempts to score another one for two points."

Lilah shrugged. "That seems like a lot of effort for only two points."

He supposed she was right. "Risky, but sometimes it's enough to determine a game."

He turned back to the television once he saw how focused Lilah became on the screen. Surprisingly, she asked a lot of questions; she didn't ask just for the sake of making conversation, it seemed that she genuinely wanted to know. It was a little difficult to focus on the game, but Kyler enjoyed it. Despite last night, and feeling like he was definitely in the friend zone with Lilah, which he'd take for now, he really liked being around her.

The vibes she sent off were a little frustrating while she sat on the couch with him, but ultimately, she was sure to keep a vast distance. He had thought about sitting in the middle when he got back from the bathroom; however, the one instance where their hands grazed over the plate of snacks and Lilah immediately jerked back, not eating for another ten minutes, totally shot down that idea.

Lilah glanced at Kyler from time to time, never staring for too long. He appeared to be intensely focused on the game or deep in thought, maybe a little of both.

She'd never tell him, she didn't know how without it coming out the wrong way, but spending the weekend with him was one of the best weekends she had in a long time.

CHAPTER 25

"I feel so bad," Alice repeated. "If I would have known that you wanted to stay over, I would have invited you to come into the city with us."

"I guess I should have made my mind up before that evening," Lilah laughed. It was incredibly difficult to try to laugh about, but she pulled it off.

Lilah and Jolee waited for Alice to finish going through her mess of a locker. How she was able to find anything in that thing was a mystery.

"At least you had fun," Jolee sighed, looking extra sleepy as they walked down the hall. "My grandmother was fired up and the most critical and bitter person I've ever seen, but at the end of the day no one said anything about it because, as my mother puts it, we don't know how long she has left."

Alice and Lilah sent skeptical looks to each other.

"Didn't she go on a senior's singles cruise this past summer," Lilah hesitantly asked.

"Exactly," Jolee scoffed. "She just gets by with saying whatever she wants because she's old."

Lilah tensed as they made their way farther down the hall, half listening to Jolee rant on about her grandmother. On her right, near a set of lockers, was Kyler and three of his friends. They made brief eye contact and he gave her a slight nod of acknowledgement.

It was strange. When it came to the hierarchy of the school, they were both at the top; however, that didn't mean that their circles blended. She was so concentrated on how to best act around Kyler that she almost missed the insult from a group passing by.

"Loser," Sean coughed, barely grazing Lilah's shoulder as he made his way in the opposite direction.

For some reason, Lilah was feeling extra snotty that morning, and while that was something so mediocre that she should have let go, she couldn't pass on the opportunity. Sean was always a jerk, and she loved putting him in his place. The best part was, more often than not, she always had the last word, and it was usually bigger and SAT quality material. Besides, he had clearly forgotten about the bet that she had won.

"Seriously," she snapped, raising her voice as she spun around. Sean stopped and turned as well, rather surprised. "That is such a pitiful insult. It's like you don't even try anymore. Then again, I'm sure you've lost quite a bit of brain activity from how often you're knocked out on the field."

Lilah saw right away that his playing ability was a trigger. He stepped closer, so close that when he hissed in Lilah's face, she could smell the old funk of milk from his breakfast on his breath. "Watch it."

"Or what," Lilah challenged, putting her hands on her hips. It wasn't the first time she and Sean had gotten into it, and it probably wouldn't be the last knowing him.

"That's enough," Kyler growled, finding it difficult to step in between them.

"Oh, so now you're taking up for the stuck-up snob over–"

Kyler quickly interrupted, realizing the predicament he was being placed in. Regardless how he felt about Sean, they were still teammates. "I'm not taking any sides, but the both of you have too much to lose if this altercation escalates and gets back to Willis.

That appeared to make Sean back down. He huffed something, no doubt another silly insult, under his breath and continued along with Cash and Louis at his heels.

Kyler turned to say something to Lilah, although right now he wasn't particularly happy with her either. What was she thinking going after Sean like that? However, when he tried to talk to her, he saw that she and her friends were already on their way. It was a bit of a relief. Anything he thought of saying to her at that moment would probably only cause more venom to bubble through her already boiling veins.

He sighed and shook his head. "I don't know which one is worse."

"Sean just can't let things go. He's worse than an elephant. He remembers everything, even the stupid stuff," Dawson said as he crammed an insanely large textbook into his bag.

Kyler cocked his head to one side and raised a brow.

"Oh, that's right. You weren't here yet," Dawson laughed.

"I guess we weren't either," Gavin added, motioning to him and Miles. Both looked as equally confused as Kyler.

"Yes, you were. It was the seventh-grade dance."

Kyler hadn't moved to Raymere Grove until his eighth-grade year, so of course he knew nothing about some silly dance the year before. Did anybody remember those things?

Miles began to giggle. "No," he tried insisting, but after thinking for a moment, "You don't think he's still upset about that."

Dawson was dead serious now. "It's Sean. Before that, I swear he had a shrine to the girl. Now he probably has her yearbook picture blown up as a dartboard."

Kyler waved his hands back and forth. "Wait. I'm so confused."

Dawson sighed, and threw his heavy bag onto his back. It was nothing for him; he could handle it. "We had a spring formal in seventh grade. Let's just say, Sean was more than a little obsessed with Lilah." Even though it was years ago, when they were just kids, Kyler found that the statement struck a nerve with him. "No offense now," Dawson began. Kyler noticed that he slightly distanced himself a step or two to the side. "Lilah has always been..." He glanced to the Gavin and Miles for help, but they were silent.

Kyler shrugged. "I'm not going to take offense. I've dealt with her mouth before."

At that statement Gavin doubled over in laughter. It took Kyler a second to realize his choice of words and how they could have been taken, that is, if you had the perverted mind of Gavin.

He playfully punched Gavin in the side. "You know what I mean." Although he could feel his face warming at the mentioning of Lilah's mouth. "Besides, she's just my tutor. I'm not going to go all caveman and try to defend her honor."

All three of them grew silent. It made Kyler uncomfortable. It was like they were in on a secret and he wasn't. He would have made a bigger deal about it, but he really wanted to know the whole story with Lilah and Sean before the warning bell rang for first period.

"Anyway," Dawson finally began again. "The dance. Lilah went with her friends and all of us jocks went together. No one really did dates at that age. Well, Sean asked her to dance, several times, but you obviously know how she is, and she ended up rejecting him, several times. Finally, near the end, I think she got annoyed with him asking and she agreed." Dawson saw Kyler grit his teeth, only furthering his suspicions that Kyler definitely thought of Lilah as more than just a tutor. "Then he tried to kiss her."

"What?!"

Dawson held a knowing smirk on his face, which caused Kyler to quickly compose himself. "So, what happened then?" He tried to hide the growing anger in his voice, but it was difficult.

"At first, Lilah just walked off." Dawson paused and Kyler waited. With Lilah, it couldn't have been that simple. Dawson laughed, the memory now replaying itself. "About a minute later, she returned with not one, but two cups of red punch and dumped them on Sean, right in front of all of his friends."

Kyler smiled at the fact that the story had a happy ending. It was something he could also absolutely picture Lilah doing. He was only further pleased that it was Sean on the receiving end of it.

"Ever since then, his whole attitude about her changed." Dawson shrugged. "The funny thing is, I don't think it was a big enough occurrence in Lilah's life for her to even remember, but I guarantee you, Sean does. I mean, he'll still admit that she's hot, but I think he hates her most because she doesn't worship the ground he walks on. I think he realized that wasn't happening that night in seventh grade."

Kyler disliked Sean just because of his attitude and the way he treated people. Sean had never been extremely accepting of him when he moved to Raymere Grove. It only got worse in high school when he started to shine on the football field. After finding out that Sean tried to force a kiss from Lilah, and that was probably the reason for his behavior toward her, it was a little different now. Now he had a really good reason to hate Sean.

* * *

"Oh, I almost forgot," Lilah mentioned Thursday after tutoring. It was already after 6:30 and Kyler had to be on his way to work. For some reason, Lilah was a little more relieved than she ought to be that he was working and not going on a date. "I had your hoodie washed. I can get it to you tomorrow."

He really didn't care about the stupid thing. He almost wished that she would have kept it. He was just about to tell her that, but came up with a better idea. "That's fine. Just give it to me at school tomorrow."

"Okay, when?"

"I guess whenever you see me," he answered. It was vague and he knew that Lilah didn't like vague.

Before she could argue with him, he opened the door to the black car waiting for her. He leaned on the door until she got in.

"I hope work isn't too bad," she told him through the rolled down window.

"Pretty much the same thing as always, but thanks." Maybe it was just him, maybe he was looking for something that wasn't there, but it really looked like she didn't want to leave yet. "Have a goodnight, Lilah."

"You too."

With that, the window went up and the car slowly pulled away. Kyler couldn't help but feel guilty. All he was doing was wasting her time now until he got his act together. If she ever found out, she'd be furious with him, and no matter how he tried to look at it, he still ended up feeling like he was lying to her. It would be so easy to tell her the truth, technically it wasn't even a big lie, but right now, his time with her was too valuable.

Plus, she didn't seem interested in a relationship at the moment, and with what her parents were going through, she might not be for a while. His plate was also fairly full, and he wouldn't be able to give her the attention she deserved. The season was almost over; he'd just wait until then. While the team had started off strong, somehow they just couldn't keep it together. One more loss and they could kiss going to state goodbye. Everything hinged on the next game.

CHAPTER 26

Lilah passed by Dawson and Gavin at their lockers on the way to her first period class. Usually Kyler and Miles were around as well. Without looking like a stalker, she glanced around the busy hall, but there was no sign of either.

Lilah: I didn't see you this morning.

Kyler: I was around.

Lilah: Well, this is taking up room in my bag. When will I see you?

Kyler: Lunch?

Unless they had any classes near each other, which Lilah didn't know if they did or not, except for the one after lunch, lunch seemed to be the only logical time. Any other time would mean she'd end up being tardy to her next class.

Lilah: Before or after? Where?

Kyler: ...

Lilah: Seriously?!

Kyler: I take it you're not having a good morning.

Lilah: Only one person is affecting that.

Kyler: So I have an effect on you?

Lilah: Class is about to start! Just tell me.

Kyler: You avoided my question.

Lilah: I hate you.

Kyler: You know where I sit.

Lilah: You want me to come to your table??? With a piece of your clothing???

Kyler: Yeah?

"What's so funny," Miles asked, looking over Kyler's shoulder toward the screen.

"I'm just messing with Lilah."

Miles gave a grunt. It was him saying something without actually saying anything.

"What's that supposed to mean," Kyler asked, a little more defensively than he probably should have.

Miles shrugged. "I just didn't think the two of you would be as close as you are."

"Don't start. She's just–"

"Your tutor," Miles interrupted. "You keep saying that, but I'm not sure that you even believe that *just* part."

Lilah hadn't responded and class was already starting. Kyler could only imagine the tizzy that she was in.

Kyler: After that scene with Sean in the hall the other day, I didn't think you'd be so scared.

Lilah: I am not scared! GOODBYE!

Oh yeah, she was mad at him. He couldn't remember if she had ever used all caps when texting him.

He sat back in his seat and waited for his name to be called at the end of the attendance. He only hoped that Sean would be around when Lilah met him at lunch. Was it juvenile? Yes. Did that change his mind any? Absolutely not.

* * *

When Lilah seemingly accepted what appeared to be a challenge, she didn't think about the part where her friends would ultimately find out, and have a million questions.

Kyler had to be messing with her. He took his time getting to lunch and he was pretty much the last one arriving at his table. Just as he sat down, he made eye contact with her. The smirk on his face made

Lilah realize that it was definitely a challenge, and she couldn't stop her heart from racing.

It was miserable attempting to eat anything. She was clearly nervous. Why was she nervous? Though she could talk to anyone, often she preferred not to. At the top of that list were the jocks and cheerleaders.

She thought about waiting until after lunch, knowing that she and Kyler had class in the same hall; however, something told her that he'd find a way to avoid her, and it was Friday, meaning she wouldn't see him for several more days. She didn't understand why he was so dead set on lunch.

Then another idea hit her. It was just a silly piece of clothing that he obviously didn't need. He had a better coat hanging across the back of his chair. In fact, he had never even asked for it back. Surely he could just wait until Monday or Tuesday when they had tutoring.

Kyler: Do I even want to know what you're overthinking?

Lilah glared at Kyler upon reading the text, and reached inside her bag, digging out the neatly folded garment, fresh with a hint of lavender from the wash.

"What's that," Jolee immediately asked.

"Since when do you wear hoodies, and especially so large," Alice chimed in.

"It's Kyler's," Lilah admitted. That was all she would admit to. Anything else would be a complete fabrication.

"What," Alice gasped. "He gave you something of his to wear." Her words were far louder than Lilah expected, and she tried to hush her up by throwing out a quick excuse.

"The library was really cold yesterday. I forgot to take it off and give it back when we left."

Jolee was more speculating than Alice. "Mhmm," was all she said. Her eyes skimmed across Lilah's features looking for signs that she was lying.

Lilah rose from the table, her knees now feeling gooey. "Seriously. It's not the big deal the two of you would like to imagine." Those were her last words as she swallowed and made her way to her impending doom.

Before she was halfway across the room to Kyler's table, Sarah and her friends, having finished lunch, approached and hovered nearby. Lilah took a deep breath, knowing that Sarah hated her and would probably have something to say.

Just as she got to the long rectangular table, standing on the opposite side from where Kyler was seated, she felt the stares of not only Sarah and her friends, but of a couple players as well.

Kyler meant to say something, but before he could even inhale a breath, Sarah was on Lilah like a vulture.

"Umm...What are you doing here," Sarah spat.

Lilah gripped the fabric more tightly, the equivalent of making a fist, and ignored Sarah's presence. She'd get Kyler back for whatever that stupidly gorgeous smile was concealing.

She outstretched her arm between Gavin and Dawson, across the table to Kyler. "Here."

Kyler locked eyes with her and watched her carefully. If there was a point when she was hesitant, it didn't show now. From the corner of his eye, he saw that her arrival had garnered the attention of most everyone at the table, Sean included.

"Keep it."

Lilah was taken aback by his statement. Keep it? What was he doing?!

"Ugh," Sarah squawked. "What is that?"

Lilah grit her teeth and glared at Kyler. She stepped closer, now invading the small space between his two friends. "It's yours. I'm giving it back."

"If you touched it, no wonder he doesn't want it," Sean spoke up from a few seats down.

Kyler never could have imagined that Sean would say something, but the fact that he did, and that he was paying attention, made it so much better.

Lilah didn't like the way Kyler was looking at her. It was the same way he had looked at her in the park that day, but she wasn't a naïve and stupid little girl, this time she knew that it was all for show. She just couldn't understand why, and despite knowing all that, a part of her wanted it to be real. She really hated him sometimes.

Kyler raised his voice slightly, making sure the now relatively quiet table heard, and leaned forward into the table. "Actually, it looks much better on you, so you should keep it."

Lilah felt her face heating. Embarrassment? Anger? Something else entirely?

Though she couldn't break eye contact from the serious look on Kyler's face, from her peripheral vision, she could tell that Sarah and her two besties, Abby and Britt, had stormed off.

The stares that she and Kyler received were alarming. Usually she didn't mind being the center of attention, but this, combined with the look on his face, was more than she could bear.

Making sure that it didn't land in any food, Lilah dropped the hoodie to the table. Acting as if nothing was wrong, that she wasn't bothered in the least, she spun around and, with her usual step, went back toward her table. The only thing about it all, something was wrong.

She grabbed her bag and apologized to Jolee and Alice, insisted that everything was alright, and left the lunchroom. At least she'd get to class early and wouldn't have to get shuffled around in the traffic coming from the lunchroom.

"Wait," an all too familiar voice called from behind her as she was halfway down the hall.

She froze in her steps. He was relentless today. She then turned, prepared to lash out at owner of the heavy footsteps jogging toward her.

"What was that," Kyler asked as soon as he decreased the distance enough for a normal talking level.

Lilah gasped, maybe a little more dramatically than needed. "Are you serious? Why don't you tell me?"

"You're mad?"

She took a step closer so that he could see the intensity of the green in her eyes. "Of course I'm mad," she spat.

He hesitated. He felt like this was one of those things he was supposed to know and not have to ask, but despite his better judgement, he asked anyway.

"Why did you do that? Why did you have to say that," Lilah insisted.

Just then the bell rang signaling the end of lunch. Kyler didn't want the conversation to end just yet, nor could they have it with the rush of people. He softly grabbed her wrist and made his way down the hall just a short distance, pulling her along to the one insert he knew would be empty, the classroom to tech apps.

This time when he opened the door to the darkened room, he was rather surprised that she didn't make a big deal or snotty remark, and instead followed him inside.

"Honestly," Kyler sighed, leaning into the back of the door he had just closed. "I'm tired of Sean, both on and off the field." He hesitated with his next statement, not wanting her to know just how much he cared. "I also don't like how rude he is to you and I thought–"

"This helped how," Lilah interrupted.

"Some of the guys said some stuff about a long time ago…" He let his words drift off for a second so that he could figure out how to continue. Lilah would think he was childish regardless how he put it.

She shook her head and gave a laugh full of irritation. "He's still upset about that stupid dance? That's why he's such a jerk to me?"

Kyler shrugged. "In fairness, he's kind of a jerk to everyone."

"And you," she shouted. "You decided whatever that was in there was a smart move." She took a step closer and jabbed him in the chest with her finger. "I'm not a game. Don't use me to irk some teammate you have a problem with." She saw Kyler open his mouth to protest and went there before he could. "Don't use his treatment toward me as an excuse. I'm not some wimpy princess that needs saving. I can handle myself!"

That much he knew. Even with everything going on in her life, she didn't need anyone saving her.

Slightly changing the subject, "I meant what I said though." Maybe it would ease her irritation with him.

Though the room was dark, Kyler could see that her hardened features slightly melted away. "About what?"

"About you keeping it…About it looking good on you." He swallowed heavily. That was about all the admission he could manage. When she didn't respond, he took a step closer, but was sure to keep enough distance. If he got too close to her, he wasn't convinced that he'd be able to keep things completely platonic. "I knew you had it when you left last Sunday. I never asked for it because I didn't care."

Lilah scrunched her face. Of course he didn't care. She was the idiot who made a big deal about it, but to her it was a big deal. Keeping something of his, something that he wore, was a huge deal. She glanced through the window opening of the door into the hall, realizing that the mass of traffic was dwindling, and the warning bell would be going off shortly.

"Well, you have it now, clean and all," she said flatly, reaching for the door.

Kyler moved to the side and allowed her to open it. They both stepped out into the nook leading to the hall.

"Is that the problem then," he began to tease.

Lilah turned toward him, not yet venturing into the hall. "Is what the problem?"

Kyler wanted to ask her. It was the same for him. He generally washed his sheets every week, but he had refrained from doing so this past week. The lavender and rosemary scent from her shampoo still hung in the fabric of his pillowcase and he didn't want to lose that just yet. He also recalled times that night when they sat outside. She had tried to hide it, but he knew that his scent on the fabric did something to her.

Lilah eyed him suspiciously as he leaned down with his backpack and dug around for something. As he was still messing around, she glanced behind her, to the hallway. It was virtually empty now. Just as she turned back to say something about being tardy, a sound of something spraying and an all too familiar smell, although now magnified, hit the small space.

Kyler rose and began backing into the hall with that charming grin on his face that probably got him out of all sorts of trouble. When he was far enough away, he tossed the garment at Lilah, which she caught perfectly.

"There, I made it better," he said with a teasing wink that shouldn't have sent her pulse racing, but it did.

The smell of his cologne hit more than just her sense of smell. All of her senses were alive, so much so that she almost missed the ringing of the warning bell.

Kyler pointed up to the ceiling, continuing to walk backwards from her. "You should probably hurry. You don't want to be late." He turned from her and walked at a faster pace than normal to class. He bit his lip to keep from smiling from ear to ear. Her wide eyes and stunned look were perfectly singed in his mind. His pulse raced from the adrenaline at being so bold with her. He honestly couldn't have asked for a better Friday up to that point.

CHAPTER 27

"What is going on out there," Coach Turner's voice boomed throughout the locker room.

All eyes were on the floor, as no one could look up at him. 10 to 24 was not the score they were hoping for when the second quarter ended.

"I'm waiting," he continued, but still no one spoke. "These last few games have all but taken your chances of going to state. This is it. If you lose this one you can forget it. So again, what is going on out there?!"

Sean was the one to finally speak up. "Maybe you should ask Kyler."

Kyler was immediately on the defense. "What's that supposed to mean?"

"You're the one who's missed the most practices."

"Not lately, besides, I have my stuff together. Maybe if you could figure out what you're doing out there."

"Enough," Coach Turner interrupted, though that didn't stop Sean.

"You're too busy failing classes and messing around with your silly little tutor that you don't even know which–"

"I said enough," Coach Turner boomed. "Shut it. No one on this team is failing. In fact, unlike some of you, West has had an A in all his classes. So back off with the accusations."

Sean sent Kyler a deathly glare and Kyler had to force himself to look away. He preferred it when everyone thought he was an idiot. Someone as vindictive and calculating as Sean would surely overthink Turner's words.

"I want us to show some teamwork this second half," Coach Turner began as halftime slowly concluded. "This win keeps us in the running to make state and though it's not ideal, it's only a two-touchdown difference."

As much as Kyler wanted to be hopeful, his hope was slowly fading. He was giving it his all, but it seemed like half the team had already given up on any chances of going to state.

"You know what I can't figure out," a sickly sinister voice whispered from nearby as they made their way back to the field. "If your grades are so good across the board, why do you still need a tutor?"

Kyler spun to face Sean head on, now more than a little annoyed with his constant mentioning of Lilah. "Maybe the reason my grades are so good is because I have a tutor."

"I call bull."

Kyler shook his head in disbelief. "What is your obsession with Lilah being my tutor?"

Sean's face turned red from embarrassment. "I'm not obsessed with..." His words drifted off as Kyler took an imposing step forward, closing their gap. Though he was much bigger than Kyler, it didn't seem to stir Kyler one bit.

"I think you're jealous," Kyler began, his voice deep and low. "Not of the fact that I have a tutor and awesome grades, but of the fact that it's her."

Sean tried to laugh it off as absurd, but Kyler knew it was fake, all an act.

"You're still harboring some ill feelings from what, like five years ago?"

Sean's face went white. "You don't know what you're talking about!"

"I do know she rejected you, quite publicly from what I heard." Kyler was poking the sleeping bear at this point.

Sean shoved his helmet into Kyler's chest. "You should learn when to shut up," he growled.

He yanked his helmet away and roughly placed it on his head as he made his way into the lights leading onto the field.

Miles caught up to Kyler as they returned to the field. "Do I want to know what that was about?"

"Sean is just a jerk."

"Yeah, we know that, but right now, he looks insane. If looks could kill, someone would be dead by now," Miles pointed out, gesturing toward Sean.

Kyler laughed it off. "Then it's a good thing that he's on our team and not theirs.

* * *

Once the cheerleaders finished another routine, they broke for a water break.

"Is everything okay today," Britt asked, sipping a blue sports drink with a straw to avoid staining her lips.

"Yeah," Sarah answered with confusion.

"You just seem...quiet," Abby added.

Sarah looked at the two girls nodding before her in unison. She inhaled and exhaled deeply and distracted herself by playing with the ribbons in her ponytail.

"I just have a lot on my mind," she admitted, secretly wanting her friends to dote on her.

Britt and Abby seemed unable to function without one another and had an identical thought process. They looked to each other before Britt, the vaguely smarter of the two decided to bring it up. "Is this about lunch?"

Sarah spun back toward them, her long blonde ponytail flopping. "What about lunch?" She knew what they were referring to but didn't want to be the one to state the obvious.

Just then a few of the junior cheerleaders came up to get beverages and the three of them attempted to quiet their conversation.

"Is this about Kyler and that dork," Abby asked.

Sarah was pleased that Abby at least referred to Lilah as such, but it didn't help that Lilah didn't wear frumpy dresses, glasses, and matted hair. No, instead she had to be one of the richest and most beautiful nerds around.

"I'm not sure what's going on between them," Sarah began, focusing her attention to Kyler on the field. "But it's not going to last. Besides, Kyler and I are perfect for each other. He's just a guy, and you know how they are. He's focused on football right now, but once the season is over, things with us are definitely on," Sarah giggled, trying to convince both her friends, and maybe even herself.

Britt attempted to change the subject that was now taking a strange and awkward turn. "So, are any of the juniors showing potential for your replacement next year?"

"I think Emory Parker shows–"

"Ugh, shut up," Sarah scoffed, cutting Abby off. "You only like her because you want to hook up with her brother. Need I remind you, he's a junior."

"Yeah," Britt chimed in. "And her twin. Kissing him would be like kissing her."

Abby's look immediately went from hopeful to pensive, now thinking Britt's theory over in her head.

"I like Rachel," Sarah finally answered. "I think she has the same leadership potential that I showed back then."

There was a fine line between leadership and whatever Sarah was, but watching Rachel chastise a good bunch of her junior equals, Rachel most definitely could be a dead ringer for Sarah's replacement.

* * *

The pain was instant.

His legs. His back. His shoulder. God did his shoulder hurt most of all. Thankfully it was his left. In his mind, he could still play.

"No, don't even think about moving," Coach Turner insisted, hovering nearby, when Kyler tried to get up from his back.

As he looked up to the darkness of the night, void of any stars because of the stadium lights, all he could think of was how much he did not want to be carried off the field.

Any protests fell on deaf ears when he tried to tell them that he was fine. Deep down he knew that he was, but that didn't mean that he wouldn't feel the pain for days to come. To his left he heard a commotion. It was Miles.

"What were you thinking," Miles screamed, shoving at Sean's chest.

The smirk of Sean's face had Miles seething. "I must have thought we were doing a different play."

"That's crap and you know it! You didn't block for him on purpose!"

Sean puffed his chest out, stepping closer to Miles, now looking for a fight. "Oh, so because the perfect star quarterback messes up, it's my fault?"

Coach Turner broke it up before it could get started by yanking Sean by his facemask. "It is your fault," he screamed, pulling Sean in a manner not suitable for a high school coach. "That's your job as left tackle! Get to the bench, but don't think that's the last of this conversation." Coach Turner all but threw Sean forward toward Raymere Grove's sidelines.

"We're going to check him for a concussion," one of the paramedics began, while two others allowed Kyler to lean on them as he walked off the field. "Nothing looks broken, but we'll check him out fully when he's off the field."

Coach Turner groaned. When he neared the sidelines, "Ellis, you're in!" Some of the other players looked at each other in confusion. Cash was next in line for the quarterback position.

"Uh, Coach," Cash began, tapping him on the shoulder cautiously.

Coach Turner ignored the players. "Ellis Parker will be starting next year," he announced. "Since we haven't got a chance in hell of going to state at this point, I'm putting him in." There were a few murmurs, but no one dared say a word about the fact that Ellis Parker just so happened to be Coach Turner's nephew. "Let's change it up a little bit. Since Sean is obviously out," he began, glaring at the most hated person on the bench. "Byron, you're in as left tackle. Miles, take a seat,"

"Wait, what did I do," Miles gasped, shocked that he was being taken out of the game.

"Nothing, but I'm putting in a couple juniors that I expect to do a lot better for the school next year after this year's miserable season."

Miles rolled his eyes. Coach Turner often went on tangents. He hadn't in a while, but that last play, and

Kyler's uncertainty in the locker room, wasn't doing him any favors.

"Deacon Garrett, you're up," he exclaimed.

Miles gave Deacon a low high five as he left the field and Deacon prepared himself to go on. Miles had watched the junior enough. He knew without a doubt that he would be a killer wide receiver next year. Maybe, just maybe, if they kept girls out of the mix, they'd actually stand a chance of going to state.

* * *

"Why are we stopping here," Rover asked with a mouthful of cookie when Antonio stopped the car.

Lilah gripped the box of cookies from Petal Pastries tightly, feeling a combination of anxious, nervous, apprehensive, and excited all at once. "My friend got hurt a little yesterday, and I wanted to do something nice."

She wasn't sure how badly Kyler had gotten hurt. Social media was nothing more than gossip and exaggerated stories; however, after looking at Raymere Grove's online edition of the paper this morning, she knew that it had to be something for them to send a replacement in.

"Boy or girl," Rover asked, and Lilah could already see the wheels turning in his head.

"Does it matter?"

Rover shrugged and continued stuffing his face with another cookie while the game on his phone loaded. Lilah hated that he was becoming so addicted to those things. Perhaps today would change that. It was a beautifully cool and crisp fall weekend, and she had promised Rover the park for long enough.

"Go ahead," Rover insisted, feeling his sister's questioning eyes upon him.

Lilah smirked and gave her brother a slight nudge. "They have a dog."

Rover hit the side button on his screen, darkening the lit up and colorful explosion of magic. "Seriously," he all but screamed. "Why didn't you tell me that?"

Lilah didn't want Rover running up to the door alone. He had no idea who the Wests were; however, before she could tell him to wait, he was already out of the car door.

Lilah realized an even bigger mistake as she stood in the doorway to Kyler's room. She probably should have let him know that she was coming.

As soon as he saw her, he shot off the bed, immediately wincing in pain, despite his best efforts to conceal it.

Lilah swallowed heavily. Kyler wore nothing but a pair of basketball shorts. His left shoulder was wrapped with some sort of bandage contraption that kept an ice pack in place. She almost dropped the box of cookies as he made his way toward her. Swallowing the lump in her throat was more than she could bear. Despite knowing that Kyler probably felt miserable, she couldn't get over how good he looked, and when he used his right arm to shift the icepack covering his left shoulder, she noticed something black and delicate etched into his skin that she had only gotten a brief glimpse of before.

Even though he was already eighteen, something about it screamed rebel in her mind, and she couldn't help but find it attractive on him. Did she just think of a tattoo as attractive? Up until recently, she found tattoos, piercings, and facial hair grotesque and un-becoming, but there was something about Kyler. He could have had all of them and more, and something told her that it would only make him more desirable.

She stopped looking anywhere below Kyler's neck. If she did, she wouldn't be able to breathe, and she'd only be in worse shape than he already was.

Kyler narrowed his eyes in skepticism, as he kept several feet between the two of them. "What are you doing here," he finally asked. He expected Lilah to say something, but she stood there with this awkward deer in the headlights look.

"I heard the game didn't go so well," she began. Looking into his eyes was suddenly no easier than looking anywhere else.

Kyler attempted to shrug, but that didn't go too well either. "We lost. I have to say some of the juniors really tried. At least we didn't lose by much in the end."

It didn't matter. 27 to 31 was still a loss.

"So are you done now," Lilah asked.

"Oh, no," Kyler laughed. He walked back toward his bed and motioned for Lilah to follow. "I was checked out. I'm just a little bruised and that's about it."

Lilah sat a full arm's length from Kyler, still clutching the box. "I meant, if the team isn't going to state, aren't you done with the season or whatever?"

Kyler realized that he still had a lot to explain to her, that is, if she wanted. "No. We still have two more games."

Lilah didn't understand, but she left it alone. There was a faint uncomfortable silence until she remembered why she had come.

She held out the box of cookies. "Oh, I brought these for you."

He took the box, but said nothing, waiting for her rambling to begin. She looked uncomfortable and he knew his silence would only worsen that. He watched her carefully until she broke.

"I realize cookies probably don't have any healing powers for whatever you're going through. Now thinking about it, you probably don't even eat much sugar during the season to stay looking like–" She quickly stopped and let her eyes fall to the floor.

"Actually, I eat just about anything. So, thanks for this."

She couldn't help it. He looked so incredible that she had to take it all in while she still had the chance. Kyler saw her eyes land for a moment too long on his tattoo and he shifted so that she could have a better look.

"It's a raven," he told her. "I honestly didn't know what I wanted, but I loved that poem."

"Poe," Lilah questioned, completely and utterly floored that he chose to permanently put something on his body based on a piece of literature.

Kyler laughed. "I know. It sounds stupid. Don't tell any of the guys."

"No, it's pretty," Lilah quietly corrected him. She reached out to touch it but quickly pulled her fingertips back after realizing how bad that looked in terms of boundaries. Kyler's next words then caused her stomach to flip.

"You can touch it. It doesn't hurt anymore obviously." There was a simple smile on his face as if he would have allowed anyone to touch his body.

Lilah hesitated, but didn't want to come across as a shy prude. It was just his side, just along the ribcage. There was absolutely nothing at all intimate about the gesture or their situation.

Kyler sucked in a breath once the dainty tips of her fingers collided with his skin, setting his whole body on fire. Lilah immediately apologized for having cold hands, but he couldn't tell her that the temperature of her hands wasn't the cause of the feelings suddenly running through him. Goosebumps soon ran up and down his arms.

When Lilah pulled away, she was stopped with Kyler's free hand clasping over her wrist. His eyes opened, meeting hers, and that's when she saw darkness in the normally bright blue. His glassy eyes appeared dazed, in another world.

"Lilah..." His voice was deep and raspy, sending chills all the way down to Lilah's toes.

Gradually, Kyler allowed his fingers to release her wrist and skim up her arm, finding satisfaction at the goosebumps now appearing across her skin. The space between them closed with each passing second, as both leaned toward the other.

Kyler's eyes clenched and he pulled his hand away when the unfamiliar laughter from downstairs made its way through his open doorway.

Whatever spell he had cast on Lilah faded as quickly as a flash of lightning across a darkened stormy sky. She bolted up from the bed, needing to put distance between Kyler and herself. She couldn't believe that he was about to kiss her, or at least that's what it seemed like. The moments between them had to mean something more and it made her crazy. She couldn't let him kiss her again, not while he was with someone else, maybe not ever.

"I have to go," Lilah managed, only realizing how breathless she sounded when the words finally came.

She could hear Kyler's steps right behind her as she darted down the stairs like the most scared cat that ever existed.

When Kyler got to the foot of the stairs, he appeared genuinely shocked. For some reason all eyes fell to him as he stared at the young kid that he had never seen before. He recognized right away that it was Lilah's brother, but that didn't help with the confusion any.

"Ky! Put on a shirt. There's a kid," his sister pretended to scold.

Rover narrowed his eyes and broke from Kyler to his sister, who was clearly uncomfortable with the situation. He could definitely have fun at her expense if he so chose.

"So, this is Kyler," Rover said in the most annoying and flirtatious voice he could muster up.

Lilah's lips tightened and she glared at him to shut up. While her brother knew absolutely nothing about Kyler, other than the fact that he had text her, she was certain that he would make something up, just to embarrass her.

"Kyler, this is my little brother, Rover," Lilah introduced. "We were headed to the park," she said, beginning to ramble. "I wanted to drop the cookies off and I thought Rover might like to meet Max. We can't stay any longer though." She began trying to motion Rover to the door. "Antonio is waiting and–"

"Wait," Rover exclaimed, not budging. "Shouldn't you go help him put on a shirt?"

Though the adult in the room, Krista couldn't help but choke on her sip of coffee at the comment.

Kyler didn't think he had ever seen Lilah's face as red as it was after that. He wanted so much for her to stay a little longer, even if it meant that her brother would be around as well, but everything was already beyond awkward as it was.

"When are you going to ask her out," Krista questioned as soon as the door closed behind Lilah and her brother.

"Never."

"Seriously? After last weekend and now this?"

Kyler sighed and shook his head. "She's just being nice because she heard I got hurt."

"Oh! Whatever! From what you told me about Lilah McCallister, I never expected *that*."

"What do you mean?"

Krista laughed in disbelief. She didn't know if Kyler wanted her to feed his ego, or if he was really that clueless. "You acted like she was a cross between Cerberus and Medusa, like she was the biggest, snottiest, brat that ever walked the halls of Raymere Grove High, like–"

"She was!"

"Well, the key word there is *was*. What I saw right now is an infatuated girl who turns to a puddle of mush when she's around you." Krista paused, scrutinizing her brother's facial features. "And if I'm not mistaken, you're not much better."

Kyler began to make his way back up the stairs. He didn't intend to spend his Saturday arguing with his sister about his relationships, or lack thereof. "You're wrong. She's my tutor until the end of the season, and–" His words stopped immediately with the cackling witch-like noise coming from his sister. There was no use with her.

He wouldn't bother telling her that Lilah made herself clear last weekend, despite whatever almost happened in his bedroom. They weren't suitable for each other. They were from two different and secretly imperfect worlds.

CHAPTER 28

The moment could not have worked out more perfectly in Sarah's favor. She laughed on the inside at how ridiculous Lilah was. Everyone knew if you went to the bathroom at least one friend was obligated to attend with you.

"Girls, bathroom. Now," Sarah insisted, rising from the lunch table.

Abby looked down at the steaming hot cheeseburger that Sarah had just told her needed to be trashed. She really didn't want to leave it yet.

"Can you wait like five minutes," Britt asked.

Sarah gasped in offense. "No!"

They both rolled their eyes but quickly rose from the table and were at Sarah's heels headed toward the bathroom. They were confused when Sarah immediately began talking about Kyler as they entered the room.

Sarah glanced under the stalls. There were only two people. One had a pair of awful looking Converse while the other had shiny black heels with bright red bottoms. She twisted her lips just thinking about those stupid perfect shoes.

She gave Abby and Britt a wink and motioned with her hand to keep going. They weren't entirely sure what game she was playing but knew not to question her motives.

"I'm sure our relationship will be a lot easier after this past Friday. I mean, it sucks that our season is almost over, but at least now Kyler and I can focus on each other, once his little tutoring sessions end," Sarah went on, motioning for her friends to do the same.

"Uh...Yeah," Britt stammered. "What's up with that? I mean, especially that whole deal with her having his hoodie."

"Oh, I'm sure they have a little something going on, nothing major of course," Sarah began, pretending to dismiss the idea that Kyler could be seriously interested in Lilah.

"That doesn't bother you," Abby asked.

Sarah managed a giggle, now looking at herself in the mirror and touching up her eyeliner. She fell silent when one of the stalls opened. She knew Lilah wouldn't be bold enough to come out, and as it turned out, it wasn't Lilah. It was the hideous pair of Converse that, oddly enough, belonged to someone on her squad. She gave Emory a slight nod and small smile before continuing back to her friends.

"Of course not. Kyler and I have an open relationship right now...Kind of like Lilah's parents."

Up to that point, Lilah had been able to take hearing Sarah's words bouncing through the room, but now she just felt sick.

"I don't feel the need to put Kyler on a tight leash at the moment. If he wants a little toy here and there, he can have it. He'll get bored eventually. At first, I didn't think Lilah would be into a guy like that, but after knowing what she has for a mother, I guess it runs in the family," Sarah laughed loudly.

Lilah felt tears sting the corners of her eyes, begging to get out. She assumed Kyler and Sarah were...something. She just couldn't believe that she had started to like him, to fall for him, to think that he'd pick someone like her over someone like Sarah, someone obviously perfect for the star quarterback. The worst of it all was being compared to her mother. Most girls would have loved to hear that, but lately she wanted to be as far from being like either of her parents. Being branded as a toy, a little plaything for some stupid jock, tore at her insides. That was not at all who or what she was.

She waited until the harsh words finally stopped and she heard several sets of footsteps leave, the squeaky door slamming shut and silencing them for now. After taking a few long blinks with deep breaths, Lilah was able to shut down any waterworks from breaking through to the surface.

She made her way from the stall to the sinks, only to realize she wasn't alone. Thankfully it was just some junior; however, upon taking a longer glance at the girl from her reflection in the mirror, she realized that the loose sweatshirt and ripped jeans only did a marvelous job at concealing what was underneath. A cheerleader.

Lilah ignored the girl and went about washing her hands. She scrubbed and scrubbed until there was nothing but a pile of foam forming a mountain in the sink that clearly had drainage issues. From the corner of her eye, she could see the girl, still there, now tinkering with making a side braid with hair that should have been cut years ago.

Not bothering to look in Lilah's direction, Emory finally sighed, attempting to find the right words. "You should ignore her. Her life's mission is to make everyone else miserable, and let me tell you, she can be a calculating and manipulative little demon."

Lilah stopped scrubbing, completely stunned by what she had just heard, and the person she had heard it from. "Aren't you one of them?" Lilah asked. She felt chills as soon as the words came out, realizing how rude she came across.

Emory huffed and turned from the mirror, now leaning against the sink with crossed arms, eyeing Lilah. "Just because I'm a cheerleader does not mean I'm anything like her. Do you always have to be such a snob?"

Lilah looked over. Had she never seen the girl in a uniform before, she never would have taken her for a cheerleader. She had this unique combination of girly and tomboy that appeared very confusing.

"Look, I get you have this stone-cold iciness about you, but that doesn't mean that what she said didn't hurt," Emory started over. "What I'm telling you is, she probably knew you were in here and just wanted to mess with you. Don't let her get in your head."

Lilah looked in the mirror and immediately had to look away. She didn't want to see the reflection of herself. "You're wrong. Everything she said was totally right. I've just never heard it aloud before." Lilah's words were quieter, barely audible over the running water.

"Yeah, well I know every guy on that team," she began confidently. Sadly, having a brother on the team and an uncle as the coach also meant that unlike Lilah, not a single guy in uniform wanted anything to do with her aside from playing catch. "What Sarah said about Kyler isn't true either." She laughed. "He barely dates and seems to have a lot on his plate." Even Lilah could attest to that last part. "I can't imagine that he would feel the need to add juggling girls to his list. Then again, what do I know? I'm just a ditzy cheerleader," Emory shrugged.

Great. This girl was being nice and comforting and somehow Lilah had managed to insult her. Lilah grabbed a paper towel. "I'm sorry. I didn't mean for it to come out like that."

"Yes, you did. I get it. High school stereotypes and all," Emory said as though she had not a care in the world. "Anyway, I have to get back to class," Emory concluded, pushing off the sink and making her exit.

Then there was silence. Lilah was all alone, the only company being that of her reflection in the grimy mirror.

∗ ∗ ∗

While Sarah knew that her actions might be considered a bit brutal, she wasn't letting go when it came to Kyler. She couldn't remember any of Kyler's girlfriends, or even him dating. It would be a cold day before she'd allow for Lilah to take that title over her.

Hopefully her words had hurt Lilah enough and caused her to think of her own actions and how she portrayed herself. The little Sarah knew of Lilah, she was certain that her goody girl reputation meant everything to her.

Now she had to move on to the next phase of her brilliant plan. She needed Lilah to focus her attention on someone else, and she knew the perfect person for the job. She liked to think that she was very observant of her social surroundings.

* * *

"Sorry I couldn't meet right after school today," Kyler began as soon as he sat his bag down at the table of the public library.

Lilah didn't bother looking up. "It's fine. Do you have to work today?"

Something about her words, in just those few, felt off to him. He bordered on trying to start a personal conversation with her, asking if everything was okay. It had been over a week since she opened up to him about her parents. Instead, "Yeah. So, I've only got an hour."

"That's great. For starters, how did you do on the test last week?" Lilah only now looked up.

He really didn't want to lie to her, but he told himself it was the only thing he had lied about. It wasn't even that bad in the big picture. He rubbed the back of his neck and averted her attention.

"Kyler," Lilah pressed. She leaned forward onto the table and crossed her arms, staring at him, waiting.

"I barely passed," he finally admitted. When he looked up, he could see the disappointment and irritation in Lilah's face. He hated that.

Lilah sank back in her chair. "I don't get it! I thought you had it. You should have had an A, a high B at the very least. Did you use your study guide we worked on?"

He shrugged. "Yeah."

Despite what she had learned from Sarah, she still felt bad for him. She knew he had a lot going on, especially with trying to work after school several days a week. "It's alright. You still passed. As long as you don't get behind on assignments, you'll be fine. Maybe we can make some extra time in the coming days."

They dove right in to wrapping up the last bits of *Pride and Prejudice*. Mr. Hughes had already hinted at an essay and his weren't the easiest. While he allowed a good timeframe in terms of completion, he also scrutinized every source and citation. Lilah was sure that the due date would fall after Kyler's football season and wondered if he'd ask her for any help by then.

"I don't know how to bring this up," Kyler began as they walked down the steps of the library to the black car waiting in the towing zone. "But how are things?"

Lilah's steps faltered and she stopped. Kyler was two steps ahead of her and when he turned, they were almost the same height.

"What do you mean?"

"Uh. With your parents and all?" He didn't know if it was a subject that he was allowed to bring up.

Lilah sighed and shifted uncomfortably. She couldn't believe that this was the one person she chose to spill everything to. Why was that again? What mystical power had he had that night? "Fine," was all she said at first, but when he didn't move, she had to assume that wouldn't be enough to satisfy him.

Above all, she shouldn't have looked in his eyes. The sincerity and care pouring from his brilliant blue irises was more than she could deal with.

"We've just been avoiding *it.*"

"Avoiding it," he repeated, turning it into a question.

"Yeah. My parents keep busy and since that news broke, we see less and less of each other." Why did she keep talking? *Fine* was sufficient. She should have left it at that.

"Well, if you ever need–"

"Antonio is waiting for me," Lilah pointed out, interrupting whatever garbage Kyler was about to feed her.

She knew without a doubt that she was being immature. She could have just asked him directly about Sarah. After all, at times it felt like they were friends. Were they? She could have asked him that too. The foolish part of her felt relief at not knowing. If he confirmed the worst, that he was indeed in some bizarre attachment with that horrible person, she didn't know how she'd feel. She didn't even bother thinking of the slim chance that he wasn't.

CHAPTER 29

Thankfully the honor society meeting was a shortened one. It's not like Lilah had anywhere to be, but staying after school for those meetings seemed redundant after three years.

The entire time she sat there, she squirmed thinking about her next set of volunteer hours. The hospital gift shop had been easy, and if she did that again, there was a chance she'd see Kyler. No. She shook that thought away. Her time with Kyler was coming to an end and it was for the best.

Instead she thought of a different assignment to sign up for if still available. Sadly, it too reminded her of Kyler.

Her hands finally quit shaking and the excitement began once she signed her name.

"The animal shelter," a deep voice said interrupting her inner thoughts.

Lilah turned to the recognizable voice. "Yes," she confirmed with a nervous excitement.

Simon's face didn't echo the same feelings. "I'm not an animal person," he said with a shrug. "There's so much hair and shedding."

His comment reminded her of her mother. That was precisely why they had never had a dog.

"I've never had a dog before, but one of my friends does, and he's just the sweetest thing ever," Lilah responded. She stepped aside so that Simon could sign up for the hospital again.

"The dog or the friend?"

Lilah could feel a tumble in her stomach. Both. "The dog," she laughed.

They both gathered their bags and began making their way from the room. Lilah knew Antonio would be waiting on her. Kyler had text her earlier that he needed to go into work early. While she was aware that he wanted to help his mom and sister, she hated that his grades were suffering because of it; however, as a result, once the honor society meeting ended, she was able to go home and have time to herself.

"Lilah?"

"Hmm?" She hadn't realized where her thoughts were when Simon woke her from them.

"Would you want to go to dinner Saturday?"

Lilah stopped dead in her tracks. Her mouth had instantly gone dry, but she was able to ask, "Like a date?"

Simon laughed, which only further lit up his perfect face full of model-like features. "That was the idea, but if you don't want to call it that, we don't have to."

Lilah felt the blood drain from her body. It would be so humiliating if the first time a guy asked her on a date she passed out. "Umm..." she began, trying to buy some time as she thought. This was something that she had wanted for a long time. To be asked on an actual date. To have Simon be the guy. The moment felt right, but something inside her didn't.

Simon was a little surprised that it was taking her so long for a one-word answer, regardless what that answer would be. "If you want to think about it–"

"What time," Lilah found herself asking.

"Around six? You can pick the place." His words were hesitant, and Lilah figured he must sense that she was still uncertain.

Despite all of that, when she got in the car to go home, it was with plans for a date that Saturday night. A date with Simon Campbell.

* * *

Kyler sat in the school library that Thursday anxiously waiting for Lilah. It had been a couple days since he had last seen her, and something felt off. She had come across as colder and more distant, which he found strange, especially after they opened up to each other so much that one weekend.

He had been thinking a lot, especially about Lilah and their time together. He couldn't pretend to need help forever, and why would Lilah want to spend her afternoons always studying? Though he never thought possible, some strange part of him liked being around her, and he needed more of that to figure out what was going on between them. He still couldn't stop thinking about that kiss that seemed to be an eternity ago. Regardless what Lilah said in that note, there was a spark, that he was certain of.

"Sorry I'm late," Lilah began sounding out of breath.

Kyler dug through his mess of a bag and found his notebook. "It's okay, I just got here too," he lied. He had been eager to leave after eighth period athletics. He didn't have work that evening and he had hoped that Lilah would want to do something after homework, even if it was as simple as him taking her home.

Throughout their session, she still came across as cold and aloof, which only heightened his nervousness. He had never been rejected by a girl, in fact, most of the time he didn't even have to do the asking. Given, he didn't go on many dates, but somehow he always found a girl attached to his side when he and his friends went out after games.

Pride and Prejudice came easy to him, but his overthinking soon made the words before him a jumbled puzzle. His concentration was only further interrupted when Lilah groaned and slammed her pencil on the table. He was just about to ask what was wrong with her when a pair of dainty hands grabbed his shoulders.

"Boo," Sarah giggled.

Kyler took a deep breath. Sarah was the last thing he needed right now. "Hey," he acknowledged, but after thinking for a moment, "What are you doing here?" He didn't mean for his words to sound as they did, but Sarah and libraries didn't mix. She couldn't even focus on documentaries in class; he had no idea why she'd be in a place where books were just longer versions of movies with lots of unnecessary words, as he remembered her saying in the past.

"I had to return a book for a project, and I saw you. I thought I'd come see what you were working on."

Lilah felt invisible with the two of them there. It only reassured her that her answer to Simon the other day had been the right one.

She hated that she was forced to listen to Sarah giggle and chatter away. A piece of her was seconds away from calling the afternoon quits when the conversation took a sickening turn.

"I thought we could go out Saturday night. There's this movie that I've been–"

Kyler quickly interrupted Sarah. Something about being in Lilah's presence and the look on her face made him unable to tolerate Sarah's flirtatiousness. "Actually, I think we have a paper to start on." He motioned to Lilah in hopes that she'd help him out. He shouldn't have.

"*Actually*, I have other plans Saturday," she responded, glaring at Kyler and ignoring Sarah.

Kyler glared back. He wouldn't tell Lilah now, in front of Sarah, but he fully had planned to ask her to do something on Saturday. He was mildly annoyed by her comment.

Sarah quickly recovered from the dismissal Kyler had tried giving her. "See, the two of you can work on your paper another time. Anyway, I was thinking that we could–"

Kyler attempted to call Lilah's bluff. "What plans," he asked as though Sarah wasn't even there. She shouldn't have been in the first place.

Lilah folded her arms and leaned into the table. "I have my honor society volunteer hours…"

"And then," Kyler pressed. He could tell in her eyes that something was up.

"Then I have a date." Her words were quick, and she had to break eye contact with Kyler after that.

Kyler thought for a moment that Lilah had gotten jealous with Sarah's presence and a sick part of him liked that. If that were true, maybe it meant that she had some sort of feelings for him; however, if what she was saying now was true, he could forget about that.

"Well, isn't that cute," Sarah cooed.

Lilah glanced up to see the fake smile plastered across Sarah's face. Deep inside Sarah was shooting her daggers, hating that she spent as much time with Kyler as she did.

"Sarah," Kyler growled, rising from his chair and causing her to stumble backward. She batted her extended eyelashes at him as he pulled her aside, but it did nothing. "Look, I really need to finish this assignment. I'll talk to you later."

A smile spread across Sarah's lips and Kyler realized that wasn't the way to let her down, if anything he was giving her hope.

"Alright, then. I'll be waiting," she giggled, hopping away like a caffeinated bunny.

He rolled his eyes and sighed. He angrily turned back to Lilah and made his way back to his seat, glaring at her as she began to slowly pack up.

"What was that," he hissed.

Only then did Lilah look up at him. He was mad. Good. She didn't like her time to be wasted, and his little chitchat with Sarah did exactly that.

"Why couldn't you pretend that we had plans rather than throw me under with some made up–"

Lilah's brows furrowed. "With the truth?"

Kyler blew out a breath. "I'm actually really glad that you're volunteering at the shelter. After seeing you with Max, I know you'll love it," he said sincerely before changing his tone. "But you didn't have to go so far as to say–"

"That I have a date," she interrupted him yet again.

Shaking his head, "Yeah."

When their eyes met again, he saw something different. The truth. She was telling the truth.

Kyler narrowed his eyes, searching her face for anything, but all it held was a firm innocence.

"Wait...You have a date Saturday?" Though he had just taken his seat again, once Lilah rose, so did he.

"I know that might sound unbelievable to you, but yes, I do," Lilah responded with a great deal of confidence, despite feeling anything but.

Kyler wasn't sure how to react. Generally, that many emotions didn't hit him at the same time. There was anger, disbelief, annoyance, and even a bit of jealousy. It felt like something inside him had broken and shattered; he had never felt so sick to his stomach.

Lilah felt a heat run down her spine. She needed to get out of the library. She couldn't have this conversation with Kyler right now. She couldn't imagine why he'd even care about her plans when seconds ago he and Sarah were making their own.

When she reached for her favorite pen that had rolled under one of the straps of Kyler's backpack on the table, there she saw their most recent English test sticking out. He must have seen that she noticed it and quickly reached for his backpack, but Lilah was a second faster.

97.

That was what the bright red numbers at the top of the page read. Not only had Kyler passed, he had only missed one question. Lilah immediately told herself that she shouldn't have been surprised. She obviously didn't know Kyler like she thought she did. Why should she have thought he'd ever tell her the truth?

Full of exasperation, "I can explain."

Though angry, Lilah was hurt. "Why would you lie to me? What do you even have in Hughes' class?"

Kyler sighed. It was almost painful to look into her eyes. Selfishly he wanted the conversation to go back to her date. "Right now, I have an A, but at the beginning–"

"I thought you were failing! I waste at least three afternoons a week helping you, and for what," she screamed, now throwing the paper at him.

They could feel the hardened gaze of the librarian. Kyler stuffed his belongings into his bag in a haphazardly fashion and before Lilah could storm out on him, he pulled her farther into the library down one of the dusty aisles. At least if she screamed at him, hopefully few people would hear.

Lilah swatted at Kyler's grip on her wrist until he let go, but he had already gotten her to where he wanted.

"Is this some kind of joke," she hissed.

"Will you just forget the stupid test!"

"No," she screamed, shoving at his chest so that he was forced to take a few steps back from her.

He needed distance from her anyway. Ever since the word *date* had been mentioned, all he could think about was doing something to make her forget she ever said yes to some other jerk. In fairness, she most definitely could, he just never thought she would.

"Who do you have a date with?"

Lilah crossed her arms and glared at Kyler. Though he came across as cool and collected, his icy eyes gave him away. He looked annoyed and angry, and it appeared to be directed at her, which only further irritated Lilah. He had Sarah; he didn't need to concern himself with who she dated. Unless Sarah was right. Maybe Kyler was stringing her along, using her as a plaything until he got bored, using her for a good grade. That couldn't be right though. It looked like he didn't even need her tutoring efforts.

Her head was a confused mess, and before she could remember what Kyler had last said, he was asking the question yet again.

"Lilah." Her name on his lips sounded more like a growl, forcing her to direct her attention to him and only him. "Who with?"

"Simon," she finally blurted out.

Somehow, Kyler knew it. Ever since he saw them volunteering that day, he knew they were perfect for each other. Despite that, he still felt angry. He felt she was making a bad decision, a wrong choice. Lilah was too unique once you got to know her, had too much fire, to be with someone as boring as Simon.

"I thought you said there was nothing going on between the two of you," Kyler continued, now taking a step forward. As he did, he could see Lilah swallow heavily from the increasing closeness of their bodies.

"That was then."

"So, the two of you? Dating?"

Lilah huffed, dropping her eyes to the floor. Uncertainty creeping up once again like it had when Simon first asked. "It's a date. Singular."

"But you obviously like him," Kyler pressed on, now standing inches from Lilah.

She felt her back hit the case behind her and a couple books fell on one of the lower shelves. A rush of chills ran through her veins. It was a feeling that she encountered often in Kyler's presence.

"I need to go," she began, attempting to dismiss the conversation, until she remembered why she was angry. That realization caused her to make a rash decision. "I think we're done here."

"Done?"

"Your season is almost over. You have this Friday and next. You're clearly doing well in your classes. You don't need me," Lilah said, as she pushed past Kyler and exited into a main row within the library.

Kyler panicked. He had never pictured the afternoon taking the turn that it had. He wanted to stop her, wanted to protest, wanted to tell her the truth, but he couldn't gather the words in the time it took her to take just enough steps that would cause him to be unheard anyway.

He sank into the shelves of books behind him. He had to fix everything. While he knew that her reasoning for being upset was the fact that he lied to her, he figured that could be solved with just her talking to him. Simon, on the other hand, that required some thought.

The first person that came to mind was Dawson.

Kyler: Hey. Do you still have that AP class with Campbell?

Dawson: That AP class?

Kyler: Come on, man. The science one.

Dawson: The science one?

Kyler grumbled to himself. How was he supposed to keep up with all the advanced junk that Dawson was in? At times it seemed like Dawson took more classes than periods allowed. Soon another text came in.

Dawson: AP Physics. Yeah, Campbell is in there.

Kyler: Awesome! I need a small favor.

CHAPTER 30

"Well," Kyler insisted as soon as Dawson sat down at the lunch table.

Dawson glanced to Miles and Gavin in disbelief. "Hello, Ky. How are you? Me? Oh, I'm great. Thanks for asking."

"Ugh. You know what I mean. Besides, I saw you this morning," Kyler groaned.

"You know," Miles cut in. "Your life would be so much easier if you would do this age-old primal thing of talking to her."

Kyler looked around to make sure no one was overhearing their conversation. Somehow things in high school had a way of always getting blown out of proportion. Sean had already made sure of that in a couple ways. Thankfully he was too consumed with something green that Louis was stirring into his milk.

"I would," he hissed quietly. "If she wasn't pissed off at me and would actually entertain the thought of a conversation."

"Wait," Gavin began, food rolling from his mouth. "Why is she mad at you?"

"Probably because he flew into a jealous rage when he found out that she had a date with Simon Campbell. Which, by the way, you have no reason to be jealous of," Miles said calmly, allowing Dawson to get a few bites in before Kyler tackled him once again with questions.

"Thanks. That makes me feel–"

Miles nudged Kyler. "Shut up. That wasn't a compliment. I think you're an idiot."

Kyler's jaw dropped in shock.

"Look at how much time you've spent with her in the last two months. You had opportunity. Don't get all cranky because you threw an interception, and the other team ran with it," Miles shrugged.

Still with a great deal of food, which made his words barely understandable, Gavin threw in, "Whoa. I like that. That's pretty deep."

"No. She's mad at me because she found out about my grades," Kyler corrected.

All three chuckled a bit, but Kyler certainly didn't find humor in it. If Lilah knew the truth, she'd be flattered, or at least that's what he liked to believe. He honestly didn't know with her anymore. She wasn't at all like the girls he knew.

"So, she flipped out because you've been lying to her that you were an idiot," Miles continued to laugh.

Dawson corrected him. "In fairness, at first he really was failing."

"Again, totally immature. All you had to do was tell her the truth," Miles insisted. "That you wanted to spend more time with her."

"It's not that easy. At least, not with her it isn't..."

"Oh, boohoo. There's one girl who isn't a complete fangirl that falls all over you and bows down to your charms," Miles continued to tease. Normally it wouldn't bother Kyler, but this time it did. It bothered him because it was just another statement that only made him further realize how different Lilah was, and how much he liked that she challenged him.

Kyler eyed a quiet Dawson, who appeared calm as could be while twirling one of his fries in a puddle of ketchup. Dawson could feel Kyler not so patiently waiting for an answer and enjoyed dragging it out for a bit.

He took a deep breath and finally put Kyler at ease, if you could call it that. "6pm, Flip's Grill."

Red flashed across Kyler's face. "Seriously?!"

Their table went quiet and several others stared, their eyes darting between Kyler and Dawson, wondering if a fight would ensue.

Miles kicked Kyler under the table and shook his head for him to calm down and not draw any more attention.

"Of all the places, he had to take her there," Kyler grumbled under his breath.

Dawson didn't know if it was the best time to correct Kyler, but he did so anyway. "Actually, from my understanding, it seemed like he wasn't too happy with the choice," he laughed. "He told Lilah to pick."

Kyler was now even more annoyed and could feel the flames creeping across his face. Lilah didn't eat that kind of food. She had never even had their food until that night in the park. Out of all the snotty places they could have gone instead, why in the world did she have to pick his place?!

* * *

Lilah couldn't help but eye the hoodie that hung on the corner of the mirror to her vanity. Even from several feet away, she could still smell the scent of Kyler's cologne. She didn't know what kind it was or how much he paid for it, but it didn't smell like the grocery store aerosol junk that the silly freshmen were always spraying in the halls. It smelled like it belonged to one of the ads that appeared in magazines, the one with a scruffy guy on a motorcycle or one with some surfer, ripped and tattooed, on a beach.

She groaned at where her thoughts were going and threw yet another dress on her bed.

"Good. That one was horrendous anyway," Rover pointed out from the doorway.

"What do you want," Lilah huffed.

"Wow. For finally being asked on a date, someone isn't in a pleasant mood."

The comment only made Lilah even more frustrated. "I just have a lot on my mind."

"Mom seems more excited than you. Apparently, this Campbell guy is going to Brown next year, or so I heard, through eavesdropping on her call."

Lilah honestly didn't know, which only made her question her choices for the evening. Volunteering at the shelter had gone so well. Her day could not have gone more perfectly. Now, getting ready for her first real date, dread was all she felt. She wanted to feel happy and giddy, but instead she felt annoyed. She plopped on her bed and sighed. What was wrong with her?

Footsteps drew closer and once the corner of the bed sank a bit, Lilah realized Rover had no intention of simply passing by her room.

"What's up?"

"Nothing," she quickly answered. "I'm just tired." That was a lie. She was on cloud nine since she left the shelter and was even more eager to talk to someone about it. If anything, she'd rather be going to a movie with Alice and Jolee.

"Then cancel."

"I can't do that. I'm meeting him in an hour. That's just rude."

Rover shook his head and laughed. "First of all, since when do you care if you're rude?"

Lilah shot up from the bed and glared at her brother.

"Okay, okay. Secondly, why go out with someone who you're clearly not into?"

"Simon is great," Lilah pointed out. Although, as she said that, she realized that she really didn't know much about him at all, or even what made him great, but that was the whole point of their date. Right? "He's at the top of our class. His parents are upstanding members of society. I mean, his dad is a lawyer and his mom dresses celebrities; that's something. Not to mention–"

Rover flailed his hands for her to stop. "Wow. I can't believe you right now. That sounds like garbage that mom and dad would say. There's a word you so

309

deserve to be called right now, but I know you'll tell mom and then I'll get grounded from video games, so I won't say it. I'm just hoping you're still smart enough to read between the lines, but in case not, it rhymes with witch."

He was right. Lilah knew that. Maybe at one time those reasons would have been good enough for her to date someone, but right now, they made her seem exactly like that word that her brother was thinking of. A part of her wondered what other language was in his vocabulary that didn't need to be there. She'd chalk it up to public school, at least that's what their dad always said.

"I guess I just thought, since recently of course, you'd look for other things," Rover said with a shrug.

"Like what," Lilah cried out in disbelief, not knowing where her brother was going with that statement or how he thought he knew what she was looking for.

"I don't know. Like...if he has a dog? If he can throw a game winning touchdown? If he makes your face turn as red as a tomato? If he–"

Lilah threw a decorative floral pillow straight into Rover's face, silencing his words, but not so much his laughter.

"Get out."

"Fine, fine," Rover managed through a fit of giggles as he rose from the bed. "Not that I give two shi–" Lilah's glare caused him to stop and seek different wording. "Not that I care about fashion or your choices, but if you want my advice, don't wear the red. It makes your skin extra pale," he concluded with a shrug as he exited her room and lightly pulled the door behind him, not completely closing it.

Lilah looked at the red dress on her bed. Rover was right. She hated it too. It was some awful designer thing her mother had bought her. It still had the price tag on it. $489. She rolled her eyes. At one point that might have meant something, but now the first thing that came to her mind was how much she could sell it for. Whatever the amount, it would make a great donation to the animal shelter.

* * *

Simon glanced around uncomfortably as the waitress sat their drinks down. Within ten minutes of walking in, the place seemed to have gotten much louder than he expected.

"I'll be back in a couple minutes to take your order," the waitress said, not bothering to ask if they were ready. She noticed that the young guy at the table was staring at the menu in contemplation with a disgusted look on his face.

"So," Lilah cautiously began, noticing immediately that Simon didn't appear too pleased with the place. If she was being honest, it was a little out of her comfort zone; perhaps her mind had been elsewhere when she suggested it. She had already noticed several other people from their school enter. "How was volunteering today," she asked, twirling the straw in her soda and taking a sip.

"I had a shift with Sophie," Simon groaned. "She talks a lot. I swear she went on and on about her five-year plan. After that, she began speculating for a ten-year one. I really wished you would have signed up for the hospital."

Lilah smiled at the compliment. At least, she thought it was a compliment. She was a little disappointed that Simon didn't ask about her day, but when he stopped talking, she decided to share anyway. "I honestly was so scared to volunteer at the shelter."

"Then why did you?"

"I just felt like it was something I needed to do. I love animals, and I think the reason I've never wanted to go to that place is because I know I'll feel guilty and sad," she admitted.

Simon looked at her like she was talking nonsense. "Seriously," he laughed. "Why?"

She hesitated. "Well, I guess I wish I could help them all, and I feel bad that we have such a big house and yard, and we don't."

"Even if they're trained, they make such a mess. Dogs dig and get all dirty. They always smell. Even if you give them a bath, they still have this funk. Then there are the cats." He shuddered. "They claw up all your furniture and jump on everything. My aunt has one that gets all over the place in the kitchen. I refuse to eat anything that she bakes for our holiday get-togethers."

Lilah swallowed heavily. She was aware that Simon probably wasn't an animal person, but she had no idea to the degree. If she married him, she'd never have a dog. Okay, so she wasn't thinking that her first date would end in marriage; however, for some reason, his feelings about animals made anything more than the date at that moment seem unlikely.

Thankfully, Lilah was saved in the form of the waitress who really needed to be wearing a nametag. "Are you ready to order?"

"I guess so," Simon sighed, as though there was something on the menu that he could manage to deal with for just once.

The waitress turned to Lilah, "What can I–"

"I'll have the grilled shrimp salad, with the dressing on the side of course, and a crab cake."

The waitress raised her brows as she wrote down his order. She always asked the ladies first, and only rarely had she run into a man that decided his request was more important.

"And for you," she began, addressing Lilah once again.

"I'll have a double cheeseburger, with..." Lilah paused and contemplated between the greasy goodness of curly or crinkle fries. "An order of curly fries," she finally decided.

"Awesome. How do you want your meat cooked?"

Lilah hadn't thought about that. Looking to Simon for advice was pointless, and she found that she was gradually wishing that someone else was with her more and more as the evening went on. Sadly, the date had only begun.

Sensing her lack of knowledge. "Let's do medium. That way it won't be too dry," the waitress said with a wink.

"Medium means that the meat is still raw," Simon piped up once the waitress left. "I'd be careful eating that."

Lilah could not believe him. Was he always like this? Had she just never noticed what a snob he was?

Somewhere deep down inside, she blamed Kyler. If she had never spent time with him, never gotten to know him, never kissed him, she wouldn't be thinking about how wrong Simon was. She felt bad for even thinking that. Simon had so many qualities that were right, on paper; however, at the end of the day, she really wished that she was at a cold park picnic table instead.

CHAPTER 31

"You do realize that this is borderline stalking," Miles pointed out as he walked through the parking lot with Kyler. He shot off a group text to Dawson and Gavin to let them know that they were at Flip's.

"We come here all the time. I've always come here," Kyler shrugged.

Miles could sense the tension in his friend and took a seat outside of the restaurant, hoping that Kyler would do the same. All he got was a confused look.

"They've only been in there half an hour. As busy as it is, they probably don't even have food yet. Sit down," Miles insisted.

Kyler sighed but did as was asked.

"I thought you would have been too tired to go out tonight," Miles stated bluntly.

Kyler scoffed. "Why would you think that?"

"Between classwork, football, and...your job?"

Kyler froze at the mentioning of the word. Miles tilted the corner of his mouth, knowing that his suspicions were true.

"My little sister messed up her wrist the other day," he began with a shrug. "My mom saw you there when they went in to have it checked."

There was an uncomfortable silence as Kyler thought of how to best address the truth.

"It's cool. I wish you would have at least kept me in the loop," Miles interjected before any words came from Kyler. He could clearly tell that Kyler didn't want to talk about it.

"It's not like that," Kyler sighed. His shoulders sank and his hands dangled between his legs. "I'm just trying to help my mom and sister out."

"It's about your dad, isn't it? It's why you never talk about him? I noticed how you clam up when people bring him up. I just never wanted to ask too much because...guys and all that feeling crap."

Kyler laughed for a brief moment. "Something like that." He then turned pensive and serious. "He didn't die some war hero," he admitted.

Miles already figured as much. Most people, in time, would have bragged or been proud and honored losing a member in such a heroic way, fighting for and dying for America. Kyler, however, never talked about his father, just that he was in the military and had passed before he and his family moved to Raymere Grove.

"He really was an awesome dad, but whatever happened over there changed him," Kyler cautiously began, referring to the Middle East. "Within two years we had financially lost everything, and my mom is still trying to recover, all while trying to provide the best for me and Krista. I didn't realize things were still pretty bad, and Raymere Grove isn't exactly the most affordable place to live."

316

Miles shook his head, understanding a lot now. "Maybe not, but it gets you seen by scouts."

Kyler gave a sincere laugh this time. "Thank goodness for last year, because this season sucked."

Miles began to laugh as well. It was still a sore subject, but they'd have to laugh it off eventually. Apparently today was that day.

"It's cool that you're helping your mom and sister out," Miles finally said, returning to the initial conversation.

"Thanks. Can you just maybe not–"

"No problem," Miles quickly interrupted. "It's just between us." He glanced to Kyler and watched as his eyes lowered to the ground and darted from left to right. With a chuckle, "And Lilah?"

Kyler groaned, bringing his hand up to rake through his tousled hair. "We happened to have an encounter when she was doing volunteer work."

"Wow. You're sharing all these personal details with your tutor, and now following her on a date," Miles began to tease.

"Okay, fine. I like her, a lot," Kyler finally admitted aloud. He could feel the heat burning through his face and his stomach flipped a couple of times. However, at the moment, he had to remind himself that she was on a date with another guy.

"Then will you do us all a favor?"

"What?"

Miles made his next words quick, as Dawson and Gavin were approaching them from the other end of the parking lot. "Tell her already!"

Like he hadn't thought about that. It was one of those things that was easier said than done. He didn't think his ego could take whatever lashing Lilah could give if what he said wasn't what she wanted to hear.

"I mean, seriously," Miles continued more quietly. "What are you even expecting with whatever this is?"

Kyler shook his head. "I don't know. Hoping to see her having a miserable time?"

"By you not saying anything sooner, you practically let her fall into the arms of someone who's kind of perfect for her." Miles gave him a friendly pat, knowing his words caused the tick in Kyler's jaw.

Kyler hated that word. More than that, he hated how true it was. Simon was like a male clone of Lilah, or at least the Lilah he knew at first. As time went on, that Lilah he met in the library that first day seemed to change. He only hoped it wasn't just his imagination.

✳ ✳ ✳

As soon as he stepped through the door, Lilah couldn't help but draw her attention from Simon. She was absolutely livid. Of all the nights, he chose this one to hang out with his buddies.

Something foreign raced inside her. Did she pick this place hoping to run into Kyler? Hoping to show him that she wasn't some ditz for him to string along? That there were guys who genuinely wanted to date her and only her?

She shook her head at the thoughts running through her head. Kyler would never think all those things. He was just some dumb jock who thought he was a gift to the female population. That's what she continued to tell herself ever since Sarah's little bathroom rant.

After noticing a slight change in Lilah, "Is everything okay?"

She nodded. "Yeah, of course." It wasn't. For some awful reason, she couldn't control the pounding of her chest when she saw Kyler walk in.

While Lilah chugged her soda, Simon glanced back to see what had taken her attention away from the conversation, not that she had been the best at conversation that evening.

"Ah. This is where they all hang out," he scoffed. Turning to Lilah, "Don't you tutor them for extracurricular credit?"

Lilah shook her head and swallowed. "Just Kyler," she said through clenched teeth. "But that's over now." She still couldn't believe he lied to her.

Simon laughed. "I bet. I heard their season sucked after the first couple games."

Lilah tried changing the subject to anything else. Kyler consumed enough of her thoughts, she didn't want him consuming her date as well; however, as soon as he walked in, an ominous feeling rose in her.

She tried not to look anywhere beyond her own table. One part of her was terrified to look up and meet Kyler's eyes, especially after the way they left things between them. Another part was even more afraid to look up and find him having a wonderful time, completely unaware that she was within a ten-mile radius of him.

* * *

Kyler couldn't take his eyes off her. She looked nervous and uncomfortable. Did Simon make her nervous? Was it a good nervous or a bad? If she said yes to a date, it had to be a good nervous.

She looked beautiful in a bright blue sweater dress, leggings, and dainty boots that didn't go too far past her calves. However, he also preferred her in jeans and a t-shirt. He honestly didn't care what she wore. He didn't know for how long, but lately he had become very much aware that he found her beautiful all the time, period.

Kyler finally brought his attention back to four sets of eyes staring at him, the waitress waiting as he was the only one who had not ordered.

"Oh. Sorry. I zoned out for a second." Miles pretended to choke on his drink and held a smug look on his face. Kyler ignored him and focused on the waitress. "Double cheeseburger, medium coke, and curly fries."

When the waitress finally left, "Aside from grabbing a bite to eat, what exactly are we doing here," Gavin asked, nodding his head in Lilah's direction. Everyone was aware as to the situation.

Kyler sighed. "I honestly have no idea."

Miles chimed in. "He's too much of a sissy to talk to a girl, so instead he's being a weirdo. I swear, if something doesn't come of tonight, I'm telling her for you."

"As long as it means he won't be so grumpy anymore," Gavin added, talking to Miles like Kyler wasn't there.

"I'm not grumpy," Kyler said quite grumpily.

* * *

Lilah welcomed Simon's idea of playing a game of pool after they had eaten. While her burger was extremely delicious, Simon barely touched a good portion of his food. He didn't even bother giving it a chance; it's like he rolled his nose up at it as soon as it came to the table.

Not only that, but he always came across as such a gentleman; however, when the check came, he asked her if she wanted to split it. Lilah could have found several different ways that he could have hinted about it, but no. His exact words were, "Are we splitting this?" She didn't know what to say. She wanted to tell him off. He was the one who invited her on this date, and so far, he seemed nothing like the guy she expected.

While she didn't want to be rude and end it abruptly, thankfully pool would at least mean that they were occupied with something other than the bland conversation, which, by the way, she found out she had very little in common with him after all.

Surprisingly pool was one thing they did have in common. While he wasn't very good, he was definitely more of a challenge than Sean.

Keeping her attention on the game of pool became difficult as there had to have been every college in the country playing on the numerous screens throughout the place. She looked to the bar area, noticing a lot of older adults now gathering and screaming.

Simon missed his shot and groaned in frustration. "Could they be any louder?"

Lilah watched the screen wondering what the commotion was. "The defense had two players called on holding. The other team is going to get a first down they never should have gotten otherwise," she mumbled to herself.

"You watch football," Simon asked. If Lilah didn't know any better, she could have sworn that there was a good deal of disdain seeping through with his words.

"No, not really." It was the truth. While she had done a bit of research on the sport so that she could watch it with Kyler, she had only watched a game that day with Kyler. Never again. Now she felt stupid for even knowing what holding was, or what the penalty was, or that the team that she couldn't care less about was now within field goal range after they were no longer forced to punt and had two back to back passes that were pretty great.

"Your turn," Simon said dryly.

Ever since halfway through their meal, Lilah had tried her best not to give any of her attention to

Kyler's general area; however, once Sean and his buddies, as well as Sarah and her squad showed up, it became the high school cafeteria packed at three small tables of Flip's Grill.

"Here, let me help you," Simon interrupted just as Lilah was about to take her shot.

She was mildly annoyed. She knew what she was doing and could have easily wiped the table, but she was playing friendly, going easy on him. She did not need his help. It was only when she obliged that she saw his reasoning for doing so.

* * *

Kyler's hands turned to fists when he saw Simon position himself around Lilah and lean their bodies into the table with the pool stick, very well knowing that Lilah didn't need some nerd's advice when it came to the game.

He took a deep breath and tried to focus on the conversations bouncing in all directions around him. He hated it. Some idiot in the place had shared too much on social media and now not only were Sean, Cash, and Louis in his presence, but if he had to hear one more screeching giggle from Sarah about something that wasn't funny to begin with, he would scream.

His chest tightened and suddenly he couldn't hear a single word around him. There was a thumping in his head from the flow of blood, and his eyes began to burn.

Their faces were too close, looking at each other too romantically. He wasn't an idiot. This wasn't some middle school dance. And Lilah wasn't about to throw punch at Simon if he continued to close the gap.

"Dude! Even I can't take this anymore," Gavin exclaimed, throwing back his soda and motioning for Dawson to follow his departure. "You too, West," he called out over his shoulder.

Gavin was a bit of a wildcard, which only sent Kyler's pulse racing as he watched his friend zigzag his way toward the gaming area.

CHAPTER 32

Simon pushed back a couple strands of Lilah's hair behind her ears. He was so close now that she could smell his breath on her. Surprisingly it was minty. She then remembered the mints the waitress placed on top of the check, the check that she ended up splitting.

She screamed inside to focus. This was what she wanted. This is what her first kiss should have been like. A proper date. Someone that made sense. So why did she feel like she was about to have a panic attack?

"You look really great tonight," he whispered.

He slid his other hand down to her waist. She felt its presence, but that was all. There were no tingles. Why weren't there tingles? Lilah swallowed heavily and waited for Simon to close the space between the two of them.

She was jolted awake and forced to take a step back when someone slammed their hands on the pool table that she had been leaning into.

"Is this table free?"

Simon didn't exactly drop his hands from her body right away, but the distance between them did increase. Oddly, Lilah felt relief. It's as if she was moments away from drowning and of all the people to rescue her, Gavin managed to pull her up to the surface, now able to breathe.

Ignoring Gavin, "Hey, man," Simon acknowledged toward Dawson. He released Lilah and took a step in Dawson's direction for a fist bump.

Lilah welcomed the space; however, it was only when she registered both Gavin and Dawson, that she bothered to look in the short distance. Right behind them, casually strolling along, although their conversation appeared intense, were Kyler and Miles.

Lilah's left hand grabbed her right forearm and she took a step back, wanting to hide in the little bit of darkness that she could find. Though she told herself to ignore the five boys surrounding the table, she couldn't help but be curious. That curiosity only got her a set of blue eyes, growing darker by the second, focused solely on her, ignoring any words directed toward him.

Kyler hesitantly took a few steps to the side while Dawson held Simon's attention. Though it wasn't as private as he would have liked, at least he was next to her, able to say something, rather than ominous looks from across the room.

"How's it going?" He cringed a little on the inside, unsure how to begin a conversation with Lilah after everything that was said, or rather left unsaid, in the library that day.

Lilah huffed. There was no way that she was going to give Kyler the satisfaction of knowing that her date wasn't exactly what she had thought it would be. "It was going great until all this." She motioned her hand around to everyone hovering about the pool table.

"Yeah, it looked like it," Kyler murmured under his breath.

Lilah turned sharply toward him. Though she kept her voice down so as not to draw attention, her anger came through loud and clear. "What exactly is that supposed to mean?"

Kyler broke any eye contact and shrugged, pretending not to care. "It just appears from the outside looking in, that you and Campbell are having a good time. That's great. The two of you seem perfect for each other." His words were dry and lacking. The part of him that wanted Lilah to correct him and argue with him was quickly disappointed.

"What are you guys doing over here," Lilah finally sighed, not wanting to talk any further about her date.

"We thought we'd come play a game, since no one else is." If he didn't know any better, he could have sworn he saw Lilah discreetly stomp her foot in frustration.

"We have this table. I'm sure one of the others is about to open up."

Kyler laughed sarcastically. "You two aren't playing."

Lilah stepped into Kyler's space and he nearly came undone. All he wanted was to tell her how beautiful she was and what a waste of time it was for her to invest another second on Simon Campbell.

"If you have something to say, just say it. Clearly you have a rude and snarky observation you'd like to make."

Feeling challenged, "Yeah, I do. Why are you letting him win?"

Lilah scoffed like the idea was preposterous, but could immediately feel her cheeks reddening. "I'm not letting him win," she insisted.

"Whatever. I've seen you play. You could have beaten him ages ago. Why haven't you?"

She looked up to meet his inquisitive and speculating eyes. Why did he of all people have to notice something like that? Why did he even care?

"I'm trying to be nice. It's a date," she pointed out. "I don't want to make it a huge competition. I know how guys can get with their egos." She arched her brow and pressed her lips into a cold line at the last part.

Kyler knew somewhere in her words she was taking a dig at him. He took a small step forward, closing their distance just a little more. From the corner of his eye, he could see that Simon was still preoccupied with Dawson rambling on about some solar thing that wouldn't take place for another insane amount of years.

Though he was close, too close for the conversation they were having, too close for just someone who was interrupting her date, Lilah didn't move.

"So," he began, his voice coming across exceedingly low and sultry, reminding Lilah of a warm summer breeze across her skin. "If I challenge you to a game, you'll go easy on me? Let me win?"

Lilah swallowed heavily, suddenly unaware if they were still talking about pool. They had to be though. She couldn't let herself think anything deeper than surface level when it came to Kyler. He already did things to her with just his presence. There was no way she was going to continue reading into his words, falling victim to whatever game he was playing.

"It's different," she managed. "You and I aren't the ones on a date." The flicker of something in his eyes sent alarms off in her head. She was so stupid for putting the both of them in the same sentence as the word *date*.

Not missing a beat, "And if we were?"

Lilah wanted to laugh, to point out how that wasn't in the realm of possibilities. Instead, she left him with one word. "Never."

Kyler gave her a satisfying smirk. Somewhere deep inside, that's exactly what he wanted to hear, because he knew that Lilah wasn't the type of person to let anyone win. The fact that she was doing so with Simon only meant one thing to Kyler. She didn't care.

He let his wild mind get the best of him. Then why would she let someone she didn't care about almost kiss her?

Kyler reached a few inches in front of him and allowed the back of his knuckles to graze Lilah's. A shiver ran through her and she fought to control her breathing.

"Lilah, I need to talk to you."

"You've been talking to me."

Kyler shook his head at how frustrating she could be. "Just us, away from here."

Lilah's chest pounded. Simple words like that shouldn't make her entire body react like it was, and yet, all she could think about was being alone with Kyler. As much as she wanted to be like one of those silly girls and fall into his arms, she just couldn't.

She took a step back, breaking the warmth from the smallest touch of his hand on hers. "I think you need to get back to your fan club," she said coldly, nodding behind her towards a few other players along with a group of cackling cheerleaders.

Kyler didn't understand and he was certain that the look on his face would tell her that before he could; however, he never got the opportunity to ask what in the world she was talking about.

"You ready," Miles asked, clapping Kyler on the shoulder.

"Yeah, I guess."

"Well, it's been real," Gavin announced, flicking one of the balls and completely ruining the game. "Oops. Sorry," he apologized, quite sincerely too.

Kyler begrudgingly left with the three of them, now only more confused than the last time he and Lilah were in the library together.

"I'm guessing you didn't confess your undying love for her," Gavin teased once they sat back down for one more round of unlimited soda refills.

"No," Kyler growled.

"Well, at least they didn't go into a full on make-out session on the table," Gavin continued.

"Yet," Dawson added with a wink.

"Come on, guys," Miles interrupted. "We can push him all we want, but the truth is, I think he's found his match. Lilah isn't going to give in to his charms so easily." Miles proceeded to pinching at Kyler's cheeks, to which Kyler swatted him with more force than necessary.

"What are we all laughing about," a bubbly voice rang out behind Kyler.

Something about the evening made him very much aware as to what he needed to do. Sitting around with his friends teasing him about not going for it with Lilah wasn't it. As Sarah made room for a seat next to him, he knew without a doubt entertaining her wasn't it either.

"Actually, I think I'm going to call it a night," Kyler announced as calmly as he could, rising from his seat.

His friends understood; however, the tiny heels clicking behind him on his way out the door didn't.

"Hey, Ky. Wait up," Sarah insisted breathlessly.

How could she be so out of breath? Didn't she have a strict workout routine with cheerleading? Kyler shook his head. He couldn't care less about Sarah's stupid workouts.

"Do you think I could get a ride," she asked once Kyler slowed for her to say something.

"I have things to do. Sorry," he declined. He tried to be as nice as he could, but inside he wanted to scream for her to just go away, especially now when all he could think about was seeing Lilah.

"It really won't take long. I'm only about ten minutes away," she went on, watching as Kyler typed something into his phone, perhaps cancelling any plans so that he could take her home.

"There," he said once he finished, and tucked his phone away. "I sent a message in a group chat. Miles, Gavin, or Dawson should be able to help you out."

Sarah grit her teeth in fury. "But, I thought," she tried once again, taking a step closer.

Kyler sighed. "Sarah, I really don't have time. I'm sorry."

Before she could protest any further, he walked off as quickly as he could. A part of him did feel like a jerk leaving her standing alone outside Flip's Grill, but he had made sure that if she did need a ride, there were several others in there who would do the favor, whether they wanted to or not.

* * *

Lilah felt her phone go off yet again. Alice's Saturday night plans consisted of binging some werewolf show and keeping tabs on her date with Simon. Jolee had been much more casual with the situation, simply wishing Lilah good luck, although the tone seemed more like she knew Lilah would need the luck, because deep down Lilah should probably not have agreed to the date in the first place. The longer the night went on, Lilah was surprisingly glad she

332

had gone out with Simon. Had she not, perhaps she would have wondered if she missed out, if she and Simon missed some bizarre chance in the universe to be together. Now, now she realized how wrong they were for each other.

She was more than a little shocked when she pulled out her phone and the message was not from Alice.

Kyler: We need to talk.

Lilah was annoyed by it. Without Kyler's presence messing with her head, she was able to think clearly. What she clearly knew, he had not only lied to her about his grades, but not even ten minutes ago he left with Sarah, only to text her something like this.

Lilah: I don't have anything to say to you.

Kyler: I don't care. I have something to say to you.

Kyler was satisfied with any response from her. If she was responding to him, that meant for a moment her phone was taking away any attention that should have been spent on Simon.

Lilah: I'm on a date. Why don't you focus on yours and I'll do the same?

He wanted to throw his phone clear across the park, when she unnecessarily pointed out that little fact. Had she not found out about his grades, she could have been on a date with him. Even that was wrong. Something before then had caused a shift in her, shortly after she brought him cookies. But what?

And what in the world did the second part of her message mean?!

Kyler: Can you meet me tonight?

He fell back across the top of the picnic table and placed his phone on his chest, hoping to feel the vibration from her response. Every second that passed without it did little in helping with his nerves.

Lilah: I don't think it's a good idea.

Kyler: Why?

Lilah: There's tension. We'll probably say things we don't mean.

Kyler: You're still mad at me?

Lilah: Of course!

Lilah wanted so badly to meet Kyler, but lately, she wasn't sure what would happen if they were alone together. As much as she wanted to punch him in his perfect face for lying to her, another part desperately wanted to feel all the feelings he gave her, starting with that kiss.

Kyler: Fine. The park. When you finish with your date.

Lilah: I'm not coming.

Kyler: The ball is yours, run with it or not.

"Is everything okay," Simon laughed.

Lilah quickly fired off one more text before putting her phone away. "Yeah, why?"

"Your face is all scrunched up and you look really annoyed," he pointed out.

"It's nothing, just my little brother," she lied.

"Were you ready to get going? I have church in the morning with my parents."

Lilah groaned internally. Of course he did! He couldn't have been more perfect, and yet, he wasn't, at least not for her anymore.

Thankfully Lilah had already made arrangements for Antonio to pick her up. She didn't want the awkwardness of Simon driving her home, walking her to the door, and then what? She had never gotten to that part. There was the almost kiss that they shared earlier, which she was a little more than relieved was interrupted. If Simon were to try again, she wasn't sure what she was supposed to do.

When he walked her out, she wanted to jump up and down at the fact that Antonio was waiting and that she wouldn't have to stand around and make awkward conversation. Though she could have been much more dismissive, she felt a little bad for wasting Simon's time. While the date didn't end with a kiss, she did give him a hug.

"Very nice looking," Antonio commented once Lilah's door was closed. Lilah only rolled her eyes and he gave a small chuckle. "Home then?"

Lilah quickly pulled out her phone. Her last message to Kyler had been to ask him where in the park, that is, if she decided to come. His response only caused her insides to fume with fury.

Kyler: Where you made the biggest mistake of your life.

CHAPTER 33

Kyler heard what he hoped were her footsteps from down the path, though he didn't turn from his spot on the bench to face her.

"Could you have been more cryptic," Lilah scoffed when she was certain that Kyler was the dark figure beneath the lamplight.

He rose and turned to face her as she continued closer. "You didn't seem to have too much of a problem figuring it out."

Lilah let out a sigh of exasperation, now standing a little more than arm's length away from Kyler. "Why were you so adamant about talking to me tonight?"

He watched her carefully, wondering where to start. While he really wanted to ask about Simon, he was terrified about what her response might be, so instead, he started with the obvious. "I needed to apologize."

"Oh, for lying to me? For using me? For wasting my time?"

Kyler ran a hand through his messy hair. He should have known it wouldn't have been as easy as he imagined it in his head. "Can we sit down," he asked, motioning toward the bench.

"No." Her response was swift, and her green eyes glared at him, sparkling beneath the light. "I don't see the point. I have a feeling this conversation won't last long."

"Fine! Yes, I lied to you a little. I started the year off with poor time management and had a hard go of it trying to catch up. No, I'm not some idiot jock like you might think. Okay? Happy? I lied, and I'm sorry, but I never meant to waste your time, if that's how you see it, nor did I ever use you."

"Why did you tell me you were barely passing? You made a near perfect score on that last test," Lilah stressed, frustration growing with the creases of her eyes.

Kyler took a step forward and swallowed heavily. No girl had ever made him as nervous as Lilah did. "You want me to be honest," he asked stupidly.

Lilah wasn't sure if it was rhetorical or not, but she answered back. "That would be a good start for once."

Kyler shook his head, a small smile creeping to his face. "I've always been honest with you, probably more than I should have. I didn't tell you that I didn't need you anymore because I liked spending time with you."

Lilah quickly squashed the little flutters that those words gave her. "Studying? You liked studying with me?"

Kyler stared into her eyes, searching. If she felt anything, she wasn't going to give it away easily. "I didn't know if I had a chance for anything more."

That's when she broke contact and dropped her eyes to the ground. Her mouth suddenly went dry and she didn't know how to respond to those words. Thankfully she wouldn't have to think about it for too long, as Kyler soon brought up a much more uncomfortable topic.

"Did you lie?"

Lilah's eyes shot up to meet his again, and she wished that she wouldn't have. The worst part of everything, he was looking at her as if she was causing him the most pain in the world.

Regaining brain function, she remembered his absurd question. "What are you talking about? What would I lie about to you?"

"The kiss."

Lilah never imagined that they'd ever bring it up. "We never said anything about it."

He held his hands out, motioning around. "Obviously it was one of your biggest mistakes."

"No," Lilah began to correct, growing agitated. "You referred to it as such when you asked me to meet you."

"Oh, sorry, accident. I believe that was what you called your first kiss," he growled. Her widened eyes made him immediately regret getting upset with her.

Lilah shook her head, trying to understand his words.

Kyler continued once he realized that he had gotten ahead of himself. "So, tell me, who did you lie to, me or your friend?"

Realizing exactly what Kyler was referring to, "How did you find that note?"

"Really? For a minute I thought you wanted me to find it. That's why I never said anything," he laughed, almost maniacally.

"What are you talking about?!"

"It was in the notebook you lent me," Kyler shouted back. Neither really knew how the shouting had begun.

"And you thought I planted it there? You're ridiculous," Lilah scoffed.

"Enough with the stupid note. Which one was it?" His voice had gone softer. However, when Lilah didn't answer him, didn't even look in his direction, "What was all that bull you told me that night about how perfect your first kiss was?"

Lilah's eyes searched the ground. Her head spun with the direction the conversation was going.

"Just answer me," Kyler annoyingly pressed on.

"The truth," Lilah began with almost nothing more than a whisper. "I told you the truth," she finally blurted out.

Kyler wasn't sure what answer he had hoped for, or which would have been worse. Now that he had it, the brief second he had to think on it did two things, make his heart beat at an alarmingly fast pace, and make his blood boil in rage.

"Then why did you go out with Simon tonight?"

Lilah glared at him. He had some nerve to question her, especially after he left the restaurant with Sarah.

"Just because you kissed me forever ago doesn't mean you have any claim to me."

Taking a couple steps forward so that he was now towering over Lilah, and not missing a beat, "And what if I kiss you now?"

Lilah's lips parted to say something, but no words came. She was utterly shocked by Kyler's boldness. The second he took another step forward, her brain screamed for her to take one backwards, but the pounding in her chest silenced the internal screaming that was telling her this could not happen again.

Kyler hesitantly reached his arm around Lilah, allowing it to rest at the small of her back. He lightly pulled her forward, and though she stumbled a bit with uncertainty, she willingly came chest to chest with him, now securely in his arms. His other hand traced along Lilah's neck, his thumb caressing her heated cheeks. She hadn't pushed him away, hadn't given him a reason not to continue, and before she could, he swiftly closed the gap between them.

His lips felt just how she remembered them, and a part of her hated how much she wanted that feeling every day for the rest of her life. He was warm and tender, silently gauging her comfort level, and despite knowing that her conscience was slowly getting the best of her, Lilah allowed Kyler to take as much of her as he wanted in those few seconds.

When their tongues finally began a dance that both seemed to know by heart, Kyler tightened his grip on Lilah, afraid that he'd wake up and find out it was all a dream. He had never felt so good being around any girl, and he knew he needed to tell her that, before she found another Simon.

Guilt finally got the best of whatever Lilah found pouring through her veins. Lust? Spontaneity? Something else?

"Stop," Lilah whispered, after reluctantly breaking the kiss.

Kyler could barely breathe, and had she not said that stupid word, and had he not been such a gentleman, he would have tried to persuade her to continue. Then he looked into her eyes and he felt a blow to his gut.

Tears.

"What's wrong? Are you okay? Did I–"

Lilah quickly interrupted as she turned her face from him, wiping away the few salty drops that had fallen. "It's just me. I can't do this."

Kyler stepped around her, forcing her to look at him. Her sadness and pain immediately transformed to anger and hatred, seemingly directed at him.

"Are you serious? That was the second most amazing kiss in my entire life. If you're going to give me that it's not you, it's me crap, you can at least explain." He was frustrated, less by the fact that she stopped the kiss and more so that she was pushing him away, for absolutely no good reason.

"I'm not like my mother. My parents' relationship is appalling, and I refuse to engage in something like that."

"Okay," was all Kyler could manage. He had no idea what she was getting at. Her parents were screwed up, he knew that, but that had nothing to do with the two of them right now.

"I'm not some toy for you to chew up and spit out once you get bored, nor will I be some dirty little secret," Lilah spat, attempting to move past Kyler and back toward the path entrance.

Kyler gently grabbed her wrist and pulled her back to him. "Whoa, whoa, whoa!" He shook his head, knowing that he didn't have much time. Lilah clearly had the fight and flight thing down. He attempted to understand what she was saying, but rather than try to reason with her, he just spit it out. "Is that what this is about? You think I'd be embarrassed being with you?"

He laughed and ran his hand through his hair, which only angered Lilah. It wasn't the fact that he was laughing at what she had just said, but the fact that somewhere inside her there was an extremely shallow little girl who was vaguely distracted by his incredibly sexy hair.

"I'm glad you find it so incredulously funny!"

Kyler took an aggressive step forward, his face not showing an ounce of humor, as his body towered over Lilah, asserting his dominance. "Where have you been? Are you blind? I'm not afraid to be seen with you! Geez, Lilah! Do you know why my friends and I interrupted your stupid date?" He didn't give her a chance to do more than shake her head. "It's because they're sick and tired of me not telling you how I feel, and honestly so am I. I'm just shocked, for you being as smart as you are that you don't see how in love with you I am."

Every part of Lilah shut down at the word. She couldn't swallow, couldn't breathe, couldn't see. Perhaps one of the lamplights had gone out and she hadn't noticed until now.

Kyler immediately let go of her wrist. The terror and fear on her face said too much. When Lilah finally managed to take a step back, he let her. He didn't mean to tell her like that. Maybe he didn't mean to tell her at all. However, doing so made him feel like a weight had lifted.

"I have to go," Lilah rapidly told him through nothing more than a whisper.

This time when she turned to leave, he didn't bother stopping her.

CHAPTER 34

Alice and Jolee shot each other looks from across the table. After meeting up with Lilah for ice cream the evening before, they knew not to mention anything more about Simon. Though Lilah hadn't said anything about Kyler, aside from insisting that he ruined her date, they knew better than to mention his name as well.

Alice had tried to convince Lilah to give Simon another chance, but something told her that Lilah had never really wanted Simon to begin with.

"Hey," Simon announced, as he walked up to their lunch table. "You said you wanted to talk to me."

Alice tilted her head and gave Lilah that look, silently asking her if she was sure.

"Yeah," Lilah began, grabbing her jacket from the back of her chair. "Can we step out into the courtyard?" She knew that Simon wouldn't be over the top dramatic, but that still didn't change the fact that she didn't want to have that conversation so publicly.

Kyler watched from across the cafeteria as Simon held the door and he and Lilah stepped out. He hadn't heard from Lilah for the rest of the weekend. His conversation with her Saturday night didn't go as he expected. He never intended to vomit out the word *love*, but he was only further irritated by how easy it was to say that to her, even if his ego took one of the worst blows he could imagine by Lilah running away and not speaking to him since. There had been so many times yesterday that he wanted to text her, only to slam his phone down in frustration. Trying to talk to someone that clearly wasn't interested in him was torture.

As if watching his line of vision when she sat down next to him, "Aww, nerd love in paradise," Sarah giggled.

Gavin rolled his eyes from across the table. "Hey, Sarah, why don't you do what all of us are hoping for and just shut it."

"Rude," Britt hissed.

"No, you all are the rude ones. All you do is talk about people. It's annoying and makes you look dumber than you probably are...or maybe–"

"Whoa, what is your problem," Sarah fired back. "I just made an observation." She then narrowed her eyes and studied Gavin. "If I didn't know any better, I'd think that you have a huge crush on little miss valedictorian."

Gavin's wide eyes met Kyler's instantly as if to silently reassure him that he had no intention of going after Lilah, although Kyler already knew better. All of his friends were very much aware as to how Saturday played out. When they first saw him at school that morning, each of them held somber looks like someone had just died.

Now here he was at lunch trying to pretend like everything was okay and seeing Lilah with Simon didn't just shatter his heart into a million pieces.

* * *

"I'm actually not surprised," Simon shrugged.

Lilah had gotten done trying to thank him for Saturday, but also making it clear that it wouldn't be happening again.

Lilah expected him to take it rather well. Along with Kyler, Simon also hadn't text her the rest of the weekend. It was she who finally text him to meet her at lunch Monday.

He laughed. "You got pretty fired up after Dawson and his friends came over, so I'm guessing that had a lot to do with it."

"No, I didn't mind them interrupting." Seriously, she didn't. Had they not interrupted, things could have gotten awkward fast with the unwanted and impending kiss.

"I don't mean the interruption. I'm guessing you have a thing for one of them, or one of them has a thing for you?"

Lilah sighed. She wasn't going to talk about another guy with a guy she was breaking up with. Although, they weren't really breaking up. One date didn't make this conversation a break-up, more like an it's not going to work conversation.

"Oh my gosh," he continued to laugh. He shook his head like he just came to some intense realization. "I knew you were tutoring Kyler, and I thought the two of you might have something going on..."

"No, it's not like that."

"Really, Lilah. It's okay. I'm not going to lose sleep over this. I like you, but I'm not going to compete with some jock. Clearly, if that's what you're interested in, you and I wouldn't have worked out."

Lilah was shocked. How had she not noticed what a snob Simon was?

Once they entered the cafeteria, and stepped away from the bitter cold, Lilah made eye contact with her two best friends. If there was such a thing as a sad smile, that's what they were giving her.

"So, friends?"

Lilah smiled sweetly. Simon would have made a horrible boyfriend, and though she didn't agree with many of his statements, she could at least agree to friendly terms with him. "Yeah, of course."

Before he turned to leave her standing at the glass doors alone, "I just don't get it."

When he took a little longer than she hoped for in forming the next string of words, "Don't get what?"

"Sarah."

Lilah tensed at the name. That was the last name on earth that she wanted to hear. That name was the only thing standing in her way with what her intentions were.

When she didn't say anything, Simon continued. "I thought that you might be into me, but honestly, it was Sarah who gave me the final push to ask you out."

"I'm sorry, what," Lilah nearly shrieked, though composed herself. She had no desire to draw any attention, and a couple band kids nearby had already taken interest.

"Yeah. She basically told me that she overheard you and some other girls, and you wanted to ask me out, but were too shy and that I..."

Lilah didn't hear the rest of his words. Her head felt like it might explode in anger.

Sarah didn't help anyone for the sake of being nice. No. Sarah always had an agenda. Everything needed to somehow benefit her. Lilah knew exactly why she did what she did. A part of her had to be scared. If Kyler's confession to her in the park was true, then Sarah had every right to be.

* * *

Kyler felt sick to his stomach when they walked in all smiles. He was certain after Saturday that Lilah would see that Simon wasn't right for her. He thought she had all but admitted that right out to him, but now here she was, giving Simon her sole focus in the middle of a crowded room.

Then that deathly glare.

Lilah's line of vision shot straight towards him and in that split second, he wished that he could have gone back to being invisible to her. She was pissed, more than he had ever seen before, and that said a lot, considering how their relationship first started. What in the world could Simon be telling her that would have her looking at him like she was about to rip his head off with her bare hands? He had never done anything to Simon. The only reason Kyler hated him was because Simon had Lilah.

Kyler's attention flew to the cackling beside him and for some reason Dawson's party flashed in his head. When he glanced back to Lilah and Simon, he could clearly see that it wasn't him that her blazing green eyes were focused on. It was Sarah.

* * *

"I really think you're making a huge mistake," Jolee insisted.

The last bell had finishing ringing only a minute ago, and Jolee and Alice were on Lilah's heels as she stormed her way to Sarah's locker.

"Seriously. It's over and done with. This isn't like you," Alice chimed in.

They were right. Lilah could be rude and dismissive to people, but she never actually went looking for trouble; however, she couldn't get over what Simon had told her.

"I just want to talk to her," she attempted to state rather calmly; yet, it still came out as a growl.

Just as Lilah assumed, Sarah and her two besties were wrapping up at her locker. She didn't intend to hurt Sarah, but a scare would be nice. Her whole body shook from rage and adrenaline when she approached the locker and slammed the door with all her might, causing the whole row to rattle.

Sarah jumped back and glared at Lilah. "Excuse you?!"

"Oh, shut it," Lilah spat.

Jolee noticed that immediately a crowd began to gather. Of course they would. Two of the most well-known girls in school were about to have a catfight. She nudged Alice to do something, to which Alice only gave her a horrified look and shrugged.

"What is wrong with you," Lilah nearly screamed.

Sarah tossed her hair back and huffed. "I have no idea what you're talking about."

"Like hell you don't."

"Maybe if you learned your place–"

"And where is that," Lilah quickly interrupted.

Sarah didn't like the fact that Lilah was making her look like she wasn't in control. So that very few people could hear, she leaned in, nearly nose to nose with Lilah. Enunciating every word, "It means, stay away from Kyler."

Lilah was furious with herself for not having the confidence to ever ask Kyler, but now, with blood boiling through her veins like the heat of the sun, "You two aren't even together, are you?"

Sarah laughed and rolled her eyes. She liked for people to believe that she and Kyler had a thing, but she had never confirmed or denied anything. Thankfully, Kyler had always ignored the rumors.

"Wow. That's it. That's why you hate me so much. He gave me attention that you wanted. Is that it," Lilah asked, suddenly feeling bolder than ever.

"We're together. We're always together. Maybe if you weren't such a skank like your mother," she began, trying to divert Lilah's attention away from the fact that she and Kyler definitely weren't together.

It was a nasty blow, but Lilah wasn't deterred. That's all Sarah had left in her arsenal. "Really, if the two of you are always together," she began. She couldn't believe she was going to say it, admit to it. It was something so special and private, and she felt bad for sharing it with anyone. Perhaps the adrenaline had clouded her judgement when she blurted out, "Then how was he able to spend an entire weekend with me?"

Sarah could have questioned her, should have called her bluff, but something in Lilah's eyes told her that it was the truth, and she spiraled down into a blinding rage.

Lilah stumbled backwards from the more than aggressive shove. Her only reason for not falling flat on her back being that Alice and Jolee were so close behind her.

She didn't know what made her do it. It was one of the most uncharacteristic things she had ever done.

Apparently, Sarah wasn't the only one in shock when she found herself brutally thrown up against the row of lockers behind her.

"Ladies," an all too familiar voice boomed throughout the hall. It was terrifying enough that the small crowd that had gathered, quickly shot off in all directions.

Principal Willis.

CHAPTER 35

Kyler was one of the stragglers getting from the field into the locker room that afternoon; however, when he walked in, the loud discussions he heard on the other side of the door went nearly silent.

Miles was the first to rush up to him. Hesitantly, "Hey, have you checked your phone?"

Kyler shot him an incredulous look. "Yeah, definitely. I keep it in my cup during practice," he said, motioning to his uniform.

Miles laughed. "My bad." Then his face turned serious and concerned.

"What is going on? Did someone die?" While Kyler was only half serious, with the way everyone was staring at him, he wouldn't be surprised if that was the case.

"Umm...Now don't freak out..."

"Dude! When you start a sentence like that–"

"Lilah got into a fight," Miles quickly blurted out.

Kyler felt like he heard Miles through a body of water between them. Lilah could definitely tell people which way to go if she wanted, but she'd never be dumb enough to get herself into a physical altercation.

He was afraid to ask, but the look on Miles' face told him there was more. "With who?"

"Sarah..."

"Are you kidding me?! What the hell," he screamed. He attempted to hurl his helmet at one of the lockers, but stopped himself halfway in. Losing his temper right now wasn't going to solve anything.

"I'm not sure on some of the details. Some people are saying it was over Simon..." Miles paused when he saw Kyler's face clench up and his knuckles turn white from his tightened grip on the helmet. He probably could have left that part out. "However, some people are saying that it was over you."

Kyler's eyes went wide, and his jaw fell open. A sick part of him really wanted that to be the case.

Dawson came up, phone in hand. "Okay, Alice just text me back. She said Lilah text her that she just got done with Willis. Her punishment is..." He stopped. Before he could even say another word, the door was already swinging shut behind Kyler.

"I don't know about you guys," Gavin began as he flung his arms around the shoulders of both Dawson and Miles. "But this is way too much drama for me."

* * *

Kyler hoped that Alice was as addicted to her phone as she appeared. He also hoped that Lilah had indeed text her immediately after leaving the office. Rather than navigating through the halls of the school, he opted to go straight to the front. As he rounded the last corner, parked directly on the other side of the street from the school entry was a familiar black car, which gave him further hope that he hadn't missed her.

Just as he started up the steps to the main doors, they swung open.

Both he and Lilah stopped dead in their tracks. Kyler hadn't been sure what he'd say to Lilah if their paths were lucky enough to cross, but now he didn't have the breath to manage the smallest of words.

Lilah was certain that her little spat, as she was going to call it, with Sarah had spread like wildfire. With the way most of her classmates were, she could only imagine what the tale had now become. Obviously, it had to be something for Kyler to be standing in front of her, covered in dirt and sweat, still in his practice gear. She hated how gorgeous she found him.

"Are you okay," Kyler managed.

Not missing a beat, "I could ask you the same."

Kyler shook his head. Only Lilah would ignore his sentiment and come back with a comment like that.

"I heard some stuff and I wanted to make sure–"

"I'm fine," Lilah quickly interrupted. She could already feel her cheeks turning red. Her conversation with Principal Willis was one thing, but talking to Kyler about her spat with Sarah would be one of the most difficult and embarrassing things in the world.

"Do you even want to know what I heard?"

Great. The gossip had already gotten out.

"Nope," Lilah said with little care, descending the steps and brushing past Kyler.

While he didn't expect that Lilah would be over the moon to see him, he also didn't think she'd be so dismissive.

Following after her, "I heard you and Sarah got in a fight over Simon." He could feel his stomach churn with those words; however, was surprised when Lilah stopped abruptly and slowly turned back to face him.

Through clenched teeth, "We did not get into a *fight*."

It wasn't exactly the response he wanted to hear.

"We had a minor disagreement," she continued.

"Over Simon?"

Lilah took in a deep breath and allowed their eyes to meet. She could see that he was scrutinizing her every response. "Partly," she admitted with a shrug as if it was no big deal.

That one word nearly destroyed Kyler, but he quickly began overthinking it. Partly meant that there was still something else that they were fighting over.

"What else?"

Sensing that Kyler wouldn't be satisfied, and desperately wanting to get home before the school called her parents, Lilah knew she needed to tell Kyler everything, or mostly everything.

"What do you want me to say? That I'm some stupid girl who got into a spat with another girl over some boy?"

Feeling brave, "Depending on who that boy is, yeah."

For some reason the comment rubbed her the wrong way.

"I mean, you shouldn't fight with any girl over a guy. If he's yours, he's yours. Ignore the rest of them."

Lilah hated that his words were, unknowingly to him, making her so angry.

"I thought he was hers." Her words were so soft and for a moment she thought that Kyler hadn't even heard them, or maybe she hadn't even spoken them.

"Wait, I think I'm a little confused. Are we talking about Simon?"

This was going to be so difficult. She felt so stupid for not asking Kyler about his relationship status the second she started to have feelings for him. "No! I thought you and Sarah were together. She's made enough comments that would lead almost anyone to believe that."

"Okay, now I'm a lot confused."

"Sarah convinced Simon to ask me out. I said yes because, call me crazy, but I'd actually like a boyfriend one day. Anyway, I went to confront Sarah about that, and then you came up." She thought she played it off rather nicely, giving him the overall gist of it all without downright spelling it out for him.

"I came up," he questioned her. His eyes were narrowed and could not have been more focused on her.

"She called me a derogatory name and told me to back off from you, and one thing led to another.

There. Happy," she concluded, throwing her arms in the air to say that that's all she had left to give him.

"No."

"Well tough, That's all I've got."

"You thought Sarah and I were together?"

With slight hesitation on her part, "You're really not?"

Kyler couldn't believe what Lilah was asking, or what she had assumed for who knows how long. "No! Never! Do you really think I'd kiss you and tell you what I did if I was with another girl?"

"She just made it seem like I was something fun and you'd eventually," she paused. Looking back, she wished that she had thought more clearly and not let her emotions get the best of her head. Maybe that's what happens when you're in love. She swallowed heavily. Her only saving grace was that she hadn't just babbled all that to Kyler.

When Lilah didn't finish her sentence, Kyler took it to mean that she probably wasn't going to. "I'm not going to lie, I'm a little pissed right now." He ran his hand through his sweat dampened hair. "You know more about me than my friends. Do you honestly think that I have time to be in a relationship with two girls? Or that I'm that kind of guy? Actually, I don't even need to be bothered with a relationship period, but I really wanted you."

Lilah's eyes shot up to meet Kyler's. "Past tense." It wasn't a question, just a statement.

Kyler had no intention of hurting Lilah, and he could see the panic in her face, but he was too hurt to think about his next choice of words. "Right now, that's what it looks like."

As if his words didn't sting as badly as they most definitely did, "Well, thanks for clearing that up." She tightened her grip on her bag and turned to leave for the final time.

He didn't know what made him do it, he should have just let her go. They were both saying too much with emotions running high. However, fueled by frustration he followed after her, knowing that this would probably be their last conversation.

"So that's it. When you're not comfortable talking about something you just run away. I tell you I love you, you run away. Now I tell you I don't want to be with you, and you run away." She kept walking, not once bothering to respond. "You know, maybe what everyone thinks is what it really is. I'm just some hot-shot quarterback that gets a thrill out of going from girl to girl, and you're some stuck-up princess living a life of luxury, and at the end of the day, our lives couldn't be more perfect."

Lilah turned to glare at him, hiding her tears for just a little bit longer. He didn't allow her to counter anything he had said. This time it was his turn to walk away.

"You should go. Your car is waiting on you."

CHAPTER 36

Needless to say, when Lilah arrived home, she wasn't surprised that a family meeting was being called. What she was utterly shocked by was the nature of the meeting.

"Wait," Rover interjected. "We have to go to some of the sessions too?"

"You will be incorporated on some occasions, yes," Jenna explained.

"Why? You two are the ones that need help!" He was not happy about the fact that he'd have to occasionally lose an afternoon of gaming.

"It's called counseling," Steven clarified.

"So, you're not getting a divorce then," Lilah asked, still completely confused by her parents' relationship.

"No. We've decided to work past our differences," Jenna answered with the sweetest and fakest of smiles.

There was nothing for Lilah to smile about. She hated how her mother referred to her affairs as *differences*.

Steven glanced down at his phone and excused himself.

"So is that it," Rover asked.

"I think so. Your father and I just want the both of you to know that we really do love you, and we're going to try everything to get this family back on track," Jenna concluded.

Lilah rose from her seat, unable to make eye contact with her mother. The statement she just heard made her want to vomit. Perhaps her mother talked it over with lawyers and discovered that she wouldn't be getting as much as she thought if she went through with a divorce.

Lilah hadn't made it halfway to the stairs when, "Lilah Rose McCallister!"

Rover, already halfway up the stairs stopped and turned to look at his sister below. "Whoa. You are in so much trouble." Just like that he took back off, running toward his room, no doubt for some video game.

There was no running anywhere this time.

Lilah made her way back into the living room where her outraged father was already filling her mother in on the details.

"It was just a spat," Lilah corrected.

"A spat? A spat?!" Steven began to pace. "A spat doesn't end up with one girl in the hospital!"

Lilah clenched her face. Hospital? There was no hospital.

"Lilah," her mother gasped. "What in the world did you do?"

"I didn't put a girl in the hospital!"

"Apparently," her dad interjected, before she could start to explain. "Lilah threw the girl into the lockers so hard that she was complaining of blurry vision and head and neck pain. Her parents took her to the hospital to check for a concussion."

"Oh brother," Lilah huffed under her breath. "She's just being dramatic."

"All this! Over some boy," her father boomed.

Some boy.

Lilah already knew that Kyler was anything but some boy.

It didn't help when her mother tried to ground her that the only thing she could come up with was taking away her books and computer. Despite the worst Monday of her life, Lilah didn't imagine the conversation she was yet to have with her mother.

Jenna stood in Lilah's bedroom doorway that evening, a glass of wine in hand and let out a sigh. Lilah knew she was there but said nothing and went on staring out her window into empty darkness, or mostly empty darkness. There were still the streetlights, and in the faraway distance she could see the black turn to blue from the city lights miles and miles away.

"Are things not working out with the Campbell boy? Is another girl encroaching on your territory?"

Lilah turned, only to glare at her mother for saying something so ridiculous.

Knowing it would irritate her mother, "I'm not with the Campbell boy. I'm not with anyone. Just to clarify, people aren't other people's territory."

"You don't have to be so snappy."

Lilah let out a sigh. "What do you want, mom," she asked, crawling out of her comfy chair near the window and going in search of her pajamas.

"I just wanted more details than what was on the message your school left."

Lilah rolled her eyes. Of course she did. Her mother was probably the Sarah of her high school back in her day. Even now when she went out with her girlfriends, all they did was gossip.

"Classic story," Lilah said with a shrug. "Mean cheerleader, football player–"

She didn't expect her mother to interrupt her with a fit of laughter.

"Oh, sweetie," she began with a sip of wine. "Please tell me this isn't over some football player."

Not liking the amount of humor her mother found with the situation, Lilah replied with, "Fine then. I won't tell you that." She didn't say another word and hoped her mother would leave her alone.

Instead, Jenna grew very serious. Lilah pressed herself up against her bathroom door waiting for whatever rubbish her mother was going to give her as advice.

"Lilah," she began with another exasperated breath. "I know he's probably popular, and muscular, and sexy right now, but think of your future. Chances are he'll end up just like the jocks that I went to school with. Don't get me wrong, they're fun at the time, but not worth detention for a week. In ten years, he'll probably be out of shape and changing the tires on the new Porsche your husband got you as an anniversary present."

Lilah was stunned. Her mother could be a snob, but she never expected her to say something so callous about someone she didn't even know.

"Trust me on this."

In that moment, Lilah was absolutely certain why her mother was staying with her father.

CHAPTER 37

"It's been days. The both of you look miserable. Dawson even said as much," Alice groaned at lunch Thursday.

"I hate to admit it, but she's right. Please tell me we're not going to have to team up with them," Jolee said, nodding towards Kyler's table. "And do an intervention," she concluded.

Lilah responded with a small laugh. "No. That's not going to be necessary."

"Right now the two of you aren't even speaking. I'm not stupid. I know who you were always texting." Alice concluded her statement by childishly sticking out her tongue.

"I'm fine. Really. Just drop it."

Alice and Jolee gave each other a look. They knew she wasn't fine. Lilah had never really admitted to ever liking anyone the way she liked Kyler. That had to mean something.

Lilah couldn't help but occasionally glance in Kyler's direction. After everything that had happened Monday, even the circumstances surrounding her parents, she had done a lot of thinking. One thing she'd never admit to anyone was that she was terrified of attempting to date someone like Kyler. In the beginning she found that she unknowingly compared herself to the types of girls she often saw surrounding his group of friends. She thought herself to be pretty and confident, but definitely not a sexy extrovert that she assumed Kyler wanted. It wasn't until she sat staring at empty night skies, surrounded only by complete silence that she realized how truly stupid she was.

Kyler had showed her who he was from the beginning. Well, if she didn't count the part that he totally lied to her about how smart he was. Instead she let rumors and her own assumptions destroy something that never got a chance to begin.

She didn't want to believe what Kyler had said to her the other day. He looked at her just like she read about in some of those ridiculous books she often found herself consumed by, just like how the men looked at the leading ladies in the old black and white movies she often enjoyed. He didn't look at her like her father looked at her mother. Nor had she ever seen him look at any other girl in school that way. Not for a second did she want to think that he meant it when he said he didn't want her anymore.

Lilah wanted to wait until the next day to say something, but not talking to him for days was driving her crazy. Her hands shook as she nervously sent off the text. Right now, all she needed to know was if they could still be friends. If they could, then maybe she had the opportunity to fix things for something more.

* * *

Kyler felt his phone go off in a pattern that signaled a text. He rarely got messages at lunch because most of the people that would message him were sitting right in front of him. For some reason, he immediately looked up, only for Lilah's eyes to quickly dart away, back to her friends.

He couldn't get his phone out of his pocket fast enough. After their conversation Monday, he never expected that she'd ever talk to him again. Worst of all, he hated that in a fit of frustration he had said things he didn't mean.

Lilah: Good luck on your game tomorrow.

It wasn't much, but it was something. Just a small something to open the door on her part. He groaned at how hopeless he was, how one simple message from her already had his heart racing.

Kyler: Thanks. It's the last one.

"Who's that," Sarah asked over Kyler's shoulder, but before he could say anything she scoffed. "What a loser."

He couldn't take it anymore. He knew that by not setting Sarah straight long ago, he had inevitably helped put himself in the situation he was currently in.

"Actually, she's pretty amazing."

Sarah sat down and didn't say another word. Kyler knew that wasn't going to be good enough.

"Could we maybe step out for a second? I need to talk to you," he asked in a way so that they wouldn't get too much unwanted attention.

"No thanks," Sarah snapped.

"Fine, if that's how you want to be," Kyler began. He took a deep breath and carefully thought how to best say it so that Sarah got the hint once and for all. "I'm shocked that you're so evil and vindictive to do what you did to Lilah–"

Sarah was quick to interrupt, a little more loudly than Kyler would have liked. "Oh, shut up! You act like I committed murder. I got a guy to ask her out, and newsflash to you, she said yes to him. So what does that tell you about her?"

"It tells me that you had her believing that in some screwed-up universe, you and I were together. It tells me that you put it in her head that she didn't have a chance with me," he growled, getting more annoyed by the second. He had days to sit and think about why things were the way they were, and this was a conversation that was long overdue.

"Then maybe you should watch the signals you send out!"

"Signals?! Being nice to you shouldn't make you think that I want a relationship with you."

Unable to deal with further rejection and humiliation, Sarah opted out of the conversation the only way she knew how. She ferociously snatched Sean's open sports drink from across the table and dumped the nearly full bottle of blue liquid right on top of Kyler's head.

She quickly got up and began to gather her things, and only became more enraged when Kyler gave up and didn't succumb to her dramatic actions.

Kyler simply pulled his messy and sticky hair back and took in a deep breath. "Thanks," he grumbled. "Real mature."

Sarah then proceeded to stomping out of the cafeteria, with Britt and Abby close on her heels.

Kyler forced himself to ignore all the attention that Sarah had managed to attract and, acting as though nothing out of the ordinary had happened, he quietly excused himself to the locker rooms. He could go without finishing his lunch, but he could not stand the smell and stickiness of Sean's blueberry drink soaking into him.

* * *

Lilah only saw the part where Sarah drenched Kyler in a sports drink. What led to that was beyond her. She watched as Kyler left the room in annoyance.

"Wow. That was..." Alice began.

"Something," Jolee finished.

They zeroed in on Lilah and waited for a response.

"Don't look at me! I didn't do *that*."

With a devilish smirk spread across Jolee's lips, "I have a feeling you indirectly did."

She had to admit, seeing Sarah storm off like a five-year-old was pretty entertaining, but she felt bad for Kyler. Though he knew how to push her buttons, she couldn't imagine what he would have said to garner such a dramatic reaction.

She hovered over the screen displaying his last text. There was nothing she could think to say after his and Sarah's performance. In fact, Sarah was hands down the last name she ever wanted in a conversation with Kyler ever again.

Then an idea hit her.

"Hey, what are you two doing tomorrow night," she eagerly asked Alice and Jolee.

Jolee gave a slight shrug.

Alice began rambling about a new season of some vampire series.

"There's something I want to do," Lilah hesitantly continued. "But I was hoping I wouldn't have to do it alone.

Jolee's eyes lit up. "Well, you have me intrigued."

Alice pretended to be disappointed. "I guess those episodes can wait until Saturday…"

"What is it," Jolee asked impatiently.

"I want to go to the football game."

Both Alice and Jolee gave each other incredulous looks before shouting in unison. "What?!"

CHAPTER 38

Walking back out on the field after halftime of his last high school career game had Kyler's stomach in knots, but it had little to do with the fact that they were losing by sixteen points and everything to do with the stupid message he saw on his phone when he opened his locker during the break.

Lilah: Please don't let my first game end in such a disaster.

It was sent shortly before halftime, right around the time that everything started to go downhill. For starters, Raymere Grove's running game had been weak all season. Though Kyler's throws were spot on, they were no match when it came to the defensive line of their opponent, Halshire High.

Now, to make matters worse, that stupid text from Lilah had his head spinning. He asked her a couple times throughout the season to come to a game, and she practically laughed at him. Scratch that, he distinctly remembered her definitely laughing at the suggestion. So why would she be here now?

Kyler sat on the bench as he watched their defense take the field. He tried from time to time to turn around and catch a glimpse of the stands behind him. There were easily a couple hundred people and he had no idea where to look for Lilah, assuming she was still at the game.

"Stop being so weird," Miles grumbled next to him.

"What are you talking–"

"Far left, about five rows up, white shirt and grey jacket," Miles interrupted.

Kyler shot him a look with narrowed eyes and a tightened jaw, only for Miles to throw his head back in laughter.

"Hey, man, wouldn't you notice a fish out of water?" He shook his head, still trying to comprehend the trio in the stands. "I never thought I'd see Lilah McCallister at one of our games."

Kyler remained silent. His heartbeat quickened at the possibility of what that could mean.

When Kyler didn't reply with anything, "Are you finally going to ask her out?"

"I don't know if that's a good idea after everything."

"Seriously?! Why do you think she's here? I can tell you one thing, it's not to watch us win, because we don't know what the heck that is anymore."

Kyler sighed at that; however, he was a little excited to see their opponents with 3rd and 17 after a nice sack from Raymere's defense.

"It's our last game. A lot of the town is here for that," Kyler admitted.

"Yeah, well it might be a lot of lasts if you don't get your head on straight when it comes to her." Miles didn't give Kyler a chance to respond. He grabbed his helmet and motioned for Kyler to do the same just as Halshire punted the ball away.

* * *

"Oh, now he's back on the field," Alice clapped. "That's a good thing, right?"

Lilah nodded, although, after watching a few of the drives in the first half, it really didn't matter who was on the field. She knew that with football, everything could change in a handful of seconds, but seeing the score, 7 to 23, didn't give her much hope in their school winning the game.

"It doesn't even matter at this point," Jolee chimed in. "We didn't go to state. I heard the team, as a whole, pretty much sucks." She shrugged and went back to a book she had brought along.

Lilah decided to keep her mouth shut and watch intently. Her friends had already given her a hard time during the first half with her little bit of knowledge about the game.

* * *

2nd and 20 after a loss of yardage from a sack by Halshire.

Kyler was livid as they got back in formation. A few choice words under his breath gained the reaction of Sean.

"Maybe if you could get rid of the ball..."

Kyler got in Sean's face. "Wow. Why didn't I think of that? Oh, maybe because I have less than a second for a window because some of you can't figure out your jobs."

"Whoa, whoa," Miles jumped in. "I'll be open this time. Just get it to me. Let's not have anyone getting kicked out on our last game."

Kyler knew that Miles couldn't guarantee that, and just like he expected, Miles was so closely covered that there was no way he was going to risk an interception. His eyes caught the flash of red and white darting toward him, but just as he was about to throw the ball away, he saw an opening.

It was risky, and a little bit egotistical, but he decided to run it himself. His goal wasn't necessarily to get a first down, and he knew there wasn't a chance in hell he'd get in the red zone, but there was no way he'd allow a loss or no gain. As he got farther down the field, he quickly started making his way closer to the sidelines. He had already been sacked three times; he knew how brutal Halshire's defense was. Not wanting to take the chance of taking another hit, he finally stepped out of bounds, the roaring cheers already telling him that he got the first down.

Miles ran up to him and jumped on him like he had won the game. "Dude! That was so stupid," he laughed. "Awesome, but stupid."

"What was that," Sean yelled as more players came to congratulate Kyler.

"That," Kyler began, catching his breath, adrenaline pumping through his veins. "Is how you get a first down."

Sean stormed off, ready for the next play, and something hit Kyler. He fully intended to tell Sean that if he couldn't do a better job blocking, he didn't need him; he could do the game himself, but suddenly, that wasn't his mentality anymore. He rolled his eyes, knowing he'd have to swallow his pride, as he jogged up to Sean.

Kyler tapped Sean on the shoulder.

"What?!"

"Look, I'm sorry." It came out quickly and Kyler felt like he had swallowed vomit.

"What..."

"I know we're all trying our best. Halshire is a really good team. I guess I just got worked up. Call me crazy, but I'd actually like to win our last game." Kyler gave a shrug, hoping that by calming his attitude and ego, Sean would do the same.

As if by some miracle, Sean sighed, his features softening, and his tense shoulders deflating. "I'm trying, man. Their guys are just so much more with everything. Stronger. Faster. Bigger."

"I get it. All I'm saying is, let's just do our best, for the team. As soon as the game is over, you can go back to hating me for being such an egotistical jock with the perfect life just handed to me."

Sean scoffed and rolled his eyes. "If you think I'm going to correct you on that, you're wrong."

Kyler laughed and patted Sean on the shoulder. He was well-aware that when Sean had a chip on his shoulder, he was useless on the field. Hopefully that brief interaction had helped.

* * *

Lilah laughed when Jolee put her book down, suddenly intrigued at what was happening on the field.

"They don't suck as much as they did at first," Jolee calmly admitted.

Lilah wasn't sure what happened after Kyler made that amazing run halfway down the field, but something in their team's attitude for the game seemed to shift. Halshire still tore their players up, but everyone worked a little better together.

31 to 29 in their favor.

Halshire with the ball just shy of the fifty-yard line.

Going for it on 4th and 2.

A minute and fifteen seconds left on the game clock.

Lilah sat on the edge of her seat along with everyone else in town.

Alice leaned in closer. "Why is it so quiet?"

"If they don't get this, we win," Lilah whispered back, unsure why they were whispering.

"Cool...What do we win?"

Lilah couldn't respond to that. Though winning seemed to be a big deal to everyone in the stands, it really didn't matter too much she supposed.

"We win not losing the last game," Jolee answered instead.

Lilah couldn't help but chuckle a little. "That."

Lilah clamped down on her bottom lip as the ball was snapped and handed off. Three seconds later, there was a messy pile of players from both teams as everyone waited for the call.

When the referee motioned that it was Raymere Grove's ball, their side of the stands erupted.

Then Lilah spent the next few minutes explaining to Alice why with no timeouts left for either team, they didn't have to play anymore, which would only risk injury or heaven forbid, an interception.

CHAPTER 39

It wasn't a game like in the movies. It wasn't like they had won the Super Bowl. When the clock hit zero, Raymere Grove had really only won their last game of the season, and possibly the last game forever for several of the seniors.

The players were excited and after a few moments of celebrating and showing respect to their opponents, they took their leave off the field. It was at this point that most of the people in the stands began to make their way in every direction.

Lilah didn't know what she was expecting. Kyler had given her a few glances after halftime, but none of which gave her any clue as to what he might be thinking with her presence there. Maybe the hopeless romantic hidden somewhere deep inside thought that he'd rush over the barrier separating the field from the stands, climb the few stairs up to her row, take her in his arms, and...

Her thoughts were interrupted with a sigh from Jolee. "Well, they won."

"It wasn't the worst. Maybe we should have come to games sooner," Alice admitted with a shrug. "I can't believe I just said that," she laughed.

Lilah nudged her. "Just so you know, they have this in college, only it's way bigger and more intense."

"So, what are we supposed to do now," Jolee asked. She looked around the stands that were becoming emptier by the second.

"You two should go," Lilah answered quietly.

They gave each other a look before Alice had to ask. "What about you? We can't just leave you here."

"I'll leave soon." Lilah put her arms around both Jolee and Alice. "Thank you both for coming. This was out of my comfort zone and I don't think I could have done it alone."

Though the girls were hesitant to leave Lilah, although they knew Antonio was only a call away, they decided to call it a night. It wasn't until just as they said their goodbyes, and Lilah received a text, that they knew they most definitely needed to head out.

Kyler: Wait for me.

Lilah clutched her phone to her pounding chest. Excitement flooded her whole body, all the way to her toes. Despite everything, this had to at least mean something to him. If he was mad at her for all her stupid thoughts and decisions, he couldn't possibly want to give her the time of day. Though it was just a text of only three words, those three words meant the world to her. She knew without a doubt that she owed Kyler the same.

* * *

Maybe he should have gone up to her right after the game; however, he felt like it needed to be a moment for just the two of them, not a good portion of the town with front row seats. Also, he smelled. Bad. While Lilah probably wouldn't have cared, he really didn't want a meaningful conversation to take place when he was covered in sweat, grass, and dirt.

He ignored all the celebration. A chuckle erupted as he dug contents from a bag in his locker and ran to the showers. He never thought after their first wins that their season would end so poorly. While everyone continued to celebrate, it was very bittersweet. Kyler knew he'd play in college, especially with the scholarships he was offered for football, but for a couple of the guys, high school and this game was it.

Kyler looked in the mirror after the fastest shower of his life and ruffled his damp hair. He grabbed a small glass bottle and gave a few sprays. Laughter erupted behind him. Turning, he saw Dawson and Miles, with Gavin in the middle, his arms thrown over the other two.

Kyler rolled his eyes and tried to hide his embarrassment.

"Aww," Gavin cooed. "Don't get shy on us now."

"You didn't have to get all fancy for us. We're just doing burgers like always. Right," Miles teased, fully knowing that Kyler was ditching them for the night.

"About that," Kyler began.

The three before him only laughed more at his seriousness.

"Don't even," Miles interrupted. "We'd be stupid to think that after all this you'd pass up a chance to *finally* get with Lilah."

Dawson felt the need to chime in. "This is *finally* right? Because you two are giving all of us whiplash."

Kyler rubbed the back of his neck and shook his head. "Yeah. I hope so."

* * *

Nerves crashed through Kyler's body with every step he took back to the field. If she bothered to come to his game, he knew there was enough there that she'd wait for him. What he didn't expect was to see her standing on the field, illuminated by the stadium lights that usually remained on up to an hour after the game.

When he was within feet of her, she turned to face him, and anything he wanted to say in that moment was washed away like violent waves to footprints in the sand.

"Hey," Lilah greeted.

His eyes went up and down her body, from a simple white button-down and grey jacket, to slimming jeans, to regular sneakers. Her hair was effortless and straight, like always, one side tucked more behind her ear than the other. Her makeup remained plain and neutral, only doing what it was intended for, highlighting her natural beauty.

Lilah played with her hands in her coat pocket. He hadn't said a word yet, which was very unlike him.

The way he was staring at her was unnerving. She had looked into those serene and beautiful blue eyes far more than she should have, but tonight was proving to be more difficult than ever, if the pounding in her chest had anything to say about it.

She bit her bottom lip, realizing that Kyler had somehow managed to find the time to shower. His damp hair was darker, the wetness hiding the bits of blonde that she found so unique in the sunlight. More than anything, she wished they could change positions. From where they were standing, the cold autumn breeze came from behind Kyler, and though he blocked most of it from slamming into her, it also meant that every breath she took was all him. Flashes of that smell ran through her head. His hoodie. His bed.

"Congratulations on the game," she managed after a few moments of them just staring at each other.

Kyler took a step toward her. "Thanks for coming."

"Well, you had asked several times before." Lilah hesitated before adding, "And I wanted to talk to you."

Kyler chuckled. "You didn't have to force yourself to sit through a game to talk to me." He was happy that the initial awkwardness from not talking for so many days seemed to fade away with every word between them.

"It wasn't that bad. We actually had fun."

"We," Kyler pressed, although he already knew the people she was referring to.

Lilah wasn't an idiot. He didn't directly ask her, and she wasn't sure if he would, but she wanted all assumptions and speculations gone. They had to be for what she needed to say.

"Jolee and Alice." She took a deep breath and rambled through the rest of her words. "I'm not seeing Simon...if that's what you were thinking. I told him that on Monday. In fact, I hear he's talking to Sophie now."

Kyler smiled at that bit of rushed information. "And you're okay with that?" He meant the fact that Simon had gone directly from Lilah to her biggest competition academically.

Lilah glared at him with an incredulous look. "Of course! Do you think I'd be here trying to..." She stopped and her eyes grew wide, her words failing her.

Kyler slowly stepped forward yet again, the space between them becoming less and less in a painfully dramatic way.

"Why are you here," he asked, his voice deep and rough.

Lilah's eyes fell to the ground. A text or even a note would have been so much easier, but with him standing right there in front of her, looking at her the way he was, it became nearly impossible to form the right sentences.

Kyler was close enough to reach out to Lilah, but as soon as he tilted her chin to look at him, that little bit of contact made him want to combust. That's the effect she had on him.

"If you were wondering, I haven't dated a single girl all year," he admitted with the faintest of grins.

Lilah sighed with annoyance, although her next words told him it had nothing to do with him and everything to do with her. "I know. I let the wrong people get into my head, and...I didn't want to be just another girl."

Kyler shook his head. "You could never be just another girl." Now would have been the perfect moment to ask her to be his, his girl, but he needed her to answer his question. "You didn't answer me."

"Answer what?" If he asked her again, there was only one thing she could say, and then everything would be out there. He could decide what he wanted.

Kyler carefully placed an arm on Lilah's waist and tugged her forward so that they were only a breath apart.

"Why are you here," he asked slowly, but her words came out before he could close his mouth.

"Because I love you."

He couldn't control the flabbergasted look on his face. He was praying she'd say something that would indicate that she wanted to be with him, and though he had said those words to her before, he never expected to hear them from her, at least not for some time.

Lilah quickly stepped from his grasp. The look on Kyler's face suggested that it probably wasn't what he wanted to hear, and now she felt sick to her stomach.

"I'm sorry," she said quietly. "I didn't mean–"

Kyler forced himself to quickly recover and he cut her words short when he pulled her back into him and stopped anything more from coming from her mouth other than a soft moan of pleasure when his lips met hers. All the tension in her body drifted away and she responded with an eager hungriness that drove Kyler crazy. Had it not been after nine and below fifty degrees, he could have stayed plastered to her on that field forever.

"Sorry," he breathed when he pulled away.

Lilah's eyes widened with a question unable to come from her lips after that kiss.

Kyler laughed, wrapping his arms even more tightly around her small frame. "I didn't mean to get so carried away, but you were about to start rambling and say something we both know you wouldn't have meant."

Lilah's cheeks turned impossibly red. "So, what now? I've never really done this before," Lilah embarrassingly admitted.

"Well, I'd first like to take you on a real date before asking you to be my girlfriend."

Lilah's jaw dropped. Okay, she had just told him that she loved him, but still, hearing that sent a whole swarm of butterflies throughout her insides.

Feeling daring, "Does that have to happen before you kiss me again?"

The most seductive and melting smile spread across Kyler's face. "Absolutely not."

He closed the gap between them once more, and this time he wasn't the one pressing for more. Lilah flung her arms around his neck and as soon as her fingers dug into his hair, he was done for. When their tongues found each other in the most familiar way, everything around them disappeared. The lights. The smell of the stadium. The frigid air. It was only them.

"Just so you know," Lilah began breathlessly. "Date or not, my answer is yes."

Kyler pressed his forehead to hers and looked into eyes that had captured his attention long before he cared to admit. "Just so you know," he began, tucking a few pieces of disheveled hair behind her ear. "It was never a question to begin with."

With that, Kyler placed the sweetest and most loving peck on her lips, knowing that if he tried for anything deeper, they'd probably be found frozen on the field the next morning.

"Oh," Kyler said, entangling their fingers as they walked off the field. "In case we're not clear, or in case you needed to hear it again, I love you too. I didn't say it back when you said it, and I know how crappy that feels when someone says something that monumental and you don't get the same," he teased.

Lilah spun around and collided into Kyler with the tightest hug she could. If she were lost in an isolated sea, he was the one something she'd never let go of, the one thing that kept her afloat, the one thing that made her feel safe, and above all, loved.

Perfect. That word was used so much, but it never meant anything until that moment. Being in Kyler's arms, feeling the pounding of his heart against her cheek, that was perfect.

THE END

EPILOGUE

It was already the second day back from winter break and Ashlyn had yet to hear from Eric. Apparently his father, a former 90s rockstar, had him for Christmas break this year. He was taking Eric around Europe, but Ashlyn knew there was still cell reception and Wi-Fi in the cities they were visiting.

Emory sat her tray down at the table alongside Ashlyn, June, and Kayla, and glanced around. "I guess the guys are done with us now that Ellis is dating Abby," Emory pointed out, after she noticed that her brother and his best friend were not around for the second day now. She was absolutely disgusted that her brother was dating one of the members on her cheer team.

"Yeah," Ashlyn sighed.

"Seriously? Are you still bummed that Eric isn't here? He said he'd be back by next week," Emory scoffed. "Although, if he didn't come back, would it really be all that bad?"

June and Kayla chuckled, but Ashlyn sent her best friend a glare across the table. She was well-aware that Emory and Eric clashed, and she hated it.

"Oh, crap," Ashlyn huffed, dismissing talk of Eric. "Here comes Sarah."

Emory laughed, already knowing what Sarah was going to bring up.

"Emmy," Sarah cooed.

"Emory," Emory corrected her. Some people might like nicknames or shorter versions of their names, for instance, Ashlyn preferred Ash; however, she was not one of these people.

Ignoring her fellow cheerleader, Sarah took a seat, with Britt following suit. "We won't be staying long." Her nose was wrinkled. She looked about the table as though it was in a completely different cafeteria than her usual table, as if it wasn't a suitable quality for her. "Anyway, Ashlyn. How are you?"

Ashlyn shook her head. "I'm going to tell you the same thing I told you in the hall yesterday."

"Yeah, yeah. Patient confidentiality." Sarah flung her hand in the air, dismissing the words. "I mean come on. Your mom is *the* therapist for the McCallisters! I'm sure you know something."

"I don't know anything about who she may or may not have as patients." Ashlyn felt like she had told Sarah those exact words the day before.

"Cut the crap," Sarah hissed, growing agitated. She couldn't believe that she was lowering herself to harassing an underclassman for information about Lilah and her family. "Her mother has blabbed it all over town. I know your mom is their therapist." She tried to reign in on her rudeness for just a second longer in hopes that Ashlyn would be on her side. "I mean, couldn't you ask her how that's going? Or do you visit her office? If so, I'm sure she has notes about–"

"Are you mental," Ashlyn interrupted. "I don't care about the McCallisters or more specifically Lilah and her *boyfriend* Kyler. It would be in your best interest not to even finish what you're suggesting."

"You know what, fine! I should have known better than come to the loser table." Sarah rose, ready to storm off. "Also, maybe you should be the one having sessions with your mommy." When Ashlyn gave her and incredulous look, "Last time I checked, your so-called relationship sucked." Sarah then spun around and stomped away with Britt in tow.

"You know," Kayla began, shaking her head. "I keep looking for that girl to redeem herself. One day I think she's going to do something to show the world that she isn't such a wicked witch, but every day, she spirals further into whatever delusional world she's the queen of."

"That's a little rude," June scoffed, garnering the attention of her three friends. With a smile, "After seeing *Wicked* on Broadway, I feel it's a little mean to compare someone as vile as Sarah with Elphaba. It's insulting to Elphaba."

"Oh, you don't need to keep reminding us that you got to see that on Broadway," Ashlyn teased.

Shortly after, the girls went back into simple conversation about the beginning of the spring semester and changes to their schedules.

Despite Sarah's craziness, her last words really hit a nerve with Ashlyn. She had been with Eric for two years now, ever since freshman year. It wasn't until his parents ultimately got divorced somewhere along the way that he started to change.

This year, all she got was a belated Christmas text from him. Though he had told her when he'd be back at school, it had still been four days since she last heard from him. She knew if he was with his father, he was up to no good, but couldn't he at least contact her?

She hated to admit it, but maybe Sarah was right. Maybe she was the one that needed relationship counseling.